FEVER

Visit us at www.boldstrokesbooks.com

Praise for VK Powell's Fiction

"If you like cop novels, or even television cop shows with women as full partners with male officers…this is the book for you. It's got drama, excitement, conflict, and even some fairly hot lesbian sex. The writer is a retired cop, so she really writes from a place of authenticity. As a result, you have a realistic quality to the writing that puts me in mind of early Joseph Wambaugh, before his writing became formulaic."—*Lesbian News*

"*To Protect and Serve* drew me in from the very first page with characters that captivated in their complexity. Powell writes with authority using the lingo and capturing the thoughts of the law enforcers who make the ultimate sacrifice in the fight against crime. What's more impressive is the command this debut author has of portraying a full gamut of emotion, from angst to elation, through dialogue and narrative. The images are vivid, the action is believable, and the police procedurals are authentic…VK Powell had me invested in the story of these women, heart, mind, body and soul. Along with danger and tension, Powell's well-developed erotic scenes sizzle and sate."—*Story Circle Book Reviews*

"VK Powell has a surefire winner with her first novel, *To Protect and Serve*. It is well-written, balancing an enchanting romance with a stimulating police procedural…Lust and love fill the novel, and the story touches us viscerally. We feel the characters' emotions, and are exposed to the intimacy that they crave…Powell has a wonderful future ahead of her as an author if *To Protect and Serve* is any indication."—*Just About Write*

"From the first chapter of *Suspect Passions* Powell builds erotic scenes which sear the page. She definitely takes her readers for a walk on the wild side! Her characters, however, are also women we care about. They are bright, witty, and strong. The combination of great sex and great characters make *Suspect Passions* a must read." —*Just About Write*

By the Author

To Protect and Serve

Suspect Passions

Fever

FEVER

by

VK Powell

2010

FEVER

ISBN 10: 1-60282-135-6
ISBN 13: 978-1-60282-135-4

THIS TRADE PAPERBACK ORIGINAL IS PUBLISHED BY
BOLD STROKES BOOKS, INC.
P.O. BOX 249
VALLEY FALLS, NY 12185

FIRST EDITION: FEBRUARY 2010

CREDITS
EDITORS: SHELLEY THRASHER AND STACIA SEAMAN
PRODUCTION DESIGN: STACIA SEAMAN
COVER DESIGN BY SHERI (GRAPHICARTIST2020@HOTMAIL.COM)

Acknowledgments

It would not be possible to do the work I love without the support and encouragement of amazing friends. Each of you brings a special gift to my life, and I am grateful.

To Len Barot, deep appreciation for allowing me to be a "writer." It makes my heart sing. And to each person in the amazing Bold Strokes family who reads, tweaks, massages, and improves my imperfect product, I say thank you.

For Dr. Shelley Thrasher, much gratitude for your guidance (subtle and otherwise), suggestions, and kindness. You help me view my work with fresh eyes.

To all the readers who support and encourage my writing, thank you for buying my work, visiting my Web site (www.powellvk.com), sending e-mails, and showing up for signings. You make my "job" so much fun!

Dedication

To the four fantastic women who shared my once-in-a-lifetime vacation: Dawn S. Chaney, Julia Huff-Jerome, Carole Morse, and Carol Place. Thank you for the memories.

CHAPTER ONE

The heavy London rain sounded like birdshot against the aluminum hull of the small corporate jet. Zak Chambers struggled not to bolt as wind gusts rocked it where it sat on the tarmac. Confined places didn't usually bother her, but any sound resembling weapons fire made her antsy. She flattened her back against the wall beside the open doorway and surveilled the area outside the plane. Satisfied that things were as normal as usual at Heathrow around dusk, she grabbed the sides of the door and leaned out, hoping the prickly raindrops that washed over her face and chest would restore a sense of control to her little piece of the universe.

Zak scraped her fingers through her thick mop of short hair, wishing the motion would contain the unwanted feelings that had haunted her for days. Then she chastised herself for her momentary weakness and returned her attention to the aircraft. In less than half an hour a new client would arrive. She still had to load supplies and review her flight plan before this ritzy hotel room was airworthy.

She transferred the last case of bottled water from the loading platform, trying not to inhale another lungful of jet fumes and saturated night air. According to Captain Stewart, this assignment would be more of a vacation than work. Some corporate do-gooder wanted to build a primary school for tribal children in the African bush and needed an escort to the site. She could hear Stewart's voice clearly. "It's a pie job, Ebony. Easy in, easy out, easy money. Take a few extra days and enjoy yourself." But this certainly wasn't the kind of assignment for which the Company had trained her and at which she had excelled for the past twelve years.

Fourteen months earlier she'd insinuated herself into the life of a bright young woman with a promising future, Mark 235. Knowing her real name would have personalized her and rendered Zak professionally impotent. She was to seduce 235 and determine how fully she was betraying government secrets. During their time together 235 was suspected of espionage, blacklisted from government work, and faced criminal charges. Through it all, Zak pretended to be a devoted lover, comforting and consoling, until she learned that Mark 235 had been framed. Then, against Company policy, Zak remained in play long enough to clear 235 before she relinquished her role. But the bitter taste of deceit clawed its way up her throat as she remembered the devastation on the woman's face when she walked out of the apartment, saying only that it was over.

Explaining was not usually possible in her line of work, but for the first time in her career Zak actually wanted to. And for the first time she needed to recharge her depleted energy, repair her bruised defenses, and rein in her frayed emotions. But she hadn't had time. She felt raw and unprepared for another assignment, especially one with the potential to stir up old feelings.

Maybe Stewart sensed her growing discontent with jobs that constantly subverted her basic beliefs. Maybe he was trying to give her that much-needed respite. If so, why this Africa assignment? More so than most, Stewart knew the bittersweet connection she had with the country and its people. It had been three years and she was in no hurry to go back, even on a drop-off. Too many things could, and often did, go wrong in Africa.

Zak pulled the remaining items from the platform, along with her worn black leather rucksack. This sixteen by twenty-four-inch bag contained everything she owned and valued. She took it everywhere. If it wasn't in this bag, she didn't need it. Less than forty-eight hours ago she took a final dip in the Indian Ocean off the west coast of Australia, packed her bag, and left the only place she'd called home since early adulthood. Though it had been the site of a mission, it had started to feel more like a home.

So maybe a hiatus was exactly what Zak needed. Time could be a friend or an enemy, and for now she wanted it to crawl slowly by while she put herself back together and figured out what she really wanted. Certainly nothing or no one kept her in London, Paris, or anywhere else she'd been in her career, so Africa was probably as good a place as any to get answers. It was, after all, where all the questions started.

Zak picked up the manifest, checked off each item one final time, and wondered about the woman she would accompany. The boss had given her very little information about the client, and the pilot was equally tight-lipped, even after she offered him a hefty bribe. He'd just smiled and said, "Some things you have to experience for yourself."

After stowing her rucksack under the seat directly behind the pilot and closest to the exit, Zak slid down the wet step railing and did a quick external check of the plane. She wanted nothing more than a quiet nine-hour flight during which she could refocus and prepare for the assignment. She needed time to stuff her feelings about Mark 235 and Africa back into a nice tidy mental compartment.

She finished her examination, scooted under the belly of the aircraft, and climbed the steps, mentally calculating the minutes of solitude before she was on the job again. "Too few," she mumbled aloud as another shower soaked her and a white stretch limo pulled onto the tarmac. "Always too few."

❖

"For God's sake, Rikki, let me close the privacy screen." Sara Ambrosini wiggled out of her lover's clutches and pushed the divider button, giving her driver an apologetic shrug.

"Fuck it. I need some farewell nooky. Fucking Africa." Rikki ripped off her shirt and pulled up her skirt in one swoop, all the while nodding toward the chauffeur. "That's one of the perks of hiring friends. Lois has seen us naked before."

"Not in the back seat of the company limo."

Rikki straddled her partner's lap, reaching for Sara's hand. "Touch me, baby."

As Sara let Rikki guide her to the desired spot between her legs she couldn't help but wonder where her lover's ardor had been the night before. Their layover, after the six-hour flight from New York, hadn't been as intimate as Sara would've liked. Rikki insisted on spending the evening at the Lair, a new lesbian hot spot, instead of enjoying the romantic farewell dinner at home that Sara hoped for. She acceded to Rikki's wishes, again.

Sara eased her fingers inside Rikki's hot opening and was amazed, as always, at how wet and ready she was. Rikki's head rolled back and forth with Sara's touch, her long blond hair sliding across her perky breasts like a windblown scarf. Grinding into Sara's palm, Rikki squeezed her own breasts and pinched the nipples until she screamed. Rikki would come in a few seconds, and Sara wondered, not for the first time recently, why Rikki needed her at all. She was quite adept at satisfying herself, or if rumors could be trusted, at finding someone to do it for her in Sara's absence.

But Sara chose not to believe the rumors. She and Rikki had been together nine months and were considering a more permanent commitment. Part of that commitment included buying a home and eventually becoming partners in the business, so trust was paramount. Rikki hated being alone, but Sara had to believe she would honor their relationship.

"Oh, yesss, baby, yes, that's it." Rikki slid her sex across Sara's hand one final time and collapsed against her. "You're so damn good."

Before Sara could respond, Rikki was getting dressed. She paused as if reconsidering, then unenthusiastically reached for the buttons on Sara's blouse. "What about you, baby?"

"I'm okay. Besides, we're almost at the airport. There's no time."

She really *wasn't* okay. She'd hoped for a quiet evening, just the two of them, to say her good-byes. Sara needed the connectedness of real intimacy, not a quickie in the back of a limo. But she wanted their last night together to be memorable for Rikki, so she'd given in.

"Damn Africa. Why Africa, of all the forgotten places in the world?"

"You know why. It's the last caveat of my mother's will. I have to go." At that moment Sara had serious reservations about leaving and prayed the flight would be delayed. At least she'd have more time to convince Rikki that everything would be fine. She reached to console Rikki, who edged away from her touch. "I'll be back before you have a chance to miss me."

"Right."

Rikki wiped a circle on the steamy window and stared into the darkening London sky with a pouty look. She was distancing. Being unattended for any length of time was abandonment and grounds for just about anything. That's how she justified her bad behavior.

"I asked you to come. Remember?"

"Right, as if. Besides, what the hell would I do in the middle of the desert with no running water or air-conditioning?"

"You're being melodramatic. I'll send you a ticket and you can visit when I get settled. You'll see."

"But you haven't been to this part." Rikki scooted closer to Sara and kissed her lightly on the lips. "I'd rather take my chances with the demons I know. Just hurry back."

"I will." Sara opened the privacy screen. "Lo, would you call the jet and give them our ETA, please?"

"Sure, boss."

"And don't call me boss."

"While I'm working you're the boss, boss." Lois smiled and picked up her cell phone.

Ten minutes later they pulled up to the hangar and waited for another downpour to subside. Rikki stroked the side of Sara's face and swung a leg over her thigh. "I don't want to fight before you leave." She ground her pelvis into Sara's firm quad. "You are so fucking gorgeous. Have I told you that recently?"

Without waiting for a reply, she continued. "You've got the greatest curves of any woman I've ever known. Your breasts are perfectly mouth-sized and my legs slide around your hips like I'm riding a wild stallion."

Sara could feel Rikki's heat rising through the fabric of her slacks. "What are you doing?"

"Just reminding you of what you're leaving—for months."

She cupped Sara's breasts and kneaded them as she slowly rode her leg. "And God, how I love it when you wear your hair back like this. You look like an innocent little freckle-faced imp begging to be fucked."

At that moment Lois's light tap on the window echoed through the limo. Sara nudged Rikki off her lap and opened the window slightly. Lois stood outside holding an umbrella and her luggage. "Sorry, boss, you have to go now."

"Shit," Rikki muttered, and rubbed between her legs. "And I was just getting juicy again." She gave Sara an evil grin. "I'll walk you to the plane."

As they approached the jet, Sara observed a figure at the top of the steps. Silhouetted against a dim light from inside the plane the person seemed almost like an apparition, smoky and indistinguishable. When she and Rikki climbed the stairs the attendant stepped aside and transformed from outline to a strikingly handsome dark-haired, rain-soaked woman. Her T-shirt looked spray-painted across her compact breasts and puckered nipples. Excess water dripped from her black cargo pants onto the floor and pooled around her polished jump boots. Even illuminated she appeared as a shadow except for the glow of her very pale complexion and the glimmer of her eyes, like light bouncing off metal.

Those dark gray eyes simultaneously captivated and startled Sara. They seemed capable of seeing through extraneous airs and pretenses and viewing only the soul. The woman's face appeared as delicate and burnished as the glazed patina of a porcelain doll. Her tall frame and lightly etched musculature contrasted to the inky GI Jane outfit to create an overall menacing image. Sara was unable to look away until Rikki elbowed her from behind.

"Sara Ambrosini." She offered her hand, which their greeter ignored, opting for a slight nod. As Sara passed the woman she detected the scent of fresh rainwater mingled with sea salt. She inhaled her two favorite fragrances and wondered how this woman managed to mix and exude them in such an enticing manner.

"Zak Chambers. Welcome aboard, ladies."

The woman's accent was predominately American with a familiar intonation Sara couldn't place. Her voice was deep and velvety like the slow beating of a skin drum, and its tone sent shivers rumbling through Sara.

Rikki's high-pitched squeal pierced the small cabin. "You're kidding, right? That sounds like a defective German handgun. Get it— Z-a-k Chambers?"

But Rikki's amusement with the woman's name didn't stop her from inching closer to inspect the goods. Her gaze oozed up and down Zak's body in slow motion, taking in every sculpted ridge and chiseled dip. "I can't imagine anything about you being defective."

"Rikki, please." Sara tried to rein in her overzealous girlfriend, whose usually lax sexual restraints had apparently unraveled. If an attractive woman was anywhere on the radar, Rikki scoped her out, even with Sara standing right beside her. Sara had gotten used to it by convincing herself that if Rikki wanted to cheat she wouldn't be so blatant.

And in this case, who could blame her? Zak Chambers *was* gorgeous—tall, lanky, and mysterious in a dangerous way. The kind of woman you fantasized about but feared meeting. Having sex with a woman like that could lead to excessive dehydration, malnutrition, and spontaneous combustion. *What am I thinking? Rikki's flirting and I'm turned on.*

"All soggy, huh?" Rikki pressed herself against Zak's side like plastic wrap to wet glass. She ran her hand down the front of Zak's chest and stopped just below her beltline. As if checking to make sure she had Zak's total attention, she then moved her hand to her own crotch. "Me, too."

Sara observed Zak's reaction to the obvious flirting with a combination of interest, embarrassment, and curious pleasure. This woman refused a handshake but allowed a violation of her personal space that was clearly intended to tantalize. But instead of slapping Rikki's hand away from her body, Zak simply stared at her with eyes that showed absolutely no emotion. Even her body appeared to shut down. Her tightly puckered nipples smoothed as if drained of all sensation.

Rikki seemed to sense the lack of effect her efforts were having on Zak and stepped back. "Do you have a gun? I didn't find one, unless there's some place I haven't searched."

"I thought this was an escort assignment, not a protection detail. Was I misinformed?"

"No, you're correct," Sara clarified.

"I mean, if necessary you could provide protection, right?" Rikki was insistent.

Zak pinned Sara with a look as convincing as her words. "Yes, I could. But I wasn't aware there would be two of you."

"Oh, no, Rikki won't be going. Only me." Sara found that idea suddenly appealing and immediately felt guilty.

"Maybe I should reconsider." Rikki gave Zak another appreciative gaze.

Sara watched Zak's concise hand gestures as she engaged in a series of nonverbal exchanges with the pilot. Then she said, "You'll need to decide soon. Wheels up in five minutes." She turned away from them, retrieved Sara's luggage in one smooth motion, and headed toward the back of the plane.

Rikki cocked her head to one side and watched Zak glide like a trained model down the catwalk. "Jeez. What a piece of womanflesh that one is. I wouldn't mind going on a trip with her anywhere. Not much of a talker, though, is she?"

Sara shook her head. "Is that all you ever think about, sex?"

"Of course not. I also think about no sex, when you're gone." She brought their bodies together and engaged Sara in a deep, probing kiss, massaging the swells of Sara's butt as she wedged her thigh between Sara's legs.

Sara had no doubt that Rikki would dry fuck her where she stood if she allowed it. "Stop."

Rikki grumbled her displeasure and pulled back. "I don't like sending you away horny, especially not with someone who looks *that* hot." She nodded toward Zak.

"Contrary to what one of us believes, lesbians aren't attracted to all women."

"You know I only have eyes for you." Rikki gave Sara a kiss and started toward the door. "I'll call you, baby, every chance I get. Love you."

"I hope that's true." As Sara watched Rikki descend the steps, she felt tremendously guilty. Before she returned, it would be clearer whether she and Rikki had a future. The private investigator she'd hired would help resolve that issue. Friends insisted that Rikki had always been unfaithful. Sara wanted to believe they were wrong.

CHAPTER TWO

Sara Ambrosini was still waving good-bye to her ornamental girlfriend when Zak pulled the hatch closed and secured the lock. One look at Rikki's long blond hair, micro-skirt, two-inch nails, and door-knocker earrings told Zak everything she needed to know. Add the tawdry seduction attempt in front of her lover and the label was firmly attached—sleaze. How did women like that manage to land seemingly intelligent lovers? And this one topped it off by bedding a rich woman. But her new client's love life was not her concern.

"Take your seat, please, Ms. Ambrosini." Zak motioned toward the back of the plane. "I've placed your things where you won't be disturbed."

"I'd prefer to sit here." Sara pointed to a seat next to Zak's rucksack. "This is my usual seat."

"Of course, this is your plane." Zak reached for her bag as Sara moved to stop her. Instinctively, Zak backed away from the gesture. It was the second time this woman had attempted to touch her. And the second time she had avoided contact. It had been impolite to refuse her handshake when they met and rude, verging on paranoid, to recoil from a simple touch just now. She had to snap out of whatever repressed emotional state she was in and get her game on. This was an assignment like any other, and the client deserved her best effort.

Sara gave her a skeptical look. "If you don't mind, I think we need to talk about our trip. That will be difficult with one of us here and the other in the back of the plane."

The request was innocent enough but something about this woman set off alarms in Zak's head. Perhaps the amber glow of her hair as it caught the dim cabin light made her appear too appealing. Or the long French braid that hung halfway down her back like a serpent lying in wait made her seem seductive. Possibly, the emerald Italian-made suit that caressed her feminine curves was just too tantalizing. Maybe it was the warmth that flowed from her dark brown eyes like hot fudge on ice cream. Or her voice that washed over Zak with the soft, soothing tide of the ocean. She stopped herself in mid-rant. So the woman was gorgeous. She'd been around many attractive women and handled herself with professionalism. Rikki was the most recent proof. But her discomfort with this particular woman was much simpler. And if she listened to her head instead of her as-of-late unchecked emotions, the reasons would be clear.

A woman like Sara Ambrosini always got what she wanted. Wealth and privilege had spoiled her for the things that really mattered in life and distanced her from other people who suffered her whims and demands. Rikki was obviously one of her entitled trophies. A woman that sexually charged, in a vulgar sort of way, constantly on the prowl, said a lot about her keeper. Sara was either a fool to think Rikki would ever be faithful or a fool who slept beneath her potential. Either way, Sara was a rich fool. Zak decided to deny her on principle alone.

"Let's put the talk on hold. I need to rest. I've just come off another job." There, that should shut her up for a while. Zak once again reached for her rucksack but Sara swung her curvy body sideways, tactically blocking her path. The cabin seemed to swallow any space for retreat as their bodies came closer together.

Fire sparked in the redhead's brown eyes and their color changed to a murky black. She straightened to her full height, which was at least three inches shorter than Zak's five-nine, and stared her down. A row of light freckles across her slightly upturned nose seemed to darken as her skin flushed. Perhaps there was more to her new client than just a pretty face and lots of money. A temper that quick usually covered a deep passion or belief in something. She waited for the eruption that followed the smoke and sparks.

"Ms. Chambers, I'm really sorry about your overworked schedule, but we do have things to discuss. I have questions about this trip, and you have been employed, against my wishes, I might add, to provide those answers and serve as an undesired, and, in my humble opinion, unneeded and terribly overpaid escort. The least you can do is answer a few simple questions. Is that too much to ask?"

While Sara Ambrosini paused for a breath, Zak replied. "No." Without seeming to hear her response, Sara continued with her apparently much-needed venting tirade.

"I've been to Africa many times in my life and feel quite capable of handling myself there. My family vacationed in Mombasa and the surrounding area. While I understand that Mombasa is not bush country, I do believe I can find my way around and communicate well enough to accomplish my goals. And furthermore—"

She stopped as if Zak's response finally registered. "No? You said no?"

As much as Zak hated to admit it, this woman would be her boss until they reached their destination, so she'd better get used to taking orders from Ms. Moneybags. And if she needed answers to her questions immediately, Zak would accommodate her. Just like the rich to disregard anyone else's needs but their own. "I said no. It's not too much to ask for information. And you're right. My failures should never be at your expense."

Her clarification seemed to take Sara off guard. The pink flush of her cheeks vanished and she heaved a deep sigh. Her appealingly proportioned body visibly shifted from fight mode to cordial hostess.

"Great. Would you like to change clothes first? You can't be very comfortable in that wet outfit. I'll start a pot of coffee."

"As you wish, Ms. Ambrosini." Zak finally retrieved her bag and disappeared into the restroom.

"And the name is Sara, please," she called after her.

Just as the pilot issued takeoff instructions, Zak returned to the cabin dressed in an outfit identical to the wet one she'd discarded. Sara was securely fastened into her preferred position by the window. Zak took the aisle seat, across from her client and the seat she'd initially intended to occupy, avoiding Sara's inquisitive look. *And I will not explain myself. Not that I could anyway. For some reason, I just can't be near this woman.* Her internal alarms continued but Zak was too tired to evaluate their meaning further. She rested her head against the seat back, enjoying the steady hum of jet engines as they climbed. Sara Ambrosini would engage her soon enough.

"Ms. Chambers?"

"Yes." Zak spoke without opening her eyes. She hadn't slept for days and hoped for a quick nap. That's all it would take, just a few seconds and she would be as good as new.

"May I call you Zak?"

"Yes."

"Can we talk now?"

The voice was tentative, quite a change from the earlier outburst. Zak reluctantly opened her eyes and turned toward her. "Yes."

"You don't say much, do you?"

"Only what's necessary." Sara studied her with a warm, encompassing stare that made Zak shift uncomfortably. The lack of rest was obviously affecting her senses, underscoring the fact that she needed a few minutes of shut-eye before they arrived or she'd be useless. "What do you want to know?"

Sara stretched across the aisle toward her, and the scent of vanilla perfume mixed with recent sex drifted past Zak. "First, I want to apologize for Rikki."

Zak shook her head to dislodge an image of Sara and her blond paramour engaged in a hot, sweaty coupling. "No need. A woman shouldn't have to apologize for her lover's behavior." Zak stopped because she really wanted to say that any woman who behaved the way Rikki did in front of Sara didn't deserve her. It was disrespectful and demeaning to both of them and to their relationship. But Zak was in no position to offer such an opinion.

Sara seemed to consider Zak's statement before she continued. "That may be true, but I seem to spend quite a bit of time doing exactly that. And while I'm groveling, I'm sorry for jumping down your throat earlier. It was unnecessary and unprofessional. I'd like to explain."

"You don't have to."

"But I need to." Sara pulled her bottom lip between her teeth as tears welled in her brown eyes. She stroked the French braid that hung down her back, seeming to draw enough distraction from her feelings to continue. "My mother died a year ago."

"I'm sorry." Zak knew that pain. She'd lost her father three years earlier, and the memory was still raw. It stabbed at her heart, deep and poisoned with guilt.

"Thank you. We were very close. When she died, she left several conditions in her will that I had to adhere to before the estate was settled. This school in the African bush is the final one. It's not that I mind honoring my mother's wishes, but I don't understand them. They seem like a series of mini tests that I'm failing miserably, like she's pushing me toward something. When this school is finally built, I have to remain in Africa to help enroll and start educating the first class. I have a business to run. Doesn't she know that?"

Zak was glad that Sara's last question was a rhetorical one because she had no idea how to answer it or how to deal with all the emotion radiating from this distressed woman. Fortunately, Sara seemed to draw on some internal strength and switched from grief back to low-grade anger.

"So I'm dealing with all this uncertainty about what my mother really wants, what she's trying to tell me from the grave, whether or not I can trust my girl—well, never mind about that, and *then* my corporate attorney tells me I'll have a babysitter on this trip." She eyed Zak contritely. "Sorry, but can you see how I might've been just a little keyed up when I came on board? Of course that's no excuse for going off on you."

Zak really hoped that question was also rhetorical, because in her opinion Sara was still more than a little keyed up. She prayed that when Sara settled down, some of the excessive talking would wind down as well. She was pretty certain she couldn't take eight more hours of nonstop chatter.

"Don't answer that question, but will you at least accept my apology?"

"Of course." Sometimes Zak truly disliked the fact that her job had converted her into an introvert by necessity. When another person was being totally honest and vulnerable, she wanted to say something comforting and meaningful. But the words hung in her throat, trapped by too much emotion and too great a risk of exposure. So she fell back on the strong, silent persona that the job afforded her.

"And I'm sorry about the whole not-wanting-to-hire-you thingy." Sara's gaze faltered and her cheeks blushed with color.

"Is it true?"

"Technically, yes."

Sara reached toward Zak, arms outstretched in a gesture indicative of an emotionally expressive person. Everything about this woman screamed honesty, openness, and sensitivity. Everything inside Zak screamed, "Caution."

"As I said, I've been to Africa many times. I don't need a bodyguard. The company insisted because of insurance liability. But I have to be able to contact people, to talk freely about their issues, and to appear at least that I understand and share their concerns. How will it look if I show up flanked by GI Jane commandos? No disrespect intended."

"But you've—"

"I've never been in the bush or around the wild animals. That's true, but how uncivilized can it be?"

"Very. You need to consider those wild animals, insects, snakes, weather, food and water issues, clothing, accommodations, security, and the political climate." Zak ticked the items off on her fingers. Sara's look was one of inquisitive amusement.

"You mean you can protect me from all those things? Perhaps I was mistaken about your services being necessary." She grinned at Zak and mischief sparked in her eyes.

Zak processed what she'd just said and found it only mildly amusing. She had to relay the seriousness and immediacy of life in Africa and prepare Sara for what could happen. "Well, perhaps most of those things are your own responsibility, but you need to be briefed and prepped. Even an inadvertent mistake could be expensive or dangerous."

Sara unbuckled her seat belt and moved to the seat beside Zak. "I'm sorry if this is uncomfortable for you, but I don't communicate well long distance. I'm from a large Italian family and we talk about everything up close and personal. Distance is a barrier I don't tolerate easily."

"I see." Having Sara so near was distracting. Her voice was like a rich liqueur flowing through Zak's system, numbing all resistance. And the perfume that wafted from her as she moved hinted of warm vanilla and sugar.

The fact that she was likening her new client to an alcoholic elixir and delicious treats was testament to Zak that she was more tired than she realized. Her internal sensors were obviously malfunctioning on the most basic levels, which was risky. She had to stay focused and remember the rules. The mission was to keep Sara safe in spite of herself, to remain objective and detached. However, like all rich people, Sara Ambrosini seemed to think the only rules that applied to her were the ones she made. "We're off track." *And you're entirely too close.*

"Are we? Feel free to brief and prep me for the next eight hours, if you'd like. But don't be offended if I nod off. Boring details are not my forte. However, if you'd like to exchange life stories, I'm all ears."

"No." The word came out with more force than she intended before she realized that Sara was only partially kidding. "Have you ever been to the Narok District of Kenya?"

"I'm not so easily distracted, but I'll play along for now. Where's that?"

Zak made note of her passenger's skills of observation. "It's where we're going. Talek Gate, to be exact, just outside the Masai Mara Game Reserve. That's the site of your school, or so I've been told. Am I mistaken?"

"No, no, you're right. I just hadn't heard it called the Nanook or whatever you said." She gave Zak an apologetic shrug. "Listen, Zak, I—"

A sharp ringing sounded from the jet's sat phone and Sara bent forward to retrieve it from the wall holder. Zak couldn't help but notice her perfectly rounded ass precariously perched on the edge of the seat. It was her job to see that this perfectly shaped ass, those luscious breasts, and that long mane of tawny red hair made it safely to her destination still attached to this highly emotional, independent woman. She had a feeling this wouldn't be the cushy assignment Stewart had described.

"Oh, hi, Rikki. It's only been an hour. Do you miss me already?" Sara raised her index finger at Zak and walked to the back of the plane.

Zak reclined the seat, closed her eyes, and within seconds dozed off with the soothing cadence of Sara's low whispers echoing through the cabin.

Mark 235 stared at her through disbelieving eyes filled with huge tears. "Why? I need you so much. Please tell me why?"

"It's just over, Gwen."

❖

Sara ended her conversation with Rikki and tiptoed back to her seat. During her hour-long conversation, she heard incoherent mumblings from Zak, which probably resulted from her high-strung guide's attempt to sleep. She'd never seen anyone rest so poorly. Her head thrashed from side to side as she muttered constantly under her breath. Sara tilted sideways to eavesdrop but couldn't decipher anything from the mishmash of mostly foreign phrases. A woman this wickedly gorgeous was bound to have secrets that kept her up at night. But she was entirely too guarded to reveal them while awake or during her restless sleep.

Intrigued, Sara scrutinized her new employee without the need for pretense or explanation. Even in repose Zak's well-honed frame appeared spring-loaded, ready to bolt into action. Her lanky legs stretched out in front of her like those of a newborn filly. Tapered hips and almost prepubescent breasts were all muscle, with nothing extraneous to encumber movement. The slender fingers of her hands coiled into fists in her lap, clenching periodically against some invisible foe. What could be so threatening that it haunted Zak as she slept?

Was it something from her past, her job? And what exactly was Zak's job? Surely she didn't spend her life escorting wealthy people around the world. That type of work didn't require any special training or skills, and obviously Zak had been part of a disciplined program for years. She had a military presence and sense of dedication. Maybe she was a mercenary on leave doing a quick favor for a friend. Sara had so many questions about this woman to whom her safety had been entrusted.

After all, the only things she knew for sure weren't very helpful. She'd been hired by the firm without Sara's input and was outrageously expensive. She supposedly had a spotless reputation and had spent considerable time in Africa. Sara had learned these facts from her attorney, Randall Burke. But Sara had surmised a few things on her own. Zak Chambers was, either by nature or design, a very private person. She exhibited tremendous powers of self-control, even down to her bodily responses, as evidenced by Rikki's failed seduction attempt. Her new escort either lived a dangerous life or was troubled by an unresolved past. Zak also seemed to have particular disdain for the rich, or perhaps it was just Sara personally. Why else would she purposely avoid a simple handshake when they met while allowing Rikki to feel her up? Though it was difficult, Sara had accepted the fact that strong, interesting women weren't often attracted to her. If they were, it was usually for her money.

But if Sara was completely honest, she had to admit she had an intellectual curiosity about Zak Chambers. People who didn't like to talk, especially about themselves, intrigued her. Such a woman surely had a lover, or perhaps several, tucked away in various parts of the world. And she had Rikki. It never hurt to look and admire a totally unattainable specimen like her new escort. Rikki would probably even approve.

Sara let her gaze travel up Zak's torso to her thick, kissable lips. They were slightly parted, revealing a tiny gap between sparkling white front teeth. Her closely trimmed ebony hair curled tightly to her scalp. If it were long, Sara imagined, it would fall to her shoulders in wavy ringlets. The drawn features of Zak's face were more relaxed than earlier, and dark fatigue circles marred the skin under her eyes. Sara wanted to brush away the signs of stress and weariness that clung to Zak's body but quickly squelched her caretaking impulse. This woman neither wanted nor needed anything she had to offer. *Remember that and you'll be fine.*

Why did the reserved and inaccessible types who had no interest in her always intrigue Sara? And how did she end up with women more pretentious than grounded, clingier than independent, and more unfaithful than loyal? A slight quiver coursed through her body and settled in her groin as she stared at Zak.

"Have you finished?" Zak asked, without opening her eyes.

"Finished?" Sara warmed with embarrassment.

"Staring at me." Stirring in her seat, Zak propped her elbow on the chair arm and rested her chin in her palm. Her steel blue gaze bored into Sara and she felt exposed.

"I thought you were sleeping."

"Obviously."

Zak smiled, something she had seldom done since they met. Her whole face seemed to glow with innocence and expectation. Sara wished she would smile more often. Just as quickly the friendly expression vanished.

"Was I out long?"

"You hardly slept at all, a bit restless. A lot on your mind?" Sara struggled to retrieve her inappropriate thoughts and disobedient eyes.

"Occupational hazard, I guess."

Sara didn't ignore an opportunity when it dropped in her lap. Besides, she probably wouldn't get many of those where Zak Chambers was concerned. "And that would be what exactly, your occupation, I mean?" Zak's initial scathing appraisal caused Sara's insides to recoil. But the look softened as she seemed to evaluate Sara for motive.

"Let's just call it security."

She wanted to ask for clarification but knew the subject was closed. "Would you like that cup of coffee now?" She rose and turned toward the small galley at the back of the plane. "Let me guess, black, right?"

Zak nodded, the corners of her luscious mouth curling slightly. "May I give you a rundown on the trip plans so you can make whatever changes you'd like?"

"Sure." Sara busied herself pouring coffee.

"When we arrive in Mombasa, I'll be gathering more supplies, checking on our flight, and arranging for transport and building supplies once we arrive in Talek. You'll have time to do some sightseeing or shopping or whatever you do."

Sara stood in front of Zak with two cups of coffee and glared at her. "Shopping or whatever I do? Do you have any idea how prejudicial and sexist that sounds?" Her temper flared in spite of the surprised look on Zak's face. "Someone in your position should be more sensitive to those types of comments. Do you dislike all wealthy people? Or just redheaded ones?"

Zak raised her arms in surrender but Sara was high on her soapbox. "Or is there something else about my appearance that you don't like, because you don't know me well enough to make such a judgmental statement."

As the startled look on Zak's face transformed to its customary mask of detachment, Sara realized she'd stepped on a nerve, or at least stumbled over it. She opened her mouth to apologize when suddenly the plane struck turbulence and pitched. So did she. The two cups of coffee she was holding flew out of her hands and onto Zak's lap.

Sara lunged forward on her knees, trying to grab hold of something, and seized the closest things—Zak's compact breasts. When she came to rest, they were so close she felt Zak's hot breath on her face. She licked her dry lips as though preparing for a kiss and startled at the thought. Sara struggled to regain her balance and release her grip, but the plane was climbing and the g-forces held her firmly in place. She cursed and blessed the laws of nature that caused this unanticipated turn of events.

Just as suddenly as it had lurched forward, the plane leveled out and she was thrown backward against the bulkhead. Her entire body hummed with a current she attributed to the abrupt change in altitude.

"I'm sorry. Are you okay? Did I burn you?"

Zak nodded, then shook her head in response, but something in her demeanor had changed. Sara stared into Zak's eyes as their stormy gunmetal melted into liquid fire. Her stoic visage momentarily evaporated into a look of sexual hunger tinged with fear, the expression so intense that Sara blinked. When she opened her eyes again, the barriers were back in place. But for a second she'd seen something Zak Chambers clearly didn't want to show her.

"I hope you've got another ninja suit in your bag."

"You need to arrange for another guide as soon as possible, Ms. Ambrosini."

CHAPTER THREE

Zak hurried to the safety and seclusion of the restroom to change, praying that the elevated temperature of her body would regulate. As she shed her soiled clothing, she scrutinized her naked breasts, fully expecting to see Sara's handprints branded there. Even though it was unintentional, that touch anchored Sara to more than Zak's flesh. The jolt that surged through her physical body was surprising and entirely too pleasant. But her touch aroused more than Zak was prepared to give, an unwelcome flicker of desire. The unresolved feelings she buried after her last assignment must be bleeding over. That was the only rational explanation. Not even Gwen had evoked such a strong response so quickly. But that had been a work situation.

Recognizing the absurdity of her last thought, Zak splashed cold water on her face. Sara Ambrosini was also business, at least for the moment. This arrangement wouldn't work for either of them. She seemed to do nothing but irritate the overemotional redhead, and Sara's openness and interminable curiosity taxed her.

Unlike Rikki, who was easy to handle, Sara posed a potential challenge. Zak was familiar with the frontal assaults of women like Rikki, with their sexual innuendos and teasing come-hither tactics. Emotions were not part of the equation and their curiosity ended in the bedroom. Zak dealt with women like this every day. Their bodies and desires, like hers, were superficial and without substance. She had wearied of the quest for physical pleasure and the uninspiring bodies and personalities that often failed to provide it.

But women like Sara Ambrosini didn't employ such blatant strategies. Her approach was unassuming, designed to lure potential partners with nurturing and sensitivity. Emotions were the agents of choice, clearing a straight, honest path to the heart. Curiosity was an endearing distraction to procure information and secure position. And unlike the cardboard cutouts Zak was accustomed to, Sara's physical form was created solely to tempt and seduce. She had curves where Zak's own body was straight and unflattering. She was soft against Zak's unyielding muscles. Her body was pure substance and, like the emotions Zak had seen in her eyes, full of dangerous potential.

She was familiar with such tactics in the context of her work and handled them with ease. But having a woman like Sara show emotional interest in her, even if it was only in her mind, terrified Zak. The Company hadn't provided the tools or the expertise to dodge such an unfamiliar and formidable opponent. Her last assignment had been evidence of that.

The long-term exposure to Gwen and their "relationship" had chipped away at the walls of Zak's resistance and left her weak. Now was the worst possible time to be sucked into another emotional maelstrom. She'd never reacted this way to someone she'd just met. Physical exhaustion during past long-term assignments had caused hallucinations. Maybe this time the symptom was physical. Whatever was happening between her and Sara, for whatever reason—fatigue, fear, or a simple personality clash—had to end now. In order to provide protection in Africa, even temporarily, she needed to be on top of her game. There were too many other inherent distractions. If Sara didn't arrange for the switch, she'd handle it herself.

Having made the decision, Zak tucked the tail of her fresh T-shirt into her cargo pants. When the soft jersey fabric rubbed against her chest, a vision of Sara's hands covering her breasts produced a moan she couldn't contain. She closed her legs to block the sudden shock of arousal and rested her forehead against the cool reflective wall of the lavatory. Zak lost track of time as she redirected the energy that had pooled between her legs to a more functional part of her body. When she felt comfortable enough to walk, she opened the door and returned to her seat without making eye contact with her client.

Sara was on the telephone in the back of the plane again, probably with Rikki, from the lovey-dovey sound of her voice. Reclining against the headrest, Zak decided to at least pretend to sleep. The flight would last several more hours, during which she hoped to rest, not be distracted, and avoid another confrontation.

"Okay, darling, love you, too."

Sara's farewell reverberated through the hull more audibly than the rest of her conversation. The small enclosure was eerily quiet for several minutes until Zak recognized hard punching into the phone key pad as Sara placed another call. She wasn't ready for what came next, even though she'd asked for it.

"Randall? Yes, we're airborne. I need a replacement guide as soon as possible. Never mind the details. Suffice it to say that it's not going to work." Her voice had an edge of sadness and her tone was more resigned than triumphant.

Apparently the other party wanted to discuss her instructions further. "For God's sake, not you too. Just get it done," she asked wearily, then ended the call and dialed again.

Sara's request jabbed at Zak's sense of duty and pride. She'd never asked to be removed from an assignment and never been replaced on one. It was like tanking the mission. She knew it was going to happen, had to happen, but the reality struck her as a failure, like she was personally deficient. She couldn't handle her *feelings* about this situation, about this woman enough to finish the job.

Sara's next conversation was entirely different. Her tone changed from strained and professional to solicitous and friendly as she shared personal stories with someone who was obviously a close friend. Zak just wanted solitude. As she sank into the haze of near sleep, Sara's voice took on a melodic quality. Her soothing whispers and soft laughter were almost relaxing, like a book on tape. Zak's eyelids grew heavy as the merry chatter continued in the background of her consciousness and she drifted off.

Sometime later a loud rumble outside the plane returned Zak to alert. The small jet bucked and wavered in the thunderstorm. She opened her eyes and Sara was sitting next to her, clinging white-knuckled to the seat, gaze terrified.

"Don't like thunderstorms, 'specially when I'm inside 'em trapped in a 'lum-i-num tube. There's somethin' not healthy 'bout that." Sara's complexion blanched, the freckles across the bridge of her nose standing out like pebbles.

"They're actually pretty safe, these aluminum tubes."

"That's easy for you to say, Ms. Ninja-Not-'fraid-of-Nuthin'." She put her hand to her mouth and giggled. "Sorry, I meant muffin. I mean nothin'. I guess several shots of vo'ka weren't such a good idea after all. Seemed like a good thing at the time."

Zak couldn't conceal a smile. Few people acknowledged their fear so readily. "Just relax. The storm will pass shortly."

"You 'lax. I'm tensed. Talk to me or somethin'." Sara poked a serious face and stabbed an accusatory index finger at her. "Oh! I forgot. You don't talk."

"Why don't *you* talk?"

"Now you've done it. Opened up that Ambrosini gas bag of gab. I'll talk your gorgeous little ears off."

She released her grip on the seat, slid out of her suit jacket, and slung it over her head. Settling back, she wiggled a hand through the crook of Zak's elbow and locked their arms on top of the armrests. The gesture was so natural and innocent that Zak almost placed her other hand on top of the joining. That realization flickered through her like a cold chill and her muscles recoiled.

"I forgot. I'm not s'pposed to touch you either." She started to move away.

"That's all right, just talk." Zak figured the least she could do was distract Sara enough to get her through the turbulence. But the tight cream-colored shell that stretched across Sara's chest disturbed her intended focus. Nice breasts were a particular fetish of hers, but these were spectacular. Sara's breasts beneath the sheer fabric were brimming cups with peek-a-boo mounds at the top, an added bonus for sucking. Zak's blood warmed at the thought and she automatically licked her lips.

"Are you ogling my tits?" The earthy brown of Sara's irises flickered with tiny slivers of green and liquid heat.

"No," Zak lied.

"Sure you were. Ever'body does. Seems to be my only redeemin' quality." She snuggled into Zak's side, wedging her breast between them. "You like me. Don't want to, but you can't help it. It's in your eyes."

Even inebriated, Sara pinned her with a gaze so intense that Zak had to look away. Maybe there was some truth to Sara's statement. She was certainly charming, attractive, and intelligent. But such thoughts did nothing but muddy the otherwise crystal-clear waters of Zak's professional life. No acknowledgment was best.

"Now where wuz I? Oh, I wuz talkin'. I'm an only child. Couldn't tell, could ya? I'm so well behaved. My parents, God rest their souls, were great. I-talian. But very un-Italian in one way. They ab-horred violence. Not very Mafiosi, huh? They were like hippie flower children twenty years after the fact.

"We always had lots of family 'round, on every holiday, every special occasion. Hell. At every meal. It was almost sacri-legious to eat alone. And we shared everything. One of the cousins got a zit, all the family and half the neighborhood knew about it. When I came out, we had a big community meetin', complete with food and drinks, to discuss it. I had to listen ad nau'seam while they disqualified every girl they knew as a potential partner for me."

The plane dipped suddenly and a flash of lighting pierced the blackness outside the windows. Sara yelled, grabbing her stomach with one hand and digging her nails into Zak's arm with the other. "Oh, shit."

"It's fine. Keep talking." Zak patted the digging hand and the nails withdrew.

"I hate this crap. Anyway, my parents made their money in oil—olive and crude. The olive-oil business was my great-great grandfather's in Italy. But Dad wanted to diversify, so he got into crude when the market was down. That was a smart move. When I was growing up, it was the thing to educate your children in Europe. I spent a lot of time in different cultures, volunteering in the communities and learning the languages."

The more Sara talked about her family and their lives together, the more sober she became, as if the memories were too important to utter irreverently.

"My dad died of a stroke five years ago. He'd arranged for my mother and me to be cared for, so we converted everything else into philanthropic ventures. I know that prob'ly sounds lame to you, but it really means something to me—what I do."

But Sara's words lacked conviction and her eyes told a different story. What could possibly be missing from this woman's life? It was perfect, by contemporary standards: power, position, all the benefits of wealth, and a more-than-willing woman. Sara seemed sad and lost in a way that Zak couldn't understand until it occurred to her that they were alike. She was running away to Africa to reexamine her life too. Both of them had some sort of connection missing in their lives. It pleased and worried her that she and Sara shared something so essential. Then she realized Sara was looking at her, waiting for a response to her last comment.

"A person should care about what they do. It helps define them."

Sara stared at her as though she'd made a unique, profound statement worthy of deep consideration. "You're exactly right."

"Ladies, we'll be arriving in Mombasa in ten minutes. Prepare for landing."

"You got me through the storm. I didn't even realize it was over. Thank you." Releasing her death grip on Zak's arm, Sara cupped her face and quickly kissed her on the lips.

Zak was so stunned she had no time to withdraw from the touch or the kiss. Both connected with her skin like water on parched sand. She wanted to freeze the moment their lips joined and drink in the softness of Sara's mouth. It was a simple gesture of thanks but so spontaneous and genuine that it registered deep inside Zak. She seldom received affection that wasn't carefully calculated for effect.

Sara withdrew her hands, bringing them to her lips as though burned. "I'm so sorry. I—"

Zak turned away, not trusting herself to speak. This woman was gently poking at things Zak preferred to keep undisturbed. Outside the window, shards of ochre sunlight sliced through the receding darkness. The sky was decorated with layers of color ranging from inky black to shades of plum, cerulean, and white. The aqua waters of the Indian Ocean appeared almost invisible under a night that refused to depart quickly.

Zak was grateful the savannahs of the Masai Mara weren't visible as they approached Moi International Airport. She could wait another day to see the country that felt more like home than her own and to acknowledge the feelings that this place demanded. Her skin tingled with anticipation as her eyes clouded and tears escaped onto her cheeks. She quickly brushed them away with the back of her hand and buckled her seat belt for landing. Even if she didn't have a job anymore, Zak would remain in Africa. She had unanswered questions and things to settle.

❖

Sara moved to her original seat and prepared for landing. Her lips stung from the kiss as she tried to make sense of it. She was prone to overt expressions, an impulse born of sheer joy at still being alive, a simple display of gratitude to a woman who knew exactly how to calm her. Rikki couldn't quiet her fears, usually resorting to shushing her like a child. But somehow Zak understood that her incessant talking would distract her just enough. The kiss was pure whimsy, so why did it feel like more?

Girding her seat belt around her, she stole a glimpse at the mystifying woman across the aisle. She hadn't responded to the kiss at all, simply stared out the window unaffected. She had reacted quite differently when Sara inadvertently groped her breasts. Her intellectual reply had been clear: *Find a replacement.* How could someone perceptive enough to intuit what would quiet her during a crisis be so emotionally contained?

She stared at the back of Zak's head as if she could absorb the answer through osmosis. Zak appeared intent on the sunrise over Mombasa as they approached the airport. A soft glow seeped in from the window, casting a rainbow of light around her. She inhaled deeply and swiped at a tear track glistening on her cheek. Sara fought the urge to comfort her, knowing that this very private woman would neither accept nor appreciate it.

Even though Zak wore the latest high-tech sat phone like an extra appendage, it never rang. She hardly spoke unless responding to a direct question or giving instructions. Controlling her feelings seemed to be like breathing. But this woman's chain mail showed scratches Sara had seen twice, and she was seldom wrong about people. What had caused Zak's uncharacteristic lapse into the emotional?

As the wheels of the jet skidded to a stop on the runway, Sara knew she might never be any closer to an answer.

CHAPTER FOUR

Royalty came to mind as Zak watched the pilot and chauffeur trip over themselves retrieving Sara's luggage. Those who orbited in the galaxy of the wealthy must be accustomed to self-deprecation. She wasn't falling into that trap, Zak thought when she stepped into the warm African air. The small dirty gray building that served as the airport terminal would be considered primitive by American standards, but it was one of the most active places in Kenya. Stalks of wiry grass stuck up through cracks in the worn asphalt, and potholes dotted the surface like a teenager's acne. Time slowed to a more manageable pace as she took in the unhurried tempo of the workers. She threw her rucksack over her shoulder and sauntered down the steps.

"Do you know this driver?" she asked Sara.

"The Mombasa Serena sent him. They always do when we visit."

"I mean do you trust him?"

"Of course, he's worked with the hotel for years." Sara gave her a look of skepticism mixed with annoyance. "Don't be so paranoid."

"Good. Would you mind getting two rooms in your name when you arrive? I'd prefer a second floor, ocean view. I'll meet you there later. I have to arrange for some other supplies and equipment."

Without waiting for a response, Zak sprinted to the nearest cab. She could finally take a chest-expanding breath without the tantalizing fragrance of Sara's perfume floating up her nostrils. As the taxi pulled away, the sights and smells of Mombasa were much the same as she remembered. The air reeked from an overtaxed septic system, too many bodies too close together, and the lingering smoke of burning wood. Smells void of temptation. This island of seven hundred thousand inhabitants bristled with activity, especially around the resort areas and the busy import/export docks.

Snippets of conversations in Swahili, Arabic, Chinese, and Italian drifted into the vehicle. The blend of distinctive dialects comforted Zak with its familiarity, but at the same time disturbed her as she recalled the history of dissidence that remained an intangible undercurrent between these peoples. But Africa was a continent of contrasts, conflicts, and contradictions.

Zak remembered the hot and cold exchanges with Sara on the plane. Did her soon-to-be-ex client find everyone as difficult to get along with, or was Zak the problem? Leaving her at the airport with a half-assed explanation certainly wouldn't help. But Zak couldn't tell Sara that she'd left the Serena Mombasa Resort persona non grata after a business stay three years ago. That would require more information than Zak was at liberty to divulge. She couldn't, shouldn't, and wouldn't tell Sara Ambrosini many things. Rule number one of the Company: Don't admit anything, don't imply anything, *don't say anything.* The less Sara knew the safer they'd both be. That thought saddened Zak as she looked out the car window and another piece of her soul locked down.

The cab driver inched along streets lined with shanty shops displaying everything from live chickens to trinkets for sale. Aggressive salesmen bled over into the narrow road, making two-way vehicular traffic precarious. A young girl ran alongside their vehicle. "Madam, look. You buy. Twenty dollars American." The child waved a fistful of bead necklaces, a broad smile lighting her dark features.

Zak handed her several bills, waved off the tendered item, and watched her run ahead to the car in front of them. She admired the ingenuity and determination of the African people. Children in this culture had family jobs by the age of six. Their chores, carrying water for the garden, pulling weeds, or herding goats, often contributed to the household income and strengthened familial and communal ties so vital to their traditions.

Memories of her family's annual working vacations in Africa when she was a child tightened her chest with feelings she had not allowed to surface in years. She and her parents had interacted like the components of a precision instrument. She had calmed and distracted the children who came to her father's makeshift clinic while he and her mother tended to their medical needs. Her role had seemed so vital that she'd briefly considered following her father into medicine.

But she succumbed to the Company's aggressive recruiting efforts, promises of worthwhile causes, travel, and generous bonuses. After her employment, her relationship with her parents had disintegrated. She had to keep her visits brief between assignments in out-of-the-way destinations to keep everyone insulated and safe. The closeness they shared slowly eroded through the years. Since her father's death she had seen her mother only twice. Back in this country, she felt the loss more profoundly and painfully.

"Where we go now, madam?"

The cab driver had stopped in the middle of the street and was waiting for Zak's instructions. She gave him their next stop and for several more hours she begged, bargained, bribed, or bought the remainder of the items on her procurement list. By midafternoon she returned to the hotel, satisfied that she'd done everything possible to make Sara's trip inland successful.

As Zak slipped into the Serena Mombasa Hotel, she took in the Swahili village resort with whitewashed walls and mangrove-beam trim nestled among gardens filled with bougainvilleas. The setting was ideal for relaxation and romance. Unfortunately, her mission didn't include either. Dodging eager employees, she made her way through the lobby toward the poolside restroom. She changed into a pair of shorts with her T-shirt, took off her boots, and grabbed a bottle of sparkling water and a *Daily Nation* newspaper on her way to the beach.

She dropped her bag against the trunk of a coconut palm, dug her toes into the warm sand, and sprawled back. As soon as she settled, local entrepreneurs swarmed her like mosquitoes. Everybody had something to sell. She waved them off and immediately regretted it. She wanted to help them all, but the entire balance of her well-stocked bank accounts wouldn't dent Africa's financial inequity. When the natives lost interest, she looked at her surroundings for the first time in appreciation instead of reconnoitering or evaluating it.

Warm salty air swept across her and brought with it the pungent aroma of fish and seaweed. The variegated turquoise hues of the Indian Ocean stretched before her, and lateen-rigged dhows bobbed lazily, waiting for their next passengers. Tourists wobbled back and forth atop camels that ferried them along the shoreline.

Windsurfers sliced across the surface of the sparkling water like gulls diving for prey. One woman in a bright green bikini that almost blended with the watery background caught her attention. She flexed and extended gracefully with the breaking waves as the wind and spray lapped at her shapely body. Such strength and control weren't easy to acquire. This woman had obviously worked hard to master the sport. Zak watched as the surfer made a few more laps then sailed toward shore.

As she got closer, Zak realized the woman was Sara Ambrosini. She beached her board and bent over to lower it onto the sand. Her bathing suit was practically see-through, but Zak didn't need transparency to appreciate the full breasts and round hips she'd admired on the plane. One more degree of tilt and those luscious mounds would tumble from her bikini top and entertain the entire resort. A slow burn started in Zak's lower abdomen and blazed between her legs. She kicked at the sand covering her toes and cursed her weakness. Couldn't Sara be more discreet? Zak had learned to slip through the world comfortable in its shadows, but obviously *low-key* didn't fit Sara's job description. She couldn't afford to be seen with Sara, or at least not be seen as too familiar with her.

Zak opened her newspaper and hid behind the pages, hoping Sara hadn't spotted her. She scanned the front page, then skipped to the local section, mindlessly skimming until a bold headline caught her attention. TITUS WACHIRA TO HEAD NAROK DISTRICT. The stirrings of arousal she'd felt watching Sara turned to irritation as she read the article.

She had seen no news of Wachira in three years, even though she'd asked her contacts for periodic updates. She thought of him every day, this man she blamed for her father's death. The fact that Wachira was not only still on the police force, but being promoted, gouged at a sore spot in her chest.

The pain she associated with this country still existed, fresh and bottomless. It swept through her like a wildfire on the arid savannah. She crumpled the edges of the paper in her fists and ripped it apart.

"Bad news?" Sara stood in front of her, water dripping from her and dimpling the sand around her feet.

Zak jumped up so quickly that Sara backed away. "Where's my room?"

"Room 210, facing the ocean, as requested."

"Can I have the key, please?"

"Well, here's what I was thinking." Sara moved into Zak's body space and leaned in as if she intended to whisper some state secret. "Why don't we enjoy the beach for the rest of the afternoon? I'll even challenge you to a windsurfing race, if that'll make it more appealing. Competition seems like your kind of thing. Then we could have dinner in the open-air restaurant. They have live music. Sound good?"

"Can I just have the key?" Why was a simple question so hard for this woman to answer?

The enthusiasm that had brightened Sara's sun-kissed face disappeared. "I just thought since we're only here for the night, we could enjoy it."

"The key." Their exchange had started to attract attention that Zak couldn't afford.

"It's at the desk along with my luggage and purse."

"You left your purse at the desk, unattended?"

"What's with you? The desk clerk knows me and is watching my stuff. I was anxious to get in the water, so I changed at the poolside restroom. I'll go get the key and meet you at the room."

"Fine, and try to be more careful. We're not in Kansas anymore."

As Zak headed toward the row of flat-topped buildings, her temper began to cool. She'd overreacted after reading the article and taken it out on Sara. Such behavior was uncharacteristic, not to mention unprofessional. And the disappointment on Sara's face bothered Zak more than it should. Maybe she'd try to make amends later. After all, Sara wasn't to blame for the emotional baggage Zak had schlepped back to Africa.

❖

"And after tomorrow, I won't be your problem anymore," Sara mumbled as she watched Zak slink around the side of the building like a stalker. She picked up the crumpled paper Zak had been reading and scanned the pages. When she didn't find anything noteworthy, she dropped it into a trash can on her way to the office. A few minutes later she was checked in and following the bellhop to her room.

When the hotel employee left, Zak stood at the top of the stairs next to their rooms. She had an unnerving habit of disappearing and reappearing without warning. "Here's your key." Sara handed it to her without further comment and started to close the door, but Zak stuck her foot out to stop it.

"I was wondering if you'd be interested in having dinner together in your room. It has a great ocean view and we can probably even hear the music from there."

Sara stared at her in disbelief. Zak had dismissed her like an irresponsible child and now wanted to have dinner. Part of her wanted to scream, "Hell no." Instead, she heard herself say, "Sure."

"Great. Order whatever you want. I'll be back in an hour." Zak started to leave, then turned back toward her. "Is that enough time?"

"Sure." Sara closed the door and scolded herself aloud. "Sure? Now you sound like your noncommunicative guide. Why didn't you just say no?" The question returned continuously as she showered and took entirely too much time deciding what to wear. She settled on a pair of beige linen shorts and a light green short-sleeved cotton blouse. *It's not a date,* she reminded herself.

She ordered her favorite lobster dish from the memorized menu and wondered what Zak would choose. In ninja mode she could probably gnaw through the elaborately hand-carved wooden door without difficulty. But she had no idea what Zak would prefer in a more conciliatory frame of mind. Sara finally settled on surf and turf with salad.

While she waited for room service, Sara dialed Rikki's cell. The background noise was so loud when she answered that Sara couldn't hear her at all. "Rikki? Rikki, are you there?"

"Yeah, baby. I'm here. What's up?"

"I can barely hear you. It sounds like a party. Where are you?" There was a long pause.

"I'm at Lois's house. She had a few people over. Wait a second while I step outside." The noise lessened a bit.

"I'm surprised Lois hasn't run you out. It's after one in the morning there." Sara thought her driver was more responsible. She'd never known her to entertain so late on a work night.

"It probably won't be long. Has that gorgeous bodyguard hit on you yet?"

Surprise and something else quivered through Sara as she considered the question. "Don't be ridiculous."

"Then she's not as smart as I thought. Hey, baby, can I call you back in a while? Things are starting to break up."

"Yeah, I'm about to have dinner but I'll be free after that."

"Okay, love ya."

Sara started to answer but the line went dead. "Love ya, too." She understood that Rikki didn't like to be alone, but why couldn't she occupy her time with family or volunteer or just read a book? Why did everything have to be a party? But that just wasn't Rikki, and Sara had accepted that fact, more or less. She moved to the balcony and let the ocean breeze take her memory back.

The last time she was here was with her mother a year ago to review recommendations for the location of the school. Instead of making site visits, her mother insisted on using a group of developers and advisers familiar with the interior of the country. The hands-off approach should have been Sara's first indication of a problem. But her mother assured Sara that everything was fine. During their stay, her energy was low, her conversations more introspective, and her attention to Sara too motherly. Why hadn't she recognized that her mother was ill, dying of cancer? With classic Ambrosini stubbornness, she chose to fight the illness alone and without extraordinary measures. She simply wanted to live her life to the fullest until the end.

That was the type of determination that drove Sara every day. The desire to honor her parents by living a full and happy life colored everything she touched. It made her impatient with excuses and negativity, hungry for the passion and excitement of life, and generous with her time and money. She wondered about her relationship with Rikki and how it figured into her life plan. She was certainly not Sara's usual type, a bit too femme and way too flighty. Their super-sexual but substantively void arrangement wasn't what she'd envisioned either. But Sara's type hadn't worked out and she'd purposely deviated, hoping for another outcome. She walked back into the room, telling herself that her decreasing satisfaction with Rikki had nothing to do with her increasing fascination with Zak Chambers.

A triple tap announced the arrival of her dinner companion. Sara opened the door and felt her mouth drop open. Zak stood in the soft light of the Arabic lanterns that lined the walkway wearing a pair of faded jean shorts and a turquoise tank top that made her skin seem more lustrous and her eyes sparkle with reflected color. She had been attractive in her stark black outfits, but Sara was not prepared for the unassuming beauty that stood before her. "You're gorgeous." The look in Zak's eyes confirmed that she'd spoken her last thought. "It's my curse for being an extrovert. Whatever comes up comes out."

Zak smiled. "May I?" She motioned toward the room.

Sara realized she'd been standing in the doorway staring shamelessly for several minutes. She blushed and stepped aside. "Of course, I'm sorry. I say that to you a lot, don't I?"

"The gorgeous part or the sorry part?"

"Now you're teasing me." Sara liked the easy banter and Zak's broad smile. It transformed her face from a mask of worry to a relaxed visage of glowing skin and dancing eyes. "The sorry part. I spend a lot of time asking people for their money, so apologizing comes naturally." She waved Zak in and watched her strut toward the lanai. "Dinner should be here shortly." As if on cue, another knock sounded at the door, and within minutes dinner was set up on the balcony overlooking the ocean.

When Zak pulled out her chair and waited for her to be seated, Sara found her action gallant and romantic. Such a simple gesture, but it seemed intimate in a way she'd never felt with Rikki. Maybe because she hadn't considered Zak Chambers in any context other than a hired, unsociable nuisance. She had a gentleness, another layer beneath the deliberately fashioned façade. A pang of guilt reminded her of Rikki as Zak filled their glasses with wine.

"Thank you for doing this," Zak said, as she dug into her salad with gusto.

"My pleasure," Sara replied, noting that it felt exactly like that. She wanted to ask why Zak had suddenly invited her for dinner but decided it was enough that she had. Besides, she was certain she wouldn't answer the question anyway. As the meal progressed Zak seemed content to let the entire evening pass in silence. But Sara wanted to know many things, and she didn't waste opportunities.

"Is everything ready for the trip inland?"

"Yes."

"Did you find all the supplies?"

"Yes."

This wasn't working the way she'd hoped. "Is there anything I need to know?"

"No."

These monosyllabic responses were starting to annoy Sara. Perhaps a change in strategy. "Can I ask a question? I know, that's what I've been doing."

"Sure."

"What was so upsetting in the newspaper today?"

Bingo. The lines along Zak's jaw tightened as she slowly rested her fork on the side of her plate. "There might be a slight problem at the site. Nothing for you to worry about. I'll brief the new guide when he arrives."

Sara's temper rose at the dismissive remark. "Ms. Chambers, I'm not some uneducated debutante who needs to be protected from the truth. This is my project, my work, we're talking about and I expect to be fully informed of any possible complications. And furthermore, I'm really tired of these unilateral decisions you've been making on my behalf. It's bad enough that you've decided to leave without any real justification—unless you consider accidental touching a terminal offense. If it affects me or this project, I expect to be consulted. Can you understand and accept that?"

"Yes." The gentleness Sara had seen earlier vanished, replaced by a piercing, unemotional stare.

"So? What's the potential problem?"

"A government official could cause trouble."

"Titus Wachira?"

"What do you know of Wachira?"

"You're not the only one who can read."

The expression on Zak's face became more earnest as her brow furrowed and the crow's-feet around her eyes deepened. "You have to promise that you won't engage Wachira for *any* reason."

"What's so terrible about him? He's just a cop."

"At best Wachira is a corrupt, self-serving bureaucrat. At worst he has deadly potential. He's without morals, dangerous. Take your pick, just promise me, please."

The urgent tone of Zak's request touched Sara. There was obviously history between the two, and it felt more personal than professional. "I promise to *try*. Guess I'll have to find a way around him if he tries to disrupt plans for the school."

"Has anyone ever accused you of being stubborn?"

"I prefer to call it resilient. It's another family curse, sort of like blurting whatever comes to mind." Sara hoped her teasing would distract Zak from the touchy subject of Wachira.

"That's as close to a promise as I'll get from you, isn't it?" Zak cut off a hefty slice of steak, stuck it in her mouth, and chewed like she was trying to digest nails.

"Yes." The tension in Zak's body vibrated from her as she sat rigidly in her chair, pushing food around on her plate that she probably wouldn't eat. Sara wanted to lighten the mood and see that stunning smile again. She poured them another glass of wine and asked, "Where did you get the name, Zak? Is there some long family story behind it?"

Zak was quiet for a few minutes, her face a study in conflict. Sara was patient, giving her most reassuring smile. "My father had a twisted sense of humor. The Bible-thumpers passing through Kenya were studying the Old Testament book of Zechariah when I was born. He insisted on naming me Zakaria. It has some connection to God and being called."

"It suits you, sort of old soul and worldly at the same time." Sara felt a sense of accomplishment at having finally tweezed one morsel of personal information out of Zak. She tried her luck again. "Have you been to Mombasa before?"

"Yes."

"Business or pleasure?"

"Boring business. Why don't you tell me about your favorite visit here?"

They were back to one-word answers and diversions. But if a recitation of her times in Mombasa would relax Zak and open her up a bit more, Sara would happily recount her entire childhood.

"It would be a toss-up between my seventh and twenty-fourth birthdays. When I was seven, my father taught me to windsurf. He said I was a natural. I had this amazingly powerful perception of controlling the elements when I was out there. I still feel that rush on the water. It's the only time I feel in control of my life anymore and like I'm doing something more than just handing out money." Sara stopped, unable to believe she'd said that out loud. "The curse again."

Zak's attention made Sara feel she was truly being heard. "My twenty-fourth birthday was the last trip my mother and I took together that wasn't work related. We walked around Old Town and Fort Jesus marveling at the three-foot-thick walls and wondering what life must've been like for people living there. Mostly we just talked for hours about the world, the absurdity of violence, hunger, and children in need. Some of the best conversations of my life were with my mother." Sara paused and felt her eyes mist with tears.

"Now it's my turn to apologize." Zak edged forward with her hands on the table as if she wanted to reach out. "I'm sorry for asking you to remember sad memories."

Sara wiped an escaped tear from her cheek. "These aren't sad memories. They're some of the happiest of my life. The sad part is we won't be able to create any more."

When Sara looked into Zak's eyes she saw her own pain reflected there. Those normally unreadable pools of steel blue were frozen with sorrow. Without thinking, Sara took Zak's hands. The skin she touched was warm, the muscles firm but vibrating with a current that was almost a tangible layer between them. A tingle like the zap of a static charge in winter shot through her body, leaving her warm but confused. With each blink of Zak's curly lashes, Sara received conflicting messages. One invited her to come closer, the other warned her to stay away. She tightened her grip on Zak's hands.

"You understand that kind of pain, don't you?" Before her mistake fully registered, Zak was on her feet.

"We have an early day tomorrow. I have to be at the airport at four to receive the supplies I ordered today. I'll see you there at six."

By the time Sara reached the door, Zak had already blended into the shadows. She stared into the darkness, rubbing her hands together to savor the lingering sensation of their touch. *What a frustrating woman—and I'm not sure why I care.* But her next thought caused even more discomfort. After tomorrow she'd probably never see Zak again.

CHAPTER FIVE

*Z*ak *moved with controlled precision as she inched her way toward the woman sleeping beside her. She was stealth personified. She molded her legs into the crook of her lover's knees and scooted in. The tiny hairs on her body extended as if to bridge the distance between them. Her objective was to get as close as possible without waking her, so close that the desire to touch was unbearable.*

She lowered her head and sniffed the caramel skin that flowed like topping over the exquisite body. The scent of sweaty sex clung to her, reminiscent of last night's activities. The pressure between her legs increased as she remembered their sex play. Dipping her head lower, she inhaled the funky morning breath that immediately made her crave a kiss.

Only in the pre-dawn hours did Zak allow these precious moments of imagined intimacy. As the woman next to her slept, she fantasized that theirs was a true relationship. But she didn't deserve this woman or the dream. She'd used her body as a weapon of seduction for so long that the programmed responses became indistinguishable from real emotion. Everything about her presence here was a lie.

"Are you going to kiss me or just stare at me all morning?" As she turned to face Zak the strands of long black hair feathered across the pillow and turned a deep shade of auburn. The round face, slightly flat nose, and dark brown eyes changed to a heart-shaped face, upturned nose with light freckles, and chocolate brown eyes with green flecks. Gwen's face slowly transformed into Sara's, smiling up at her, waiting to be kissed.

Zak backed away and abruptly fell onto the hard tile floor of her hotel room. She'd drifted into a restless sleep on the sofa only an hour ago. After bolting from Sara, she reprimanded herself for having dinner with her. She had issued the invitation because of guilt, and a moment of sentimentality nearly caused her to divulge personal information.

Something in Sara's voice when she talked about her parents tugged at Zak's heart. Such love and devotion was rare these days, especially in families. It reminded her of the way her own family used to be. And Sara's lack of control over her life struck a chord in Zak. They seemed to share a bond, a mutual search for the missing piece of themselves.

Without considering the repercussions, she had gazed into Sara's eyes and was torn between the need for a real connection and the fear of making one. She only hoped Sara couldn't see how much she wanted to confide in her. When Sara touched her hands, the contact registered not only in Zak's body but in a place untouched for years.

In her previous life she wouldn't have hesitated to explore her conflicted feelings about this alluring but annoying woman. But in her previous life she wouldn't have hurt a woman like Gwen either, not even if it *was* her job. While she knew that Gwen wasn't in love with her, they shared a link, a trust that had been broken. The more she put her life on hold for work, the more she felt like a Company instrument instead of an individual. Could her feelings atrophy from disuse?

Maybe her lack of sleep was contributing to this unproductive foray into the emotional. She needed to remember for just a few more hours that she didn't know this woman well enough to feel anything for her except irritation. One more day and she'd be free. Then she could sort through these residual emotions, rest, and get on with a less distracting assignment. She untangled herself from the blanket she'd thrown over herself and headed to the bathroom.

After a hot shower, Zak was at the airport by four and had everything ready when Sara arrived at six. Her client wore appropriate bush-country attire and negated the necessity for the sermon on brightly colored or stark white clothing that attracted animals and insects. The snug-fitting cargo pants, khaki-colored camp shirt, and lightweight jacket were mundane but still managed to elicit appreciative stares and comments in Swahili from the attendants.

Zak nodded a morning greeting, but they packed and settled in the plane without conversation. The short forty-five minute flight from Mombasa to the Keekorok Airstrip inside the Masai Mara National Reserve featured none of the energy of the flight from London. Sara seemed withdrawn and preoccupied. While the change was more comfortable for Zak, she was also disappointed. She had hoped their last day would be cordial and filled with new experiences for Sara. But this way was probably best. The less notable their interactions, the fewer memories she'd have to forget or try to hide.

❖

Sara watched Zak settle her black-clad body into the plane seat and wondered why she'd been compelled to touch her last night during dinner. Ever since that touch Sara felt off balance, a little confused. This detached, evasive woman wasn't like anyone she'd ever met, but something about her intrigued Sara. Her Catholic guilt kicked in and she'd tried to call Rikki back twice but had to leave a message both times. Then the reforming Catholic in her revolted. She hadn't done anything wrong. She'd simply reached out during a moment of shared pain when Zak dropped her guard.

Their connection was brief but tangible. This silent treatment must be her punishment. Somehow it seemed worth it. To look into those steel-colored eyes and know that she'd been understood had validated her in a brand-new way. But their link had been tenuous, and in a few hours Zak Chambers would be out of her life.

The plane started to descend and Sara looked out the window for the first time since takeoff. A huge expanse of orange dirt and dry scrub grass stretched to the horizon, and a herd of wildebeests ran from the noise of their engines. An occasional solitary tree broke the view out across the plains. Tiny lines crisscrossed the savannah in all directions. As their descent continued, the lines became narrow paths. She tried to find some sign of civilization as the plane neared the ground.

"Where's the airport?" Her voice sounded forced and unfamiliar.

"Straight ahead. Keekorok Airport."

"But I don't see anything except—" One of the narrow paths became a single-lane road full of ruts and bumps. A strip of packed red clay and rocks, lined on either side by a single shrub and a windsock, served as the landing strip. "Oh, my God."

The wheels hit the ground and Sara grabbed the seat arms to stop the jarring of her teeth. "You have got to be kidding." She thought she heard a soft chuckle from Zak as a wave of dust engulfed the plane. She dug her nails into the seat fabric, her fingers aching. At least if the plane couldn't stop immediately it had plenty of room out here to coast. She tried to think on the bright side, then realized they'd slowed to a stop. To the left of the makeshift runway, a concrete platform topped by a sheet of tin housed two backless benches. A rock-and-sod building with two doors advertised the facilities for gents and ladies. "You might've warned me," she grumbled, but Zak was already headed to the door.

"I don't see our trucks or supplies. That probably means your new guide isn't here either. Call your people and see what's happened while I collect our things."

"Yes, master." Sara executed a mock salute and dialed Randall's number. When she finished her conversation and exited the aircraft, Zak was standing under the shelter with their luggage, hands on her hips, looking expectantly toward the plane.

Sara took a deep breath and almost choked on the dry powdery dust that still hung in the air. The sky was crystal blue without a single cloud and the temperature felt like springtime. Two people wandered near the toilets but she could see no one else: no cars, no homes, only the vast savannah. She stepped off on the ground and walked slowly toward Zak.

"This is the airport?" Zak nodded. "My attorney said the guide should be here with our supplies. That's obviously not happening."

"What's the guide's name?"

"Roger Kamau."

Zak flipped the phone from her waistband, punched the keys, and spoke in a language Sara didn't recognize. But the intonation of the dialect sounded perfectly natural. The familiar cadence she'd detected in Zak's speech when they first met was obviously an African derivative. What else didn't she know about Zak Chambers and would probably never learn?

When Zak ended the call, she asked, "What language is that?"

"Swahili. We'll have a ride in a few minutes. I'll give you the lat and long of our overnight location when we arrive so you can forward it to the guide. Maybe he'll find us by morning."

"A ride? What did you do, call a taxi out here in the middle of nowhere?"

The smile that Zak gave her was devilish. "Sort of. You might want to utilize the facilities before we get started." She nodded toward the primitive rock building. "We have another hour's ride, which will seem like four."

Sara considered her options. "I think I'll wait."

"Suit yourself, but it doesn't get any better." She sat down on the shelter's raised concrete floor, feet on the ground, and reclined against a post.

"What does that mean?"

"Since we don't have our supplies, we'll have to spend the night along the way. The accommodations won't be exactly top drawer."

Sara sat beside Zak on the floor and took in her demeanor. Some of the tension that usually marred her alabaster complexion with worry lines was absent. But the hypervigilance of the hunter and the hunted was still apparent in her steadily shifting eyes and spring-loaded posture. "You love this country, don't you?"

"Why would you think that?"

"You're slightly more relaxed. Don't get me wrong, you're still revved higher than a jet engine at take-off, but something's different." Sara thought Zak might ignore her comment completely as she surveyed the surrounding area again.

"It's easier to see what's coming on the savannah. The threats aren't camouflaged as friends or amiable associates. Life simply consists of varying degrees of danger."

"That sounds rather pessimistic. When I look around, I see potential. It seems beautiful, wide open, and wild. I can almost taste the excitement. The people I've encountered in Mombasa through the years have always been cordial, helpful, and eager to work. Nobody rests. Nobody takes their livelihood for granted. I assume it would be the same in the bush. Where's the danger in that?"

"They can't afford to take anything for granted. They have to work every day just to survive." As Zak spoke, her eyes sparked with intensity. Her usually throaty voice pitched an octave higher and words flowed from her effortlessly. "A middle class is just beginning to develop in Africa. You're usually rich or poor, and the rich want to keep it that way. Danger is inherent in that type of unbalanced socioeconomic environment, not to mention the government's corrupt attempts to bilk everyone."

"I was right. You are passionate about this place. It's good to know you have that kind of energy about something. I was beginning to worry about your soul, Ninja." Sara smiled and nudged Zak with her shoulder. "Careful or I'll start to think you're a nice person."

"Ndugu, ndugu!" A dust cloud moved toward the platform from across the savannah, a voice calling from somewhere inside it. *"Ndugu."*

She and Zak stood and looked toward the approaching vehicle. "What's he saying?"

"He says 'sister' in Swahili. That's Ben, our ride."

The rust-colored Jeep was still skidding to a stop when a young man vaulted out the driver's door and charged toward Zak. He was tall and lanky, like Zak, well toned but not muscular. His complexion was deep brown and powdered with dust from the road. The red plaid shuka wrapped around his waist complemented his high cheekbones, forehead, and bead-braided hair.

"Jambo! You are home." He grabbed Zak in a bear hug, swept her off her feet, and swung her around like she was a featherweight.

"Ben, I can't breathe."

He released her but they danced around, throwing fake punches at each other like kids on a playground. So this was Zak Chambers unrestrained. Her cheeks glowed pink with excitement. The blue of her eyes seemed to blend with the endless sky. Her brimming smile was genuine, the small gap between her front teeth making her appear almost childlike. Vitality oozed from her like heat from the blazing sun. She was exquisite. When the pair's enthusiasm finally waned and they stood simply staring at one another, Sara cleared her throat and stepped forward.

"Oh, yeah, Ben, this is Ms. Sara Ambrosini, my client for the day. Sara, Ben Owenga."

"Pleased to meet you, Mr. Owenga."

"Ms. Sara Ambrosini. I am called Ben." The heavily accented consonants of his language sounded warm and welcoming. Its rhythm was almost musical. "Just Ben."

"And I'm Sara." She sensed the young man's kindness and liked him immediately. "You and Zak are friends?"

Zak shot her a cautionary glance, her lapse into celebration passed. "That will have to wait. We need to go." She was obviously not thrilled about Sara's question. But she wouldn't be able to muzzle everyone on the African continent, and Sara could be patient when necessary.

"And where exactly are we going?"

"To our village. You are guests." Ben smiled, his teeth shining like a nightlight against his dark complexion.

As Ben and Zak loaded their luggage and supplies, Sara thought how fortunate that she'd be spending her first night immersed in the culture. She was anxious to find out about life in the rural areas where her school would be located. Surely the people of Ben's village had retained some of the traditional ways of life, even if they'd modernized others.

One thing that had definitely not been upgraded was the roads, if they could be called roads at all. They had no regulatory markings, no names or speed-limit signs. The dirt path Ben followed was barely wide enough for two vehicles to pass, but they hadn't seen another car since they left the airstrip thirty minutes ago. Every bump, ridge, and rut in the road jarred her like a jackhammer. No spot on the well-worn backseat offered a suitable cushion. She gripped the door handles on either side, trying to stabilize herself while Zak and Ben engaged in an animated conversation in Swahili, apparently oblivious to any discomfort.

Ben turned toward her. "You like African massage?"

"Massage?" It felt more like torture.

"Yes, no charge." His hearty laughter filled the vehicle and Sara smiled in spite of her aching bottom. As hot air swirled in through the open windows, bringing a fresh coat of orange dust, she searched the vehicle's gauge panel for an air-conditioning control with no success. She was suddenly very glad Rikki had chosen not to accompany her. If the rest of their trip was anything like this, it would've been difficult to remain optimistic with Rikki's constant complaints.

Sara shifted in her uncomfortable seat and stared at a group of men stretched along the side of the roadway like a conga line. Each one swung either a pick axe or a hoe in time to an inaudible cadence. "What are those men doing?"

"Planting fiber-optic cable whereby the Internet comes," Ben explained. "Very good work. Start at daybreak, end when night comes."

"And where are they going?" She motioned toward the steady stream of people walking on both sides of the road. "Is there a festival? They're carrying bags and baskets full of things." Sara thought they looked like a colorful parade headed toward a destination far off in the distance.

"Some go to work. Some to sell goods in town. They start very early."

"Amazing. Even on Sunday?" Sara said, almost to herself.

"Every day."

When she returned her attention to the inside of the vehicle, Zak was watching her with the amused expression one might give an inquisitive youngster. "We're almost to the village."

Within minutes they arrived at the top of a small flat hill overlooking the savannah for miles on either side. Branches of thorn bushes provided a border that encircled several mud huts measuring about five feet tall. A group of men, all adorned with brightly colored wraps and beads, gathered outside the border under an acacia tree that provided the only sliver of shade. Small children chased each other inside the makeshift fence while women sat in the shadows of their huts engrossed in some type of manual activity. Sara was surprised about the cultural detour since Zak had been so anxious to get to their destination.

"We are home," Ben announced as he parked the jeep and waved his arms proudly toward the meager surroundings. "*Karibu.* Welcome."

Sara tried to contain her shock and appear gracious and appreciative as she exited the vehicle. Apparently she failed miserably.

"Close your mouth, Ms. Ambrosini," Zak whispered from behind her. "Breathe and don't swat at anything larger than you are."

She grabbed Zak's arm and pulled her closer, keeping her voice low. "Where will we sleep?"

"Ben has offered us one of his huts. That's an honor."

"*One* of his huts?"

"Yes, he has three, one for each wife."

"Surely there's a hotel or rooming house nearby. I'd hate to inconvenience anyone." Sara had been camping many times and was quite capable of adapting to most things, but this setup gave new meaning to the term "roughing it."

Zak seemed to be enjoying her discomfort. "I'm afraid not. Besides, it's an insult to refuse his invitation."

"Ebony!" a female screamed. Sara searched for the source and saw a tall, mocha-skinned woman running toward Zak with her arms spread wide. The red garment draped around her body barely covered her ample breasts that nearly escaped with each step. "Ebony."

"Imani," Zak whispered, and started running too. As they neared, both stopped within arm's reach. Imani stared into Zak's eyes and raised her hands to touch her. Zak backed away slightly, and Imani stepped toward her again. The tension in Zak's posture seemed to drain away as Imani slowly cupped her cheeks. Neither spoke for several minutes as she explored Zak's face, head, neck, arms, and hands. The gentleness of her caresses seemed intimate. Sara wanted to look away and give them privacy but couldn't. When Imani finished her examination, she raised Zak's arms and placed them around her waist. They hugged like lovers parted for too long, close and tight. The two were obviously good friends. The ache in Sara's gut made no sense.

After what seemed an embarrassing eternity, the women parted and walked toward her arm in arm. Zak introduced them, her gaze leaving Imani for only seconds at a time. "Imani is Ben's sister. Their father is chief of the village. You'll meet him later at the celebration."

The woman was even more striking up close. Though her complexion was lighter than Ben's, the similarities were obvious. Her skin was flawless, lips full, and eyes the color of a gold cat's-eye marble. Her dark hair was curly and clipped close to the scalp, similar to Zak's. And when she smiled, her entire body radiated congeniality. Sara immediately understood Zak's attraction but not her connection.

This woman's touch seemed to have transformed Zak. The stiffness that usually resided in her shoulders and back had disappeared, replaced by a more relaxed stance. The woman who resisted physical contact clung to Imani like a lifeline. The eyes that constantly scoured her surroundings for danger now rested solely on the woman at her side. Sara fought a wave of jealousy, wishing she was the object of Zak's attention.

Sara nodded, still enthralled with the sudden changes in Zak and the familiar interactions between her and Imani. Surely this relationship ended at friendship. Homosexual activities were taboo in Africa, especially in the more traditional areas. Suddenly she didn't want to leave Zak here while she traveled deeper into the savannah.

"Let's go meet everybody," Zak said, walking toward the interior of the compound.

Children flocked around them, a halo of flies encircling their heads. They pulled on their clothing and laughed as Zak and Imani spoke to them in their native language. The entire village lined up to welcome them. Zak evidently knew many of the older folks and some of the kids. Everyone called her Ebony. When Ben joined the group, he handed Zak her rucksack. She opened it and sat down on the hot ground. Children climbed on her, screaming with delight as she pulled pencils and note paper from the bag and passed them out.

With Zak occupied, Sara sat next to Ben on a thatched rug he'd thrown on the ground. "You've known Zak a long time?"

"Oh, yes, miss. She came to us as a child."

"As a child? I don't understand."

"Her family lived in our village three months every year, to help with the medicines. Me, Imani, and Ebony were very young. She is family." His rhythmic tone was friendly and soothing.

"How did she get the name Ebony?"

"Imani called her as Ebony. She must tell the story."

While Zak and Imani played with the children, Ben shared tales of growing up with a gangly little white girl as part of their Maasai family. Others gathered around and added their memories of the outgoing, enthusiastic, strong-minded child who wanted to do everything. She struggled with the language but spoke fluent Swahili by her second year. The women taught her to fix meals, string beads for sale at the market, and help build the cow-dung-and-urine huts. The men were reluctant to share their tribal ways, but year after year she returned more determined than ever to learn. Eventually she was allowed to make weapons, use the spear, and tend the herds. At fifteen, the age that Maasai recognize adolescent boys as men, Zak was finally allowed to hunt with the warriors. It was the first time a woman had been allowed to join any Maasai tribe on a hunt. As Sara listened to their stories, her picture of Zak Chambers became clearer.

Her willpower had certainly helped her assimilate with the Maasai. Learning to live off the land surely contributed to her self-sufficiency. Her disdain for wealth and possessions was obvious, as it appeared that everything she needed was in her old rucksack. Zak's love of this country and its people was ingrained in her as surely as the heat was integral to the environment. Then why the lone-wolf mentality? It was apparent that these people placed a very high value on family and communication. Maybe it was about her birth family.

"So, Zak has been coming here every year since she was a child?" she asked Ben.

"Not for three years now. Until then, every year."

"What happened?" Even though Sara was sure Zak would think she was snooping, she couldn't stop herself from asking.

Ben looked at her and his big brown eyes suddenly appeared very sad. He stared out across the savannah. "She must tell the story." His statement resembled one of Zak's evasive answers, but from Ben it seemed to convey respect. His affinity for Zak was palpable.

She smiled at him as a group of women and older men gathered around her. "Where are all the young boys?"

"They tend the herd, sometimes very far from village. Come back at night." He launched into the responsibilities of young men in the tribe as Sara watched Zak and Imani with the children. They were almost like a teaching tag-team, entertaining one minute and instructing the next. Occasionally Imani brushed against Zak's shoulder or touched her hand, and then their eyes would meet for a second. The more Sara learned about Zak Chambers, the more questions she had.

"Time to make fire." Ben rose and spoke in Swahili. The women gathered twigs and limbs from the surrounding area and piled them into the fire pit in the center of the enclosure. "Night comes, animals too."

Sara had been content to listen to stories and watch Zak as the day slipped by. A huge orange sun was dipping across the plains, painting the sky a contrast of red and blue. The vast expanse of earth absorbed the setting evenly and reverently, unlike the jagged gnawing of the city skyline at sunset. She'd never seen an evening so alive, though nothing moved as far as she could see. The enormity of the sunset nearly took her breath. As light slowly faded from the sky, the subtle shifts in color and mood mesmerized her. The sight was magnificent, and she suddenly wanted to share it with someone she cared about.

She dialed Rikki's cell, oblivious to time differences or cost. She was anxious to enjoy this amazing event with her lover. She'd never felt so connected to the enormity of the universe and wanted to experience it with the person who shared her life. With each unanswered ring, her enthusiasm waned. When the message began, Sara hung up.

"It makes you realize how insignificant we are in the big picture, doesn't it?" Zak stood behind her, watching the last glow of light leak from the sky.

"I've never seen anything so beautiful. And it certainly puts things into perspective."

"We should move closer to the fire. The ceremony is about to start."

"Ceremony?"

"The traditional Maasai welcome dance. Afterward we'll eat and rest."

Every member of the village seemed to have changed from mundane everyday wear to more colorful, festive attire while she watched the sunset. Men on one side of the fire, women on the other, they began a rhythmic humming combined with a chant and echo. The men jumped straight up in the air and the women shook the bead plates around their necks and stomped. Zak sat next to her on the ground and explained the significance of the bright clothing, beads, weaponry, and the purpose of each new performance.

The participants' bodies rippled with energy and a sense of respect for the perfectly choreographed dances. The drumbeats vibrated deep in Sara's chest and the chanting called forth images of primitive ancestors performing the same ritual. She was caught up in the culture and revelry and in watching Zak's reaction. Zak appeared mesmerized. She tapped two sticks against a stone in time to the drums and mouthed the words of both the chant and echo. It was the most animated she'd seen Zak Chambers since meeting her. Life in this place agreed with her. Sara was disappointed when the music and dancing stopped.

Then food was brought to the fire, blessed by the chief, and passed to the elder men first. As they waited their turn, Zak moved closer and whispered, "The meat is guinea fowl, so it's probably safe."

The bird tasted like roasted duck and the corn paste was similar to mashed cornbread. The meal was delicious, or maybe she was just starving from the day's activities. After they finished eating, everyone sat around the fire and sipped from a gourd that passed from person to person. When it was Sara's turn, Zak said, "I'd pass on that if I were you."

"Well, you're not me and I don't want to seem inhospitable. Besides, I want to try everything." She took a big gulp and was immediately sorry. The thick iron taste stuck to her tongue and almost gagged her. She could barely swallow without heaving the rancid mixture back up. Her face must've been telling because Zak gave her an I-told-you-so grin. When she could speak again, she asked, "What *is* that?"

"Milk and cow's blood. It's a staple and an acquired taste."

Sara felt the color drain from her face. Her stomach churned as much from the knowledge of what she'd drunk as its actual taste. She watched Zak and Imani down some of the offensive elixir and thought she might faint. They laughed together, then engaged in an animated conversation in Swahili, probably at her expense. After the gourd made its final pass around the circle, the group started to break up. Couples paired off and disappeared into their huts with children in tow. Chief Owenga, Ben, Imani, and Zak huddled together discussing something in Swahili that sounded serious.

Ben handed Zak a folded piece of paper and when she opened it, her entire demeanor changed from relaxed to anxious. Though Sara couldn't understand Zak's words, she recognized the angry tone. Imani placed a hand on her arm as if to calm her and nodded in Sara's direction. They continued in hushed voices until the headlights of two vehicles flashed through the camp.

The Maasai night watchman escorted a short, red-faced man and an African into the compound. "I'm Roger Kamau, the new guide." He directed his comments to Sara. "I've brought two vehicles and the supplies. Randall sends his regards."

After a round of introductions, Zak offered Roger a seat near the fire to discuss the takeover, as she called it. As Sara listened to Zak explain the preliminary details, she realized their association was being terminated. Maybe she was just feeling helpless out here in the middle of nowhere, but the idea of turning her safety over to this man made her as queasy as drinking cow's blood.

"Do you speak Swahili?" Sara hoped for any excuse to send him back where he came from. Zak might be annoying and stubborn, but at least Sara felt safe with her.

"No, but I don't think that will be a problem. The primary language in Africa is English."

"We'll be in the bush country." Sara felt like a dog with a bone.

"I'd feel more comfortable with a native speaker." Zak gave her a quizzical look. "We can talk more about this in the morning. I'm not feeling well." The milk concoction did another flip in her stomach.

"Of course, Ms. Ambrosini." Roger rose as Sara did and wished her good night.

As she moved away from the fire, Sara realized she had no idea where she was going. Before she could turn to ask the question, Zak and Imani flanked her. "There," Imani said, pointing toward a hut near the back of the camp. She gave Zak a look that Sara was too tired and sick to interpret and disappeared.

Zak pulled back the animal skin covering the door and waited for her to enter. "I know this isn't exactly what you're used to, but it's only for one night. The sleeping section is to the left as you enter. Someone will keep the fire going inside, so you should be warm. I suggest you sleep in your clothes."

"I'll be fine. Where will you sleep?"

"I'm taking over rounds."

"You're not going to rest?"

She shook her head. "I'm not very good at it anyway. And don't go outside the compound for any reason. The thorn-bush fence, campfire, and guards are here for a reason. Wild animals do attack villages from time to time."

"Good night." Sara ducked her head and entered the hut, crouching inside to get her bearings in the darkness. Smoke drifted up from a small fire to the right of the doorway and out a hole in the ceiling. She choked on the dense fog, fanning to catch a clean breath. By morning she'd smell like a smoked Italian sausage. To the left was a mud half-wall that partially separated the entry area from a sleeping space. An animal skin that covered the hard-packed ground served as the bed. The entire structure was smaller than her closet at home.

Sara was suddenly grateful for her long pants and shirt sleeves, mentally noting to check her body for hitchhikers in the morning. She took off her jacket and fashioned it into a pillow as she tried to get comfortable in the cramped space. Bouts of nausea that sent her stumbling from the hut and voices that grew louder and more heated through the night interrupted her attempts to sleep.

❖

When Zak thought Sara was asleep, she pulled the folded piece of paper Ben had given her from her pocket and handed it to Roger Kamau. They sat alone by the fire so she felt comfortable questioning him. "Have you seen this?"

Roger examined the paper in the dim light. "It's a copy of Sara's driver's license, passport, and social security card." His gaze swept around the campsite and back to the fire. He was clearly avoiding eye contact.

"I didn't ask what it was. That's obvious. Have you seen it before?" Roger shifted uncomfortably, a stall tactic to compose a plausible lie. These documents had been out of Sara's possession only once during this trip. Apparently the staff at the Mombasa Serena Hotel wasn't as loyal as Sara thought. "You have. Where?"

He dug into his coat pocket and produced an identical piece of paper. "It was given to me when I was assigned this job."

"Why?"

"I'm not sure." Roger's face paled. The man didn't lie well or think very quickly.

"You live in Nairobi?"

"Yes," he answered tentatively.

"Who gave you this information?"

"My boss. He works for the National Parks Service. He got a call from Ms. Ambrosini's attorney looking for a replacement guide."

"And?" Zak was growing impatient with the cat-and-mouse game.

"I guess he wanted to be sure I reported to the right person."

Zak had her hands around the man's throat in an instant. He was bug-eyed and red-faced, sputtering for breath. "I'll give you one more chance to answer my questions, and then I'll feed you to whatever wild beast is hunting tonight. Are we clear?" She waited for a nod and released him.

Roger took several deep breaths as his facial coloring returned. "Some people in government want this project to fail. This paper has been heavily distributed, warning against assisting in this endeavor."

"What does the government have against a new school that won't cost them anything?"

"They're not against the school or the Ambrosini Foundation."

That left only one possibility and Zak balled her fists against her building anger. "Then what? Say it."

"The opposition is twofold. One is a personal issue with you. Apparently you have a very powerful enemy in the Kenyan government."

"Then you're in luck, Mr. Kamau, because your job is to replace me. And your first and only loyalty is to Sara Ambrosini. What's the second issue?"

"I'm not sure of the details, but I do know the influential, wealthy opponents are land-hungry."

"Your job is to take care of Ms. Ambrosini. If I hear that you've let her down in any way, I'll hunt you to the ends of the earth. Do you understand?"

The prominent Adam's apple on Kamau's throat bobbed as he swallowed. "Yes."

"Then we understand each other. Good night." Zak walked toward Ben, who stood at the camp entrance.

He passed his spear and club to her, relinquishing the watch, and headed to his hut. "Be well, Ebony."

This was the first time since her arrival that she'd been alone, and she relished the night. As she patrolled the camp's perimeter, she rolled the hand-hewn spear shaft between her palms and remembered whittling and fashioning her own weapon many years ago. The scents of scorched earth combined with the evidence of human habitation and the layer of wood smoke that clung to the air. The sky was top-heavy with stars, their brilliance undiminished by the artificial lights of civilization. In the distance a hyena's musical whoop broke the silence with its modulated up-and-down pitch. Part of the thrill of Africa was the primal sounds of animals that survived by their instincts. Adrenaline surged through Zak's body as she acknowledged the challenge and potential this country always represented for her.

And this new turn of events was certainly challenging. She felt like she was in a time warp, living three years earlier. One corrupt man in a position of power was instrumental in her father's death. It had never been proved, but she knew it in her gut. Now he wanted—what, to ban her from Kenya, to eliminate her entirely? And what of this competition for the land? Who was behind it and why? She'd fled the country before in deference to her mother's wishes and her father's memory. Was she willing to simply leave again?

She was thankful that the decision to terminate her job with Sara hadn't been related to this new development. It was best for the school project and for Sara personally if she wasn't involved. She refused to place Sara in danger, so she couldn't explain to Sara why she would be in jeopardy. Ben and her other contacts could keep an eye on Kamau and make sure he lived up to his obligations. She would have Stewart investigate the land issue and smooth the way for construction. It was best all around that she was leaving.

When she rounded the backside of the camp, Zak detected movement inside the fence. She crouched behind a clump of thick thorn bushes and listened. Gagging and heaving sounds confirmed that Sara's stomach was still upset. Zak allowed her privacy and when Sara returned to the hut, Zak buried the remnants so they wouldn't attract animals. She was almost back at the entrance when a vehicle started and spun away, stirring up dust and rock. Watching the truck's taillights disappear, Zak felt a sense of dread.

CHAPTER SIX

Cramps gnarled Sara's legs and her stomach seized as she struggled to wake the next morning. She tried to straighten her legs but couldn't in the confined space. A strange bouquet of manure, garbage, and smoke assaulted her. Then she remembered where she was and what she'd done last night. Her mouth tasted like the air smelled, rancid and unclean. She shivered at the recollection of the foul concoction she'd drunk and the unpleasant consequences. After that, she could handle anything.

"He is gone. What will you do?" a man's voice asked outside the hut.

"It's really not my problem anymore, Ben." Sara's body dimpled with goose flesh as she heard Zak's husky voice. "Sara, are you awake?"

She mouthed her reply but nothing came out. Her tongue seemed plastered to the roof of her mouth. She grunted, "Uh-huh."

"I've left some bathing and drinking water by your door. We need to talk, soon."

Sara listened as Zak and Ben walked away, then retrieved two bottles and the small bucket of lukewarm water from outside. She downed one of the bottles immediately, feeling like she might vomit again but needing the hydration. Choosing not to consider what might be living in the bucket, she splashed the murky liquid on her face and began to wake up. She used the second bottle to brush her teeth and tongue until they felt almost normal.

The sun had just begun to finger the skyline as Sara threw back the skin opening of her hut. Muted shades of orange, pink, and lavender striated the eastern sky and bathed the camp in a gauzy film of light. The compound hummed like bees in a bottle. Sara wanted to watch as the seemingly unrelated activities transformed into the daily life of these industrious people. But Zak, her hair wet and wearing a fresh gray ninja outfit, was bearing down on her like an unstoppable freight train.

She spoke as she walked. "You need to call and make arrangements for another guide."

"Good morning to you, too," Sara replied.

Zak stopped in front of her and stared, her azure gaze sweeping over her like the heated winds of Africa. "You're pale and probably dehydrated from throwing up. Drink lots of water."

"You say the kindest things to a girl first thing in the morning." Sara shook her head like she hadn't heard Zak properly. "But back up. What do you mean I need another guide?"

"He's gone. Took off in the middle of the night."

"Kamau?" When Zak nodded, Sara felt calm for the first time since seeing the man yesterday. "Oh, really, that's too bad." A smile crept across her face.

"I assume you have a plan B since you're smiling about this unexpected turn of events."

By this time Ben and Imani had joined them and waited for Sara's answer. "I was hoping you'd stay on."

"No."

The quick response took Sara by surprise, like Zak hadn't even thought about it. "Why? Are you still upset about my touching your—"

"Absolutely not," Zak snapped with an irritated frown. "It's just not possible."

"Anything is possible if you want it to be. If I have to wait until Randall finds another replacement, we'll be behind before we even get started. Will you at least consider it? I need you, Zak."

Ben and Imani had been watching the exchange in silence and now their gazes rested on Zak. "I'm sorry. I can't." She spun and walked away.

Sara started after her, but Imani raised her hand to stop her. "I will go."

"She is the most stubborn, inflexible woman I've ever met. What's the big deal? If it's the money, I'll pay her more."

Sara asked the question to no one in particular, but Ben, shuffling his bare feet in the dusty ground, replied. "Ebony does not wish your money. She wishes you safe."

"I'll be safer if she's with me. At least I know her, a little, and feel comfortable with her."

Ben's glance shifted from her to Zak, as if struggling with his thoughts. "She knows things you do not. It is safer without her."

If Zak's friend thought she'd be safer without her, something had evidently gone terribly wrong since they arrived. Zak's previous objections to the job had given no hint of danger, just annoyance. She watched the exchange between Zak and Imani, though she couldn't understand anything they were saying. At first Zak assumed a quiet conversational posture, and then her body tensed as if she had become more confrontational. A few minutes later she balled her fists at her sides and the tones became more audible and insistent. The only sound Sara could distinguish was a word Imani used and Zak repeated as they looked in her direction. *Mpenzi.*

"What does that word mean, *mpenzi*, Ben?"

He looked at the ground as though embarrassed and walked away.

❖

Roger Kamau's departure hadn't relieved Zak's discomfort. It was unexpected but not unwelcome. Neither his character nor his abilities impressed her. But she dreaded the discussion with Sara about his replacement. She knew Sara would ask her to stay. Zak had made her initial decision to leave quickly, in the heat of excitement and emotion. This one would require more thought, an objective threat assessment, and the thing she feared most, an honest evaluation of her feelings.

This woman already stirred up uncomfortable emotions that made no sense. Her very presence was distracting and her persistence annoying to the point of irritation. But her ability to ask for exactly what she wanted, which initially chafed, now left Zak with a pathetic-puppy-dog desire to grant her wishes. Her hard exterior shell seemed to melt in Sara's company, which was a dangerous tendency, especially in such an unforgiving country. One idealist in their midst was too many. She needed to remain on point.

When Sara asked her to stay and said she needed her, the protector in Zak sprang to life. Just like in the plane during the thunderstorm, she wanted to say yes and shelter Sara from any harm. But in this case, she was also a threat. Wachira gave no thought to collateral damage. The look in Sara's eyes was warm and pleading, its draw entirely too enticing.

Zak refused and walked away before Sara could spot her reservations. But Imani knew her better than Sara and saw what she tried to hide.

"Why do you refuse her, Ebony?" Imani asked.

"I'm part of the problem now. Kamau practically admitted there's a vendetta against me. And Wachira hates me, so anyone close to me is a target. Besides, you know how hard it is for women traveling alone."

"You never cared for this before. Take Ben, if you worry. He knows the years you missed. He needs more work." She inched closer to Zak and lowered her voice to a whisper. "Why do you resist? She is like you. You care for her."

It wasn't a question. Imani saw things no one else could. She'd always had that gift. It was Imani who first realized that Zak's feelings for her went beyond friendship. Their long discussions on walks to the river to fetch water helped Zak accept her lesbianism. But her heart had been broken as she gradually understood that because of her cultural traditions, Imani could not reciprocate. They had been lovers in every sense except the physical, constant companions, confidantes, and steadfast supporters through the years. When Zak needed to escape, she often returned to Africa and Imani.

"It's not like that," Zak struggled to explain. "I mean, yes, she's like me, but—"

"Your lover, *mpenzi*?"

"No, not *mpenzi*. She has someone else."

"You care for her. It shines in your eyes, Ebony."

"I'm just worried about her. That's all." Imani's probing gaze held Zak's until she had to look away.

"Do not do this again. Do not separate the heart from the body. It kills too slowly."

As Imani walked back to camp, Zak paced and tried to make a decision. She wanted to help Sara and she wanted to know her better, but was it worth risking Sara's safety to satisfy her own selfish desires? Why did her decisions always seem to involve two choices that were just as right as they were wrong?

❖

Sara watched Imani disappear into the swarm of bodies busy with morning chores, leaving Zak by the compound entrance. She paced back and forth, kicking up a cloud of dirt with each step. Turmoil radiated from her. Sara knew Zak had a tormented history. It clung to her like the orange dust of this place stuck to fresh sweat. She didn't want to be the cause of one more problem or regret in this woman's life. At the same time, she didn't want to make this journey without her. Right now she felt exposed and alone in a country that offered little comfort. Zak was all she knew. And even with her frustrating, arrogant, and detached ways, she somehow made Sara feel safe. That was almost as frightening as any danger the bush presented.

She approached Zak and said, "I'm sorry. I'll phone Randall immediately. I don't want to cause you any more difficulty."

The expression in Zak's eyes as she turned to her was a mixture of pain and sadness. "It just wouldn't be safe for me to accompany you any farther."

"Can you at least tell me why?"

"It's best if I don't."

"Then I have to assume it has something to do with Wachira. When the new guide arrives, his office will be our first stop. I need to know what I'm facing."

Zak's pale skin blanched whiter. "You promised."

"I did no such thing. I said I would *try* not to engage him. But if there's some sort of danger, he should be aware of it, don't you think?"

"I've already told you, he's part of the problem."

Sara moved closer to Zak and stroked her arm. Zak flinched at the initial contact, then relaxed into the touch. "I need someone I can trust. Granted, I don't know you very well, but I believe you'd honor your contract. We could play this revolving-guide game for days without finding a suitable replacement. Whatever issue you have with Wachira,

I'm willing to face it with you and put the full weight of Ambrosini Philanthropic behind you."

"I can't ask you to do that. It's my issue." The cobalt blue of Zak's eyes softened as she held Sara's gaze. "I'd be putting you in harm's way. I couldn't live with that."

"Could you live with me getting eaten by a lion or raped by a marauding band of criminals? Would that be easier? I doubt it, because you like me."

Zak looked pained. "Don't talk like that."

"Then say you'll stay on. I'm not trying to blackmail you or make you feel guilty, but if it works, I will. I'll concede that I'm not an ideal client and I'll even try to do better. Just, please, don't leave me out here alone."

Zak paced a few more laps as if considering Sara's request. When she finally stopped in front of her, Sara held her breath. "I'll stay under one condition."

"Anything."

"You must do exactly as I say with no exceptions."

Sara didn't suppress a wicked smile. "That sounds much more promising than I'd hoped." Was she flirting or negotiating?

"I'm serious."

"You usually are. Very well, I'll do as you say." Without thinking, she hugged Zak appreciatively and felt her body stiffen. "Sorry." She backed away. "I'm very grateful, and I promise to *try* to be a good girl."

"Get your gear together. We'll leave right after breakfast. And I'd like to ask Ben to go with us. He has more recent knowledge about the area. Plus, he has a truck and we need another vehicle. Are you okay paying him?"

"Of course." Sara paused, wondering if his sister would be joining them as well, if she possessed some talent that Zak required on the trip. The thought unsettled her in a way she didn't want to consider. "And Imani?"

"What about her?"

"Will she accompany us too?"

"She has responsibilities here."

"A husband and children?"

"No." Zak headed toward the truck stacked with supplies that Kamau had brought the night before.

As she walked away, Sara tried to make sense of her feelings. She was relieved that Zak was staying on while simultaneously confused about her own insistence that Zak do so. There were probably capable men who could easily handle the job, but she wanted and, if she was honest, *needed* Zak for reasons she couldn't articulate. Her gut simply refused to let her go, which triggered guilt. She and Rikki were lovers and she wouldn't cheat. So why did she have this intangible connection to a woman she hardly knew? And why did Zak's friendship with Imani seem so intimate and threatening?

Maybe the heat, dehydration, and nausea were playing tricks with her mind. At least now she had a little more time to sort through everything. Zak would be with her a few more days, and she couldn't think of anything more pleasant than being submissive to the mysterious and attractive woman—figuratively speaking, of course.

After breakfast Sara tried to call Rikki again without success and left another message. It had been a whole day since they'd spoken, and that wasn't like Rikki, who needed constant reassurance and stimulation. The former Sara could provide long-distance; the latter gave her reason for concern.

She said her good-byes to everyone at camp and headed toward the truck. Zak and Ben were talking in low tones, and as she rounded the corner Zak hid something behind her. "More secrets? What've you got there, Chambers, weapons of mass destruction?" The look on Zak's face said it all. "Weapons? We need weapons?"

Zak produced a menacing long gun that looked like something she'd seen in a Rambo movie. It had a magazine hanging out the bottom with enough ammunition to clear the camp. Ben was holding a couple of handguns that he quickly slid inside the sash of his shuka.

"Have you ever used a weapon before?" Zak asked.

"No. Do you really think that'll be necessary?" Sara knew her eyes were bulging in disbelief.

"I can't take the chance. Forget you saw these. We could get in real trouble if anyone knew we had them."

"I wonder why?" Sara mused as she tried to regulate her rapid heart rate while she heaved her luggage into the back of the truck.

Imani ran toward them waving a small leaf-wrapped package in the air. "Food for the trip." She handed it to Ben and hugged him as they spoke softly in Swahili. Next she hugged Zak, but not with the chaste family-type hug she'd given her brother. Again, it was too close and intimate for Sara's comfort. When they parted, she stroked Zak's cheek and said in English, "Be well, my Ebony." She shook Sara's hand and wished her a safe journey. Sara wanted to be outraged but she had no right, and who could blame Imani? It wasn't easy to cultivate the closeness these women shared. It had taken years of God knows what to forge such a bond. She was suddenly ashamed of her childish jealousy. And that's exactly what it was: jealousy.

"Where do I sit?" Sara asked, looking back and forth between the two trucks.

Ben answered with a smile. "On the rifle, with Ebony."

Zak clarified as she climbed into the driver's seat of the supply truck, "He means you ride shotgun with me."

In less than four hours they arrived at their destination in Talek Gate, a wide expanse of grassland beside the Talek River. Sara wasn't sure how Zak knew they'd arrived since this particular plot of land looked the same as every other for miles around. But a couple of flicks on her GPS and a double check of the map seemed to convince her. The river itself resembled more of a mosquito breeding ground than an actual flowing body of water, but Sara tried to remain optimistic. At least she wouldn't be sleeping in a dung-and-urine hut tonight.

The three of them assembled a huge tent, which was to serve as the dining hall and Ben's sleeping quarters, while a troop of baboons protested the invasion from their perches in the acacia trees on the opposite side of the river. Sara organized supplies in the cooking area as Zak and Ben started erecting another canvas cabin, probably for sleeping, but Sara saw only one. It looked as though Zak noticed the same thing. She went to the truck and rifled through the remaining equipment.

"Damn incompetents. Where's the other tent? I specifically asked for two large and one small one." Ben shrugged and continued unloading the remaining supplies. "There's not enough room in the mess hall for our stuff and both of us."

A twinge of excitement shot down Sara's spine as she thought, "Guess that means you're stuck with me," and apparently said it out loud. Both Ben and Zak turned to her. Ben nodded like that made perfect sense while Zak shook her head emphatically.

"We need to ride into Talek Town and spread the word about our construction jobs. I'll check around and see if I can find another one." She was obviously not happy about the idea of spending the night in the same dwelling with her.

"What's the matter, Ninja, afraid I'll bite?"

Zak's glare said she didn't see the humor. "We've got work to do before nightfall."

They set up the camp stove and a small wood-burning boiler for heating bath water. Ben stuffed the unit with wood and started a fire, then filled a container on top with water so it could heat while they were in Talek.

The main road was actually closer to camp than Sara imagined, just a few hundred yards beyond a small incline. Like the other paths she'd seen that served as roads, this one was a narrow, rutty stretch of loosely packed dirt. As they drove toward town, small concrete dwellings with tin roofs sprang up periodically in the middle of nowhere. Children stood in bare yards wearing scant or no clothing, waving and shouting words the dust clouds of their vehicle absorbed. Older folks averted their gazes or merely ignored them.

Farther down the road, a group of people gathered around an animal carcass. Some were on cell phones while others slashed off portions of the animal's flesh with large knives and machetes. "What are they doing?" Sara asked, trying not to look at the carnage.

"A car probably hit and killed the cow," Zak explained. "Everybody in the area comes to get the meat. If they leave it here, the meat goes bad quickly in the heat. They don't have refrigeration. So they call their friends and relatives and everybody eats well tonight."

The crimson hands, slabs of raw meat, and rusty sick smell of fresh blood made Sara queasy. The metallic taste of last evening's delicacy returned as she stifled a dry heave and turned her attention to something less evocative.

She needed desperately to talk about anything except the sight she'd just witnessed. A line of old telegraph poles stood like bent soldiers, some holding their ground, others bowing toward earth. Wires hung from their tops and danced on the slightest breeze. "What happened to the telegraph poles?"

"Elephants used them as scratching posts." The image made Sara smile. As they approached a strip of tin shanties along the road, Zak announced, "We're here."

Sara studied the crude brightly painted buildings and tried to imagine them as stores. "This is the town?"

"Yep, think of it as a yard sale or thrifty market."

Ben nodded toward some men lingering in the doorways of several of the shops. "I will ask for workers."

"Stay with me, please," Zak instructed Sara as they exited. While Zak checked every building in the strip for another sleeping enclosure, Sara tried to identify what they were selling and for how much. The conversion from Kenyan shillings to dollars made her head hurt. They both finally gave up and headed back just as Ben returned.

"They will spread the word," he said as they climbed back in the truck. "Materials arrive tomorrow and work begins. Last day of rest." As Ben drove, he started singing a lively African song and Zak, to Sara's amazement, helped out. *"Jambo, jambo bwana. Habari gani? Hakuna matata."* After the first verse, Zak quickly translated for Sara. "Hello, greetings, sir. What's new? There are no problems."

She watched the interaction between Zak and Ben and marveled at the difference between this woman and the one she'd met on the plane. She was much more relaxed and animated. The human shell was filled with vitality and emotion, and she was glowing from the inside out. How easy it would be to care about this Zak Chambers. As the two friends continued to sing, the catchy tune and lyrics enticed Sara to join in. Soon they were all belting out the words, laughing and bouncing through another African massage.

When they reached the top of the incline near their destination, they stopped mid-song. Their small encampment beside the river bank was a hub of activity. Several vehicles had parked around the tents, and blue-clad police officers rifled through their supplies. Boxes had been emptied onto the ground, and their clothes littered nearby bushes like scarecrows.

Zak bolted from the truck, running full-tilt toward the officers and yelling in Swahili.

"Not good," Ben muttered.

CHAPTER SEVEN

The Kenyan police officers turned their AK-47s on Zak and ordered her to stop. She froze, realizing they were serious and would have no problem filling her full of holes.

"On your knees, hands behind your head. Now!"

Zak complied, an image of her father in the same position flashing through her mind. She scanned the officers for Wachira and, not finding him, felt a little less threatened. "What are you doing here? We just arrived. We haven't done anything wrong." In her peripheral vision she saw Ben and Sara approaching and wanted to warn them off. Sara's expression was a combination of horror and outrage.

"Silence." The lieutenant of the group stepped forward. "We know who you are and when you arrived. And we do not need a reason to be here. You are on *our* land."

Not breaking eye contact with the man, Zak forced her voice to reflect a composure she didn't feel. African authoritarians didn't like having their power questioned. Deference was the better tack and she needed to calm the situation before Sara launched into one of her rants on social injustice and oppression. "You're right, sir. But why did you go through our things?"

The man's face never changed, but he motioned for his men to lower their weapons. "We were searching for identification to verify your papers and purpose."

"If I may, Lieutenant. Sorry, I don't know your name."

"You call me Lieutenant."

Neither the police force nor the military wore name tags, another method, Zak surmised, by which they could deny complaints. "Yes,

Lieutenant, if I may get up, I'll produce my identification, as will my friends." She indicated that Ben and Sara should do the same. The look on Sara's face said she wanted to do more than show her ID, but Zak gave her a cautionary stare.

"Do so," he responded.

As Zak rose, she assessed their situation more fully. The lieutenant was a huge man in height and weight, his mass appearing entirely muscle. His skin was so dark it seemed to absorb the ebbing sunlight around him. Dark close-set eyes that showed no signs of life topped a wide nose and broad lips. This man had to be one of Wachira's henchmen. They shared the same lack of respect and human courtesy. He was accompanied by six more officers, all heavily armed. This was more than a simple document check. They were here to make a statement.

When Zak and the others offered their passports, three officers took them and retreated to their vehicles. The lieutenant addressed Sara. "So you are the Ambrosini woman who wishes to build a school for our poor, underprivileged children?" The fact that he knew this without looking at her credentials concerned Zak even more.

Sara's chest rose and fell as she took a deep breath and released a shaky sigh. Zak started to answer for her, but Sara waved her off. "Yes, sir. I've visited your country many times over the years and wanted to help. What better way than to educate the children, don't you agree, Lieutenant?"

His gaze swept boldly over Sara's body before he answered. "Yes, indeed, children." A few minutes of strained silence passed before his men returned with their passports and the group moved away from them, whispering among themselves. One of the officers waved a passport in Zak's direction and the lieutenant stabbed her with his lifeless glare. Then he spoke to Sara again. "It seems we have a small problem."

"I wonder what that could be," Zak asked, no longer concerned about her tone or its implication.

Several of the lieutenant's men edged closer to her, their posture more aggressive. "I was addressing Ms. Ambrosini." The lieutenant remained focused on Sara. "We have no building permit or architectural plans on file for your school and no record that you paid the fees to begin work."

Zak started to move closer to the lieutenant but his men

immediately surrounded her. "I get it, more cash." This had Wachira's money-grubbing signature all over it. If he could make a few extra bucks and irritate her at the same time, he'd consider it a good day.

Sara touched Zak's arm, her eyes pleading with her to be quiet. "Lieutenant, I paid the fees and filed the necessary paperwork, but I understand that things get lost. May I retrieve the copies from my luggage? I certainly want to comply with the law."

Her voice was smooth and silky like she was asking the man to dinner, not for permission to look for documents. And it seemed to be working, because the corners of the lieutenant's mouth actually turned up in a small grin. "We do not accept copies, only originals, and they seem to be missing from the office."

"Then may I please have some time to rectify the problem? I'll take care of it first thing in the morning."

"We do not wish to be unreasonable."

"Thank you, sir," Sara replied.

With a nod from their leader the officers returned to their vehicles. The lieutenant slapped the side of the jeep in which he was a passenger as they drove away, and it stopped abruptly. He pointed at Zak but directed his comments to Sara. "Get a new guide, Ms. Ambrosini. This one is a liability to you and your school." The caravan was swallowed in a swirl of dust.

As the vehicles topped the hill and disappeared from view, Sara glared at her, hands on her hips. Zak imagined one of her probing questions or long tirades perched on the tip of her tongue, but she wasn't in the mood to listen. "I tried to tell you this wasn't a good idea." She started retrieving their supplies and clothes, which were scattered across the ground. Sara followed.

"Leave it alone," Zak said over her shoulder, "and stay away from him. I'll take care of the permit and the fee tomorrow."

"I don't take orders from you, Zak." Her tone was neither angry nor critical but held the same tolerance and control she'd demonstrated with the lieutenant. How could a woman who was normally verbose and emotional be so calm? She had every reason to be furious with her. Zak placed her and the project in jeopardy and talked to her like she was an unruly teenager.

She didn't want to see the questions or accusations in Sara's eyes, but had no choice but to face her. Instead of the recriminations she'd expected, there was only concern. Her usual defensive remarks stalled as she realized the untenable position she'd placed Sara in. "You're right, but you agreed to do as I say."

"That was before I realized what we're up against."

"You still have no idea."

"Then school me. I deserve that." She followed Zak as they gathered their belongings.

"Corruption is everywhere, Sara. Just let me handle it."

Sara grabbed Zak's arm and forced her to make eye contact again. "If you won't tell me what's going on, I can't trust you or your ability to handle anything for me. For all I know you're just a white female version of the lieutenant and Wachira."

The comment pierced Zak's heart like a spear. Of all the insults Sara could use, she'd chosen the ones that inflicted the most damage. Having her abilities and her loyalty questioned was hurtful enough, but being compared with those two vile men ripped at her like an injured animal. She pulled from Sara's grasp and walked toward the mess tent. ————

When Zak entered the cooking area, Ben was making arrangements for dinner. "Did they damage anything?" she asked.

"No."

The lack of further comment was unlike her friend. Ben usually stated his opinion, and he was certainly in hearing range of her conversation with Sara. Right now, Zak needed an objective view. Her feelings about this place, about Wachira, about Sara were clouding her judgment.

"Go ahead and say whatever's on your mind. You think she's right, don't you? Do you think I should tell her everything and let her make her own decision?"

"Grief and anger blind. You forget how to be with people." Ben's stance was tall and erect, his eyes never leaving Zak's. This was his preferred method of delivering what he considered unpleasant news, with honesty and respect. "Tell her. She can help."

"I'm afraid. What if she gets hurt? I couldn't live with another loss like—"

Sara entered the tent and approached Zak, her brown eyes watery with tears. "I'm so sorry for what I said. It was cruel and thoughtless. Please forgive me."

Zak could hardly bear to see her in such distress. Sara's remark had hurt, but Sara's regret and plea for forgiveness touched Zak's heart. She was the one who should be asking for Sara's forgiveness, telling her the truth about her past with Wachira and the potential impact on the school project. She should be finding another guide and removing herself from this assignment. But something inside her refused to let logic and reason lead her. "No problem. Let's forget it. Help me gather some firewood?"

As they left, Ben said, "This one is strong," and Zak knew he wasn't talking about her.

It was almost dark by the time the wood was collected, the camp secured with the wire-mesh consistency of thorn bushes, and a fire blazed in the center of their space. They sat on canvas chairs, ate the vegetable medley Ben had prepared, and watched stars populate the pitch-black sky. No one spoke as the baboons grunted and settled down for the night and a Maasai herdsman drove his cattle to the riverbed to drink. Zak heard lions in the distance, taking down their prey. She'd almost forgotten how quickly things could go from peaceful to deadly in this country. The reality had always been invigorating, but now it was daunting in a way that threatened her professional and personal stability.

How had her past in Africa become so entwined with Sara Ambrosini's present? Their current situation was precarious and could turn lethal just as quickly as a lion's hunt. Tomorrow she'd contact Stewart and find out who the other players were in this game they'd stumbled into. She needed to know what demons she was fighting besides her own.

❖

Sara hugged Ben good night and followed Zak toward her tent. The beam of the lantern she carried was powerful and flooded the area. When they reached the entrance, Zak spoke for the first time in hours. "There's a pallet on the floor under your sleeping bag, which should make it comfortable enough. We've put a washtub and a latrine bucket in the back. Unzip the flap in the right corner for the water hoses. The green one is cold, the red one hot, or probably lukewarm. Be stingy with both. Use only the bottled water to brush your teeth and drink."

This was the most Zak had spoken since her hours-long briefing on the plane from London. She rattled off her list as she looked around the roomy sleeping quarters and waited for Sara to light the two lanterns. She seemed in a hurry to issue her instructions and leave. When she paused, Sara asked quickly, "Where will you sleep?"

"I have first watch. After that, I'll toss my bag under your overhang."

"Outside? Why don't you come in? There's more than enough room."

"I prefer the outdoors. If you need anything, just call. You have a flashlight on the table over there. Sleep well."

Sara knew Zak hadn't recovered from her tactless comparison to Wachira. She avoided eye contact during dinner and spoke only when directly addressed. Sometimes Sara's careless tongue could damage more severely than others, and today had certainly been one of those times. It was obvious how much Zak despised Wachira, but Sara wasn't terribly concerned about how that animosity might affect her project. She'd dealt with corruption in other countries and knew how to get what she wanted. Her interest was Zak and how to help without seeming like a meddlesome outsider. Tomorrow she'd start taking care of herself. At least Zak wouldn't have to worry about Sara's problems and her own.

A stiff breeze pushed against the sides of her canvas home and it recoiled with a sharp flapping noise. It echoed in the spacious enclosure and reminded her how alone she was in an undeveloped country with two strangers. She checked her cell phone one last time before shutting it down. Still no message from Rikki.

Sara took a quick sponge bath, climbed into her sleeping bag, and pulled it up around her neck. She'd been warned about the cold nights on the savannah, and already the air held a chill. Where was Rikki and why hadn't she returned her call? The wind continued its rhythmic lapping against the tent sides, and in the distance a nocturnal creature emitted a lonesome howl. She drew her knees up to her chest, scrunched into a tight ball, and imagined her lover next to her, warm and comforting. But as she drifted into sleep it was Zak Chambers's face she saw, not Rikki's.

The next morning the aroma of brewing coffee roused Sara from her restless slumber. She'd tossed and turned most of the night, fighting images of Zak and Rikki and trying to ignore the pitiful moans of animals too close to their site. She splashed cold water on her face and brushed her teeth before joining Ben at the campfire.

"Morning, Miss Sara." Ben poured her a cup of coffee from a large pot sitting on the coals.

She accepted and wrapped her hands around its warmth. "Good morning, Ben. Where's Zak?"

"Running."

She looked out across the flat plain toward a sunrise that promised to be spectacular. "Physically running?" Ben's nod and cagey smile said her implication wasn't lost.

"She runs far."

"And often, I imagine," Sara said without thinking. They watched the sun top the horizon and sipped their coffee in silence. She respected this young man and his devotion to Zak, but she also needed answers. "Ben, can you tell me anything about the animosity between Zak and Wachira? I'm worried for her."

Ben looked around as if searching for eavesdroppers, picked up a stick, and doodled on the ground. "Stories have many sides. With time they change. Ebony was hurt. She blames Wachira."

"Is he to blame? Was it his fault?"

"Maybe some, not all."

"Can whatever it is be resolved?"

"Only when guilt and reality meet, and Ebony does not wish this to happen. It is easier to hold on to the past."

Ben's answer reminded her more of a Zen koan than an explanation, but it was all she would get.

Zak was running toward them, sweat and the bright red color of exertion drenching her body. A pair of khaki-colored shorts and a tank top clung to her wet frame, outlining every nuance of femininity. Sara tingled with excitement as she stared in unapologetic appraisal, then asked, "Good run?"

"Great." Zak sounded barely winded. "There's nothing like seeing an African night change into day. It's easy to imagine outrunning all your troubles, leaving them in the darkness."

"Good luck with that," Sara replied as she started toward her tent. Zak seemed almost sad as she walked away, but Sara was probably projecting. "I'm going to change clothes and get ready for the day. Don't hold breakfast. I'm not hungry." Turning to Ben she added, "Thanks for the coffee."

She changed while listening to Zak and Ben discuss the day's activities. It was interesting to hear them talk about her project like she wasn't a part of it. But the decision she'd made last night to take care of her own problems remained firm. When Zak went to shower and Ben was busy making breakfast, Sara made her move. Her window of opportunity was small so she acted quickly. She zipped the note she'd written earlier into the opening of her tent and ran up the side of the incline, over the top, and out of sight.

Luckily the road was only a short distance from camp. The morning sun was already sucking the color out of the sky as heat rose around her. Zak had told her in one of her long-winded briefings that bus taxis on the back roads provided rides to the locals. She'd said something else about them, but Sara wasn't interested in the details. While she walked she passed several people with canvas or burlap-wrapped bundles on their backs heading toward town. Everyone smiled in greeting but gave her a quizzical look. They talked to her in English and told stories about the items they were taking to market. She wanted to ask about transport but felt silly when she looked around at the vast nothingness that surrounded them.

About thirty minutes later a car horn sounded behind her. When she turned, she saw a small panel van with people hanging out of every door and window. It skidded to a halt next to her and the driver said something in Swahili. She shook her head and asked for a ride, though she didn't see how she could possibly fit inside the already overcrowded vehicle. He motioned for her to get in and, miraculously, people scrunched closer together, making room. She wedged between two young men who smelled like they hadn't bathed in weeks. Every bump in the slotted highway jostled the passengers back and forth against each other. She felt uncomfortable as something Zak said about shady taxi drivers and thieves filtered into her mind. Sara clutched her purse against her chest as the men on either side pushed and rolled against her. At the first stop, two passengers got off and the driver motioned Sara to a seat in the front of the van.

"I am Joey," he announced. "Where you going, madam?"

"The County Development Office. Is it far?"

"No, madam, but you ride here." He looked toward the other passengers. "Not in back."

Joey reminded her of Ben with his kindness but he looked barely old enough to drive, his face round with the fullness of youth. He certainly drove like a typical teenager, however, looking over his shoulder, talking, and running people and animals off the road. He wore jeans and a blue work shirt that hung loosely from his shoulders and was long at the sleeves, making him appear even younger and smaller. She almost wanted to mother him, but a worldliness in his eyes assured her he didn't need it.

"Is this your taxi?" she asked.

"Taxi? Oh, matatu, my father's. He is sick. I drive until he returns tomorrow. Then I look for other work. Must work."

"What else can you do?" Sara thought about the school and their need for labor. Maybe she could offer him a kindness in return.

"Many things, miss, anything. I work hard. You have work?"

"I might." She gave him a business card and the young man's face burst into a broad smile. "Give me your number and I'll call you."

"Very good, miss." He stopped in front of the County Development Office, scribbled his number on the card, and handed it back. "I pick you up later. Wait here."

The small office reminded Sara of a one-room schoolhouse without any of the tools. A long table sat in the middle of the space and four people worked busily around it, each with a phone to her ear and a notepad and pen in hand. One antiquated computer hummed noisily against a wall surrounded by metal filing cabinets and bookshelves filled with loose-leaf binders. In spite of their outdated equipment the clerical staff was quite helpful, especially when Sara encouraged them by strategically disseminating cash.

She paid the fees and filled out the necessary forms again, and the clerk assured her the documents would be filed by the end of the week and her permits would be official. They even provided an expedited permission slip to begin construction since the original had been lost. Zak Chambers couldn't have done it better or faster. Satisfied with her progress, Sara asked about a place to get a drink, certain a coffee shop was out of the question. The supervisor offered the use of their break area until her ride returned.

Sara settled into a straight-backed chair in the shade of an umbrella acacia, the CDO's break area. The afternoon heat was stifling, without the slightest breeze to disperse a ring of flies that buzzed around her head. She closed her eyes, hoping time would pass more quickly if she didn't watch, then remembered that she'd turned her phone off so Zak couldn't contact her.

When the phone powered up again, she had three messages. The first was from Rikki, apologizing for missing her calls and explaining that she'd had trouble getting through. The next one was from Randall Burke, a text message with a picture attachment. His message was cryptic, very unlike him. The only thing that flustered Randall was her love life. He tiptoed around the subject like an overprotective father, not wishing to invade her privacy. He knew she'd hired a private detective, and if he was worried, that wasn't a good sign. She opened the picture file and waited for the slow, laborious download. Sara had been amazed at how many people in Africa had cell phones. She'd even seen herders on the savannah propped against their staffs talking on them, but receiving pictures or large clumps of data was sluggish at best. Her gut already knew this wasn't good news or Randall would've called and delivered it personally.

When the file finally popped open, her breath caught in her throat. The pictures showed Rikki in various stages of sexually explicit behavior with two different women. The caption for one read, "Night of return from London," and the other said, "Trip to Vegas next day." She trapped her bottom lip between her teeth to keep from screaming aloud. Tears clouded her vision and she was grateful for the obstruction. She couldn't really call what she was feeling pain, or even surprise. She was just angry for being so gullible, for not believing friends who tried to warn her about Rikki, and for not trusting her own instincts. Jesus, she'd even made excuses for Rikki's behavior, justifying her flirting and rationalizing her preference for parties over spending time with her. Was she so desperate for companionship that she'd settle for crumbs and pay for the privilege?

She stabbed at the Clear button until the file closed, then listened to her last message. Whatever it was, she needed the distraction. Anything to keep her from thinking about Rikki and her own stupidity. Zak's deep, throaty voice was too calm and polite as she stated, "Sara, this is dangerous. Come back, now." A short pause was followed by a single word, "Please."

More than anything Sara wanted to be with Zak, to hear her soothing voice tell her that everything would be fine, that she wasn't a complete fool, and that she deserved better. But that wasn't what Zak would say at this moment. She'd have to justify why she left without telling her and promise never to do it again. It almost seemed worth it right now because Zak made her feel safe and important in a way she didn't understand.

"Okay, miss?"

When Sara looked up, Joey was standing in front of her. Her vision was blurry and she realized she'd been crying. "I'm fine, thanks. Can we go now?"

"Yes, miss. You ride with me, then I take you home."

"How long?" Sara didn't really care. She just wanted to stop crying, and being around people she didn't know seemed a good cure.

"We finish when night comes. Okay?"

"Okay." Sara took her honored seat in the van beside Joey, and as he drove he talked about his family, their small farm, their cattle, and his hopes for the future. It was as if he understood that she needed the distraction. She nodded from time to time, which was enough encouragement to keep the prattle going. Shadows grew long as the sun headed toward the horizon and more passengers got off.

When the last female rider disembarked, Joey said, "One more stop." A short distance farther he stopped and seven men, older, stronger, and rougher looking than Joey, climbed on board. Sara felt immediately uncomfortable. What had she gotten herself into now? If she had the chance, maybe she'd listen to Zak next time.

❖

"Sara?" Zak called as she walked toward her tent. "Sara, the construction materials are on the way. The truck should be here in about—" When she saw the slip of paper sticking out of the canvas flap, she cursed under her breath, already sensing something she wouldn't like.

She uncurled the note and read:

Zak,
    I've gone to take care of the fees and permits. Will be

back soon. Wait for the materials as you've planned. Don't
worry. And don't be mad.
    Sara

Waving the note in the air, she asked Ben, "Did you know about this? Did she talk to you about it this morning?"

He shook his head.

"She's gone—to take care of things herself. I've never met such a stubborn and independent woman. How did I get into this mess?"

"You chose it."

Zak read the note again, hoping it might give her a clue of what Sara had been thinking. "She doesn't know anything about the country—how to travel, who to contact, nothing."

"I believe Miss Sara is strong. She will find her way."

Zak grabbed a small backpack, filled it with bottled water and snacks, and threw it over her shoulder. "Well, I don't plan to sit here all day and hope for the best. I'm going after her. Will you be okay waiting for the building materials?"

Ben nodded and started to say something else.

"I know what you're thinking. If I'd told her the truth, this might not have happened. I'm not so sure."

"I will call when she returns." Ben gave her one of his you-don't-know-anything-about-women looks and returned to his breakfast cleanup.

Zak mumbled under her breath as she climbed into the truck and drove toward the road. "With my luck she's gotten a ride in a matatu and has already been robbed, assaulted, and dumped by the side of the road."

She drove over the rutted roads like she was on a racetrack, the truck bouncing from side to side. She focused on the path ahead of her, scanning the savannah for any conveyance that might have given Sara a ride. It had been just over an hour since she left, but many things could happen in Africa in that time. Why didn't Sara trust her or at least respect the warnings she'd given her?

Zak had been very specific about the dangers of riding in a matatu, the small vans that teenagers and unlicensed taxi drivers used. These people were reckless and their vehicles had not been inspected for proper equipment to transport passengers. Often the drivers operated while dangerously overloaded just for more money. To make matters worse, thieves and rapists utilized the matatu to find victims. The papers were full of these incidents daily.

Worst-case scenarios played in Zak's mind as she veered off the road to dodge a goat. If anything happened to Sara, she'd never forgive herself. The woman was a royal pain in the ass, but she wasn't quite the spoiled rich girl Zak dubbed her when they met. She'd proved that she wasn't just a pretty face. Sara didn't back down from a challenge and she didn't expect other people to handle her problems. And if her interaction with the police lieutenant was any indication, Sara was also a pretty good negotiator. She read people very well, too well in some instances.

Zak remembered their plane ride from London, and a wave of anxiety and desire swept through her like heat bouncing off the plains. She didn't understand what about this woman captivated her. She'd tried to blame her response on lack of sleep and residual feelings about the assignment with Gwen, but neither of those rang true. But she had to find Sara and keep her safe.

Her phone rang and she grabbed it, praying Ben was calling to report that Sara had returned. Captain Stewart's gravelly voice killed that hope.

"Ebony, how are things going?"

"Uh, well."

"That good, huh? I heard this girl was a handful. As long as you haven't lost her in the bush country." Zak used her customary silence and waited for Stewart to fill the gap. "Anything I can do for you?"

"As a matter of fact, yes. There's some sort of rivalry for land in this area. Sara, I mean, Ms. Ambrosini, believes she has permission to build her school here, but that may not be the case. Can you have someone look into it and get back to me? It's possible the dispute is between two corporations with ties to the government."

"This is supposed to be a pie job. What have you gotten yourself into?"

"I'm not sure yet. We've already had the fees, plans, and permits mysteriously disappear, along with a visit from a hefty police squad."

Silence on Stewart's end indicated that Zak had provided too much information. "Is this related to your past with a certain police commander?"

"I hope not, but it's possible."

Stewart cleared his throat with a rumble Zak had come to recognize as a precursor to an attempt at authority. "Do I need to replace you? You're not exactly objective when it comes to Wachira."

"I'm fine, really. Just get back to me soon with the information. And thanks, Captain."

Stewart disconnected without further comment, but Zak had a feeling her cushy escort job had just been upgraded to active-case status. She wasn't sure how she felt about Sara, but she wasn't happy about having her involved in any aspect of a Company mission. Zak checked the County Development Office for Sara first. The painstaking task of retrieving information from a clerk, who referred her to her boss, who had to get permission from another boss, took far longer than Zak imagined. She had to wait until after the lunch break for verification that Sara had been in and even longer to confirm that she had refiled the architectural plans, resubmitted the necessary permits, and paid the fees. Each step of the process involved another clerk. No one knew how she arrived or left.

Next she staked out the police station, choosing to observe from a distance instead of go inside. She wasn't ready to face Wachira and didn't want to further jeopardize Sara or her work. The small strip of stores near the station had very little activity and no one who even slightly resembled her wayward charge. Her patience wearing thin, she called the police station and asked if Sara had been arrested. The officer who answered gave her an ominous reply, "Not yet."

She called the hospitals close enough to serve the area, but Sara had not been treated or admitted. What good was it to be part of an international group of spooks if she couldn't find one missing woman? She could have Stewart access Sara's sat phone and get a location. But that would require giving her boss more information than she wanted. It was best to handle this one alone. Besides, she'd called her phone and it went straight to voicemail. She'd probably turned it off, in which case a locator wouldn't help. And it wasn't like she was trying to find someone in New York City or London. There were only so many places a lone white female could go. Eventually someone would notice her and Zak would get word. As long as she wasn't hurt. The thought made her stomach lurch.

It was late afternoon and the sun was already low in the sky when she started driving back to the campsite. Ben hadn't called, which meant Sara hadn't returned. How could she go back without her, without any idea where she might be or if she was okay? The restraint that had kept her calm throughout the day slipped, and Zak felt something akin to loss. She hadn't allowed that feeling in years. It was suddenly too fresh and too powerful. She stopped in the middle of the road and pounded the steering wheel until the pain inside changed to rage. Anger, she could handle. Anger was easy. It swept through her, consuming everything except the destructive urges to lash out, contain, and deny.

Zak had no idea how long she sat in the roadway willing herself to bury the emotions Sara Ambrosini had forced back into her consciousness. In three years no one had elicited such a response. No one had come close to breaking the code that gave access to her feelings. How had Sara gotten so close so quickly and, more importantly, without her permission? But Sara obviously didn't require her permission. It seemed that she came and went at will—into Zak's professional life, into her African world, into her thoughts, deeper into her life—and then out. Where was she?

As dusk milked the last rays of light from the sky, Zak cranked the truck and started again toward camp. She had no idea how to face Ben with the news about Sara. He thought Zak was capable of anything. And what would she say to Randall Burke about losing his benefactor? When she topped the hill overlooking their tent site, Zak slammed on the brakes and the truck skidded in the sand before stopping too close to the Talek River.

Sara and Ben stood in front of a large fire surrounded by a group of men who were shouting and waving their arms. Zak's instincts took over. Her friends were in danger.

CHAPTER EIGHT

Sara watched Zak slide out the driver's side of the truck and roll into the bushes. The long rifle she kept behind the truck seat was slung over her shoulder. She wasn't sure if Ben saw Zak snaking through the underbrush like a commando, but she needed to warn the men who stood around her before—

The rat-a-tat of automatic-weapon fire echoed through the darkening sky. "Hands up," Zak ordered.

The group of startled men did as they were told while Ben and Sara just stared and shook their heads.

"What?"

"Put the weapon away, GI Jane," Sara said. "They come in peace." She couldn't imagine Zak acting so irrationally. The woman she'd met on the plane was calm and cool under the worst of circumstances, but twice since they'd arrived in Africa, Zak had overreacted. Was she trying to protect her? The thought warmed and confused Sara, but right now it looked like Zak wanted to kill her.

"Who are these people, Ben?" Zak asked.

"Miss Sara found them to help with the school." He waved his arms toward the group. "They need work, Joey and his friends."

"Where are the building materials?" Zak still addressed Ben, refusing to look at Sara.

"Truck broke down. Be here tomorrow."

"I'm sorry." Zak directed this comment toward the puzzled-looking men and walked back toward the river.

"Zak, wait." Sara ran after her but her longer legs kept her well ahead. "Would you wait, please? We need to talk."

Zak whirled, her face an ivory, expressionless cast. "Actually, we don't." Her muscles were tense, hands balled at her sides, and her entire body seemed to vibrate with suppressed energy. The blue of her eyes had turned to cool steel and pierced Sara with their intensity.

"I messed up today, and I'm sorry." She would've tried anything to get Zak to talk to her, and groveling seemed appropriate.

"Not now, Sara."

"You can't keep doing this, you know."

"Doing what?"

"Walking away every time you feel something, burying your emotions, pretending they don't exist." She was right. The shocked look in Zak's eyes was verification enough. But saying it aloud was a mistake. That damned curse.

Zak's cold stare almost made her back down, but Sara recognized it as just another layer of protection.

"You have no idea what I feel."

Sara turned her palms to the sky in her Italian family's symbol of eureka. "Exactly, and that's my point. If we'd talked about what's going on with you, I wouldn't have felt it necessary to handle everything on my own. I respond to trust and openness, not ultimatums and secrets." The fight drained from Sara as she remembered the pictures of Rikki. "Besides, I could've used someone to talk to tonight." She started to walk away, then turned back. "I'm sorry again that I left without telling you. And I'm sorry you were worried." Sara ran from her and didn't look back.

The large canvas enclosure felt like a circus tent as Sara lit the lanterns and looked around. She paced back and forth, trying to gain some sense of self in a vast country that made her feel insignificant. This trip had caused only difficulty and chaos. The moment she'd left London her girlfriend started screwing around. Since meeting Zak Chambers she'd done nothing but annoy, disobey, and upset her. Even her work was delayed by lost paperwork and greedy officials. Maybe all this was a sign to forget the school, go back home, and start over.

But she couldn't leave without fulfilling her mother's final wish. That was unacceptable. The school meant too much to her mother, the foundation, and the children of Kenya. She owed her parents more than a symbolic gesture. Quitting would imply that a few problems were stronger than her determination. She'd never given up so easily, and this wasn't the time to start. Her personal issues would have to wait. No matter how uncomfortable she was or how awkward Zak felt, she was in until the end.

"Sara?"

The soft, husky voice that usually caused goose flesh stopped Sara's frenzied pacing. Zak's tone was reverent, almost pleading, and it wrenched at Sara's heart. "Yes."

"May I come in, please?"

Sara unzipped the flap and stood back, allowing her entry. As Zak stepped inside, her distinctive fragrance of fresh rainwater and sea salt tickled Sara's nostrils. How did she manage such a scent in the middle of dust, sweat, and flies? The question was as intriguing as the woman.

"What is it, Zak?" Sara wasn't in the mood for games. If Zak had something to say, she'd have to do it on her own. She deserved that much. She sat down on a folding metal chair and watched Zak stroll the length of the canvas-clad room. As she walked, her muscles began to relax and she slouched ever so slightly. It took all Sara's energy to keep from asking questions to help her get to the point. But Sara sensed this was important and something Zak needed to handle alone.

After a period of pacing in silence, Zak stopped in front of her. The beautiful alabaster complexion of her face was tight and drawn, her eyes hard and dark. "I believe Titus Wachira had my father killed three years ago."

Sara crossed her hands over her chest as her heart raced wildly. "Oh, my God." She saw the pain buried in Zak's eyes. Zak took a halting breath. Her lips parted slightly, and her bottom lip trembled. This formidable woman suddenly looked helpless and alone. Sara's heart ached for her.

The muscles along her jaw worked as she struggled to continue. "He was a doctor. We came to the bush for three months every year to help with health care. My parents wanted to build a clinic not far from here." She started pacing again, her right thumb digging into the side of her finger. "Are you beginning to see the problem?"

"The police, here."

"They went to my father's site too. A hundred people were there to help lay blocks and build the clinic. Wachira and his men showed up to stop them. When the workers refused, he gave the order to fire. My father was the only one hit—and killed. What are the odds?"

For the first time since she'd met Zak, Sara was speechless. She went to her, placed her hands on her forearms, and looked into blue eyes now drowning in tears. She had no idea how to comfort her for such an inconsolable loss. Small fragments of things she'd seen and heard fused in her mind. Zak's overreaction to the police presence made perfect sense in this context. Her desire to protect her friends was entirely understandable.

"How horrible that must've been for you."

Zak's arms tensed under Sara's touch. "I wasn't there." Tears escaped and slid down her cheeks. "I could've helped my father, but I wasn't there." She whispered the words through clenched teeth, as if saying them fully formed would be too painful. Zak dropped to her knees. "I wasn't there."

Sara sat in front of her and wrapped her arms and legs around her crouching form, cradling Zak's head on her shoulder. "I'm sorry. I am so very sorry." She rocked them back and forth, Zak's tears soaking the fabric of her shirt.

Then Zak gave one final gasp, shook her head, and pulled away from Sara's embrace. She would not be comforted. It was as if she thought she didn't deserve it. "I should have been there. It's my fault."

"You had no idea what would happen. And I'm sure you had a good reason for not being with him."

"No, I didn't. I should've been with my family."

It was obvious Zak wouldn't relinquish her guilt. She felt responsible in some way for her father's death, and Sara couldn't change that. And it was certainly not the time to ask why she wasn't there when her father died. "Is that why you've been so on edge since we got here, the memories?"

Zak nodded. "This place burrows under my skin and makes me crazy, like a fever. I'm hypersensitive to everything and everyone, especially you. I feel I have to protect you, to make up for past mistakes. But I know it doesn't work that way." Zak captured a tear from Sara's cheek on the tip of her finger and brought it to her lips. "When I couldn't find you this morning, I was so scared. You make me feel things I don't want to." She trembled. "There's something about you." Her eyes never left Sara's as she added, "I'm sorry. I shouldn't have said that. You're my client and you're with Rikki."

"Not anymore."

"Am I being fired again?"

"No, I mean the Rikki part. It's over."

"Why?"

"Think about what happened when you met her. Now add two women who didn't resist and pictures to prove it."

"I'm sorry." Zak stroked the side of her face and flames shot through her. "That's not true. I'm not sorry at all. She doesn't deserve you."

Sara wanted to kiss her so much that her body trembled with desire. "Thank you for saying that." She edged closer and wet her lips with the tip of her tongue. "Now will you please kiss me? You so want to."

The pain in Zak's eyes melted into passion as she licked her lips and inched forward. Just before their mouths met, she pulled away. "I can't."

Sara stared at her in disbelief. "Of course you can. There's no reason to stop."

"You don't know me, Sara."

"Then for God's sake tell me and let's move on. I know you want me. And the feeling is very mutual."

"Don't care about me. It's not safe, especially not here." Zak was on her feet and headed for the door.

"I already care more than I should and I'm pretty resilient. But I can't take your constant running away."

"There are too many things I can't tell you. I would put you in danger."

The determined, almost urgent, look on Zak's face told Sara she shouldn't push further.

"Fine, I'll drop it, for now. But I don't give up easily. Soon you'll be begging me to kiss you and more." Sara thought she heard a sexually frustrated moan as Zak unzipped the flap and ducked out. "Nope, it won't be long at all."

"And don't leave again without telling me. Please."

When Zak closed the tent behind her, the temperature seemed to drop twenty degrees. Just being close to her gave Sara hot flashes that weren't age related. Though she'd tried to lighten the mood, everything she said about her feelings was true. She wasn't sure how it happened, but she did care about Zak, more than she'd realized. Rikki's betrayal gave her permission to admit her attraction. Her body hummed with arousal. And Zak had almost admitted she cared as well. "There's something about you," she'd said. But Sara didn't really need a verbal admission. Zak's eyes and face were like a canvas on which each feeling was clearly painted.

No one else seemed to notice, but to her it was obvious. Zak cared, but her attraction came with a price. The reason for her ambivalence was keeping them apart. Sara tried to imagine what could be so compelling. Was it just the potential danger from Wachira? That seemed too simplistic. With an exasperated sigh, she fell onto her sleeping bag and wiggled inside. It could be any of a thousand things she didn't know about Zak. But she was certain of only one; she didn't plan to stop until she found out.

❖

Zak joined Ben by the fire as he threw another log on top and embers shot up like sparklers on the Fourth of July. "Where is your band of merry men?"

"Home. They come tomorrow to work."

"Did Sara approve all this labor, paying for it, I mean?"

Ben nodded and handed Zak a lukewarm Tusker from the small cooler beside his chair. "You need a beer."

"You have no idea." She clicked her bottle against his and downed half of it in one gulp. "Where did she find all those guys?"

"Joey was matatu driver. He brought them." Ben took another sip and studied Zak for a moment. "She did okay today. Not your way, but okay. She did it for you and her."

Zak wanted to protest but Ben was right. She'd practically left Sara no choice by keeping quiet about Wachira. Obviously this woman wouldn't abide secrets or lies. Taking care of the project issues herself was yet another indication of Sara Ambrosini's capability and resilience. She wasn't like anyone Zak had ever met. All that intelligence, independence, and determination combined with emotional sensitivity was more than she'd expected.

"I'll take watch," Ben said, finishing his beer and rising from his chair. "You sleep."

Zak nodded as he moved toward the perimeter to begin rounds. She stretched toward the fire, and the heat crawled up her legs like the warmth from Sara's body had done earlier. Real desire had followed, a hunger she seldom acknowledged. Passion pulsed in her veins like toxic venom, seeking to consume or to be remedied. The intensity was so powerful she trembled trying to contain it, which had taken all her willpower. She'd wanted Sara's kiss but something more frightening than physical surrender had also happened.

Telling the story of her father's death had released emotions that demanded attention. Unlike times past, they didn't just bump against her well-constructed defense system and tumble off. Like thieves they crept upon her, robbed her of logical reasoning, and rendered her vulnerable. And in her weakness, she'd allowed Sara to soothe her momentarily. But the comfort was too cathartic, giving her an undeserved sense of peace. The guilt over leaving her father unprotected while she went on assignment would not be so easily appeased. She'd been unable to share that part of the story with Sara. How would she feel about a woman who abandoned her family responsibilities for a job? To a woman still fulfilling her deceased mother's requests, that answer seemed obvious. And what about the lies of omission required in Zak's work? Sara had already proved she wouldn't tolerate deceit of any kind.

As Zak pushed away from the fire and prepared for bed, she told herself that her decision not to engage Sara physically had been the right one. It was easy merely to have sex, but the kind of emotional commitment a woman like Sara wanted, and deserved, had never come easily for Zak. In fact, it had never come at all, which was enough reason to keep her distance. Detaching kept her defenses intact. She didn't need to lie, and Sara's dreams survived so someone more worthy could fulfill them. Zak's last thought was as cold as the sleeping bag she pulled around her, as hard as the ground she settled on, and equally unsatisfying.

Zak edged closer to the front of Sara's tent to block the breeze whipping around its sides. Low moaning came from inside, and Zak imagined Sara taking her physical needs into her own hands. The visual sent shocks of renewed desire through her. She slid her hand between her legs but was unable to touch the deep-seated ache that pounded there. Instead, she rocked herself to sleep listening to Sara's moans and wishing she was the cause.

CHAPTER NINE

"Oh no, no, no. Help!" Sara dropped the water hose and jumped out of the small tub. She was reaching for a towel to wrap around her shivering body when Zak burst into the tent waving a club and scanning the area for intruders.

"What happened?" She looked like a cartoon character frozen in frame as Sara let the towel she held drop to the floor.

"There's no hot water." She motioned toward the offending hose, aware and grateful for the subtle shifting of her breasts as she moved. Zak's gaze was glued to them like they were a couple of delicious desserts.

"Uh, sorry." Her stare swept down Sara's body and returned to her chest. The normally colorless skin of her face and neck flushed pink.

Now Zak had some idea what she had to offer if and when the opportunity presented itself again. "Guess I should've checked before I climbed in, huh?" She tried for her most innocent face, then bent slowly to retrieve the towel. Her full breasts hung like ripe fruit waiting to be plucked, and her rounded ass mooned the heavens. Zak watched every move. As Sara tucked the towel around herself, she thought how uncharacteristically slutty she was acting. This was more Rikki's style, but she didn't want there to be any doubt in Zak's mind that she wanted her. The look of discomfort on her face said she'd succeeded.

"I'll get to work on the problem." Zak stroked the club in her hands like the shaft of an erect phallus as she spoke. When she glanced at Sara and realized what she was doing with her hands, she turned abruptly toward the door. "Breakfast in five minutes."

While Sara dressed, she gloated over the uneasiness she caused Zak with just the slightest effort. That level of anxiety usually implied feelings close to the surface that should spill over eventually. But it wouldn't happen quickly, not with Zak, and not today. This day she had to build her mother's school. Excitement shot up her spine as she threw back the flap and stepped into the dimly lit morning.

Her footsteps caused a scurry of activity in front of her and she stopped. A herd of zebras dotted the edge of the riverbank. Their grayish-black stripes blended with the still-darkened sky and made them appear as dissected creatures bowing their heads to drink. She watched in amazement as they continued their ritual, giving her only a cursory glance. On the opposite side of the river, a group of elephants lumbered slowly toward the water, their trunks and bodies swaying in opposite directions. A troop of baboons camped out in the trees chattered in protest as the morning drinkers invaded their peaceful retreat.

"Coffee?" Ben asked from fireside.

"Please." She turned reluctantly from the wildlife. "Does this happen every morning?"

He nodded. "And night. They all come. We are very near the game reserve."

"I guess my sleeping hours and their drinking times don't exactly coincide, do they?"

Zak chuckled behind them. "They don't understand bankers' hours." She placed fresh scrambled eggs and bacon on the long picnic table that served as a dining surface and motioned for them to join her.

Sara dug into a huge bowl of fruit, grabbed a piece of charred toast, and started eating, amazed at how hungry she felt. "Is it the air or am I just ravenous this morning?" She glanced at Zak, trying to relay her double entendre with a sultry look.

"By tonight you'll be hungry enough to eat raw warthog but too tired to try," Zak replied. "The construction materials should be here shortly, and if your workers show up, we'll be laying the foundation."

"Have you ever actually built anything like this?" Sara asked.

"No, but Ben has worked on several projects. He knows everything about it. Besides, building a square structure with cinder blocks and tin isn't too difficult."

Ben raised another forkful of eggs. "Done in a few weeks, with no delays."

"Really?" It didn't seem possible, but they weren't constructing a three-story multiroom public school in the States either. A twinge of disappointment crept into her consciousness. Had she wanted it to take longer? She searched her motivations for leaving New York. Was she running away from something? An extended absence would've almost guaranteed Rikki's infidelity. Was that what she'd unconsciously hoped would happen? She dismissed the idea. No one wanted their lover to cheat. But she'd never been good at endings. She held on forever or until the other person gave up.

"Trucks." Ben pointed. "Time for work."

The vehicles traveled toward them across the savannah like a line of ants weaving and following the scent of food. Sara's heart swelled with happiness. She was proud to oversee the fruition of her mother's dream, but the sadness at not being able to share it with her was almost overpowering.

"She would be very proud." Zak placed her hand on Sara's shoulder and gave her a comforting squeeze. "You should be as well."

"Thank you."

Behind the trucks, Joey and his seven day laborers hung from the openings of his father's van waving and shouting. Sara breathed a bit easier. She'd been unsure if they would come back after Zak's erratic behavior yesterday. This project just might get off the ground after all.

Ben referenced the building plans, stepped off the approximate location for the foundation, and poked sticks in the ground to mark the corners. While Zak directed the trucks to a staging area, Sara cleared the breakfast remnants so as not to attract animals. She finished and quickly joined the offloading process, unwilling to miss the physical labor that would make this project literally her own.

As they unloaded the trucks, morning haze gave way to the scorching heat of midday. The men seemed comfortable in their long pants and sleeved shirts, accustomed to the sweltering temperatures. Zak zipped the lower section off her cargo pants and shucked her shirt. Her long, muscular legs and streamlined upper body flexed and extended beneath the shorts and tank top, making Sara glad her rote task didn't require much concentration. After their near kiss the night before, she'd gone to bed visualizing those strong limbs clamped around her, riding her like one of the wild beasts of Africa. Another wave of heat unrelated to the temperature swept over her, and she averted her gaze from Zak's body. If she didn't focus on the school instead of the woman, she'd work herself into a sexual frenzy before lunch.

But something about the way Zak moved and directed the activities around her commanded attention. As they worked, she engaged each man just enough to get a sense of his particular strengths and, armed with that information, assigned tasks. She divided the workmen into two groups, one to help Ben dig the foundation and the other to continue unloading materials. The unloading group finished their job and moved to Ben's location for orders about construction. When noon approached, Joey helped Sara prepare lunch while the others continued their tasks. Their band of eleven had transformed from a group of strangers into a well-coordinated workforce under Zak's direction.

Throughout the day, Sara marveled as the school took shape and at the contrast with the world around them. They were building an institution of learning in an environment rich with the very essence of life and death. Their progress was swift in a place where time seemed to almost stand still. As a herd of giraffes sauntered past in the distance, their long necks stretching in a rhythmic cadence, she wondered if she was doing the right thing. Education was valuable and essential for the advancement of a culture, but was it her place to decide when that should occur? Would the school disturb the balance of nature in this area in a destructive or non-beneficial way? She'd had that discussion with her parents so many times and still had no definitive answer. She could only trust the people who had lobbied for the facility and hope her efforts would be helpful.

Sara became lost in the melodic humming of the men as they worked and in the repetitive stacking of cinder blocks one beside the other in time to the rhythm. When she occasionally glanced at Zak, those sky blue eyes stared back at her. What was Zak thinking, her gaze concentrated but quizzical, though her work pace never faltered. She worked more efficiently than the men, each movement a steady progression toward the finish. The exertion of physical labor seemed to energize Zak while her own body slowed as the day wore on. When light started to fade from the sky, Ben spoke to the men in Swahili and walked toward her. "You pay the men now."

"Now?"

"They get paid daily," Zak explained as she stopped work and approached her. "It's not you. They've had their pay withheld too many times to trust anyone. Do you have enough cash?"

"It's not a problem." She retrieved the money and gave each their agreed-upon payment for the day's work. "Aren't you staying for dinner?"

Joey shook his head and waved as they walked toward the van. "Family waits. Tomorrow, miss. *Asante*."

The three of them waved the others off and turned their attention to the day's work. Sara was amazed at the double layer of foundation blocks that extended above the top of the ground. She'd been so intent on her own little task that she hadn't considered the bigger picture. "I can't believe how much we accomplished today. Thank you." She turned to Ben and Zak and felt another wave of appreciation threaten to bring her to tears. "Is anyone hungry?"

"Crap. I forgot to check on the boiler." Zak started toward the rear of the mess hall. "Sara didn't have warm water this morning. I better figure out the problem or we won't have any tonight either."

"Guess that means you and I will be cooking again." Sara hooked her arm in Ben's. "Does she do this often?"

"Always," Ben answered. "Ebony does not cook so good."

Zak examined the huge gash in the side of the water hose leading from the boiler to Sara's tent. There didn't appear to be any damage to the unit itself, but the cut was too clean to be made by an animal. She checked the ground surrounding the boiler, but after a breezy day and eleven people walking around the site, chances were slim that she'd find a track. An intruder would've found their camp an easy target. One person on night watch couldn't effectively cover the area. Besides, their efforts were directed at four-legged prowlers, not the more dangerous two-legged variety. She removed the other hoses and coiled them together, leaving only the one for the meal-prep area intact. When she returned, Ben and Sara were serving dinner. They took their plates and huddled by the fire, eating and watching the sun ease toward the horizon.

"When you're ready for warm water, tell me or Ben. One of

the hoses has a hole in it so we'll have to switch out." Zak hoped her tone didn't relay the concern this incident aroused. They'd already had a run-in with the police. If someone was purposely sabotaging their equipment, the stakes had been raised. She thought about her conversation with Captain Stewart and hoped she'd have an idea who the players were soon.

Sara didn't seem to notice her preoccupation, but Ben gave her a questioning look. She'd fill him in before night watch. Zak picked at her food in silence and replayed the day's activities. Sara had contributed her share of manual labor like everyone else. It shouldn't have surprised Zak after her insistence on handling the documentation issue. But the sight of this petite, fair-skinned woman toiling in the African sun alongside nine natives was surreal. She handled herself admirably, resting only when they rested and drinking only when they did.

Sara had easily related to the men as well. She didn't have the type of perfunctory conversations with them that Zak had to determine their skill levels. Sara talked with them about their lives and what mattered to them. Working her way along the line, she stood shoulder to shoulder with each one and engaged him in a direct, caring manner. The warmth that developed between them was almost tangible. It reminded Zak of conversations she'd had with people before falsity and secrecy became a part of her life. She missed those conversations and envied the ease with which Sara managed them.

As the day progressed, Zak's respect for Sara rose with each block she set in place. In fact, Sara constantly amazed her, requiring steady revision of the spoiled-rich-girl label Zak had attached to her initially. And every time she'd glanced at her today, Sara was looking at her with those chocolate liquid-center eyes that tugged at her heart and lower parts of her anatomy. The thought of how much she wanted to kiss Sara confused Zak. It wasn't like she was sexually deprived or in desperate need of physical release. Her strong pull toward this woman made no sense.

A loud screeching noise sounded next to her and Zak startled from her memories. A small black-faced monkey crouched near her chair, eyeing her untouched dinner and protesting her hoarding. She set the plate on the ground and watched the creature devour the food while Sara and Ben cleaned up.

"You know better," Ben growled. "Now the whole family comes."

"She's just a softy," Sara added as they washed dishes and flicked water at each other like frisky siblings.

"I'm going to take a splash in the river while you kids play. It's probably warmer than the boiler anyway." Zak found a section of the bank surrounded by whistling acacia trees with a clear stretch of water, took off her shorts, and waded in wearing only her sports bra and boy-cut undies. The water felt nearly hot against her skin, but it sliced away the day's dust and sweat as she ducked under the surface quietly and quickly.

Her time was limited. A large crocodile that rested on the opposite bank waiting for dusk and feeding time would not tolerate her long. He'd want to investigate the fuss and taste the intruder that dared to invade his space. Crocs were known for their stealthy attacks and, when on the move, their lunging strikes. She took a final dip just under the water's surface and started backing out of the river just as the croc stirred.

"Hey, thought I'd join you for a sunset swim." Sara was about to step into the edge of the water as Zak neared the bank.

"No!" She looked toward the opposite side of the river but the croc was already mobile. "Get out, now."

Sara stood ankle deep in the water staring at her like she'd lost her mind. "Why?"

Zak grabbed her around the waist and struggled up the bank. Sara's feet had barely cleared the water when the crocodile lunged at them, his jaws slamming with a ferocious snap. Zak fell backward into the acacia bushes at the crest of the hill with Sara on top of her. As she landed, Zak heard a gunshot and Ben yelling at the croc in Swahili.

Stabbing physical pains down her backside alternated with a sexual ache every time Sara moved. Her thigh pressed into Zak's crotch and sent shivers through her. The cleavage of Sara's soft breasts cupped her chin and made breathing difficult. She wasn't sure which was more excruciating, the injury or the desire.

"Croc is gone," Ben assured them. "Everybody okay?"

"Croc? What croc?" Sara's eyes were huge as she stared at Zak for an answer. "What just happened?" She tried to get up and Zak grunted in pain. "Are you all right?"

"Not really."

Ben helped Sara to her feet. "Big croc in the river. Feeding time now."

"You mean I was almost dinner for a crocodile? I didn't even see him."

"Ebony saved you." Ben smiled broadly. "Now you help her."

She looked at Zak, her gaze taking in the nest of spiky bushes that surrounded her. "I am so sorry, but thank you for rescuing me."

Zak examined the situation, her body surrounded by needle-like protrusions, and realized that her skimpy undies and bra were almost transparent after her dip in the river. Her nipples were rigid, the black triangle between her legs pronounced. Sara's gaze wandered over her body again, taking in the obvious exposure and her precarious predicament.

"Can you get up?"

Zak was reluctant to move, knowing that as soon as she rose some of the thorns in her back would come out. "I can, but I'm not sure I want to. That's going to hurt worse."

Ben looked back toward the river, affording her the respect of not gawking at her revealing attire. "Acacia thorns very sharp, very painful," he said. "I get medicines."

Sara offered her hand and Zak slowly rose from her prickly bed. As she straightened, the fabric of her sports bra and undies tugged and irritated the impaled objects in her skin. Some of the stickers had come out and blood trickled down her back. She gritted her teeth to keep from crying out.

"My God, you're bleeding." Sara started to touch her but Zak raised her hands in defense. "Like it or not, you'll need some help getting those things out of your backside. You look like you did battle with a porcupine and lost."

"Ben can—"

"Ben most certainly cannot. It wouldn't be fair to put him in that position. I'll take care of you. Get over yourself and get in here."

Sara held her tent flap open so Zak could walk inside without bending. "Lie down on my sleeping bag." She lit the lanterns and placed them on the floor near the bedroll. When Ben brought the first-aid kit and her rucksack, Zak heard a whispered exchange between the two but couldn't make out what they were saying.

"Do you need something for pain?"

"No, just do it. Take them out quickly. It'll hurt less." Zak clenched her teeth each time Sara plucked one of the embedded thorns from her flesh. One by one she picked them out of her shoulders, her back, her buttocks and legs. Zak's discomfort alternated between pain from the stickers and pleasure from Sara's hands as they rested gently on her body while she worked. It seemed to take hours for her to complete the extraction.

"There, I think I've gotten them all. It's hard to tell in this light if any points broke off in the wounds. When you stop bleeding, I'll have another look. Take off your clothes."

"What?" Momentarily forgetting her predicament, Zak looked over her shoulder at Sara. Realizing she was still in nurse mode, she added, "I'll be fine. Thanks."

Sara shook her head at her like the uncooperative patient she was. "Those punctures have to be swabbed with alcohol and an antiseptic applied or you could get an infection. God only knows what's in that water you bathed in, not to mention on the points of these prickers. Now get out of those clothes or I'll cut them off." She waggled a pair of blunt-looking scissors at Zak to emphasize her point.

"Jeez, Florence Nightingale you're not." She stripped off her bra and undies quickly, trying to shield herself from Sara. But her nurse wasn't paying attention to her body at the moment. She was busy digging through the first-aid kit. When Zak stretched out on the sleeping bag, the polyester fabric was cool against her breasts and belly. She wanted to throw it over her back and let the chill ease the fire that tormented her injured skin.

"Ouch." She jerked at the alcohol's sting as Sara swabbed her back. "A little warning would've been nice." She flinched again. "Talk to me or something." Sara was being unusually quiet but her touch remained a constant gentle stroke.

"I don't believe I was ever in love with Rikki."

Zak almost choked on a breath. "What?"

"We've only been dating for nine months, and something about it never felt right. My friends told me she was cheating, but I didn't want to believe them. To me a promise is a promise and you don't go back on it just because you're horny or you've been inconvenienced. I think I knew deep down, because I hired a private investigator to follow her while I'm away. And as you know, it didn't even take twenty-four hours for her to find another playmate. I have to talk to her and end this charade. I'm sure she'd love a free trip to Africa as long as it's in a four-star hotel."

"Why would you do that? Bring her here, I mean. Why not wait until you get back?"

"Now that I know the truth, I just want it to be finished. Maybe it's my pride, but the thought of her screwing around while everybody thinks we're still together is a bit much. It was different when I didn't know. I could at least feign ignorance. It'll be worth the expense to fly her out here and tell her face-to-face. I deserve that at least."

"You deserve much more than that," Zak muttered before she could censor her thoughts.

The smooth swabbing continued, as did the heartfelt chatter. "I can't seem to keep a lover. Maybe I'm fundamentally flawed in that department. Or maybe I'm trying to funnel my passion into the wrong things." Sara paused as if considering her last statement. "Maybe that's it."

Sara's alcohol dabbing stopped and Zak's skin cooled. She'd almost forgotten her own pain as she wondered about the underlying sadness in Sara's voice. It conveyed so much doubt and self-deprecation. Zak wanted to reassure her, to relate the multitude of characteristics and abilities she'd observed that were worthy of pride and appreciation. But Sara's hands returned to her and arrested further cognizant thought.

Sara straddled her body and vigorously rubbed her hands together, spreading the pungent antiseptic cream over them evenly. Then she delicately applied the ointment to each individual wound. Her strong fingers feathered over the injuries, then fanned out to smooth the tension down Zak's rib cage. She massaged the unaffected section of her lower back with a firmer touch and let up again at the swell of her butt. Sara touched her skin gingerly, almost reverently, with strokes that eased the flesh and calmed the senses.

For some reason too complex to decipher or too simple to consider, Zak melted into the tender caresses and her body drank as though famished. These touches held no motive other than to heal. They worshipped her with gentleness and compassion. This kind of connection sought nothing in return. Her body completely relaxed and she drifted into a place of quiet safety that she hadn't experienced in years. The tempo of Sara's fingers kneading her body lulled Zak with their mantra—Sara, Sara.

❖

Everything happened so fast. Sara had merely wanted to commemorate their first workday with a celebratory dip. She had no idea there was danger in the river. Zak literally saved her life, and her reward was a painful bed of acacia thorns. When she saw the damage they caused, Sara was heartbroken.

This was the second time she'd caused Zak pain, and she wasn't sure which had been worse, the callous comparison to Wachira or the backstroke into needle-sharp bushes. She only knew that she had to make it right. In spite of her stubborn objections, Zak allowed her to tend her injuries. And during that nurturing process Sara realized how deeply Zak Chambers and everything that concerned her affected her.

The thorns that protruded from Zak's alabaster skin looked cruel and obscenely invasive. Each one she removed with a quick flip of her wrist stabbed her heart like a saber. Blood oozed from the puncture wounds and painted an ugly trail down Zak's back. When she breathed, the protrusions rose and fell like a live entity, taunting her with their ability to attach to the woman Sara seemed unable to reach.

As she cleaned and dressed Zak's injuries, the ache inside robbed her of words. She felt responsible for Zak's pain and incapable of making it better. And when Zak asked her to talk and distract her, she launched into a tirade about Rikki, the one person she didn't want to think or talk about. She was angry with herself for being so careless in a place full of the unexpected. No wonder she couldn't keep a girlfriend. She attracted the ones she didn't need and couldn't attract the ones she needed.

Zak seemed to relax as Sara finished caring for her wounds, but Sara couldn't stop touching her. She gently massaged the tight muscles around her injuries and caressed the small of her back where it dipped before rising to her perfectly bowed ass. Her legs were like a sprinter's legs with sinewy, well-defined hamstrings and calves. Sara traced her fingers up the back of Zak's legs and savored the line of gooseflesh her touch aroused. She knew she should stop, but the pleasurable sensations the caresses produced in her own body hijacked the thought before it reached her hands.

Zak didn't move or object to the unnecessary explorations. She seemed almost too relaxed, her breathing too deep and even. Sara wondered if she'd fallen asleep but doubted the pain would have allowed that. She edged forward to be sure. Zak's eyes were closed and her face so peaceful that it might have been a painting on canvas. Sara carefully stretched her body lengthwise behind Zak's, careful not to touch the red, irritated puncture wounds. She wanted to understand what miracle had released the tension that she carried and to absorb some of the tranquility that enveloped her. For just a few minutes she longed to lie next to this woman who went to bed hours after she did, rose before the sun, and never seemed to rest. She inched close enough to feel the heat radiating from Zak's body and was overcome with a sense of belonging. As she drifted into sleep she wondered what it was about this woman that called to her on such a fundamental level.

She felt like she'd been dreaming for hours when someone whispered, "Sara, wake up." Zak was standing over her sleeping bag fully dressed. It was still dark outside, but the tent was aglow with light that cast ominous shadow figures against its sides. Something was wrong. Zak was motionless, but her anger radiated across the space and frightened Sara.

"What's going on?"

"Get dressed, now."

"Please, what is it?"

As Zak straightened, she uttered a single word like it tasted sour in her mouth and had to be spat out. "Wachira."

CHAPTER TEN

"Wake in the camp." Zak would never forget that sickly, phlegm-coated voice, weak but cold as metal in a blizzard. "Wake in the camp and come out," Wachira repeated.

She motioned for Sara to stay put, then let herself out. Ben would make himself scarce unless needed. His run-ins with the police, mostly on Zak's behalf, had left him in an untenable position. But if she needed help, Ben would be there. She scanned the campsite, saw him crouched behind a giant termite mound in the shadows, and motioned for him to stay. She walked toward the officers, her revulsion surfacing with each step.

The man she hated leaned against the front of a police jeep, his arms akimbo. His five-five frame looked even smaller against the grill of the large all-terrain vehicle. He was dressed in a full command uniform decorated with medals he probably didn't earn. The eight-point duty cap added another inch to his height and was pulled low to hide most of his face. Zak imagined he wore the outfit to make himself look taller and more important. How could a man so physically lacking generate such fear in so many, she often wondered. But seeing him again, staring into his lackluster eyes, she understood perfectly. His blood was circulated by a mechanical device. Titus Wachira had no real heart.

Wachira was partially surrounded by at least twelve men that Zak could see and numerous vehicles, the headlights all trained on their camp. Her first impulse was to charge him with all her physical force and hope to hit him once before the guards aerated her with bullets. Muscles in her body strained for release as sharp pains shot down her backside, reminding her of the acacia-thorn ordeal and moderating but not obliterating her urge for immediate action.

The thought of her father probably kneeling, possibly prostrate in front of this evil man made Zak shiver. Her hatred and rage had been building for three years, coiling tighter and tighter inside her like pressure inside a rocket launcher. She'd rehearsed her first meeting with Wachira since her father's death so many times that it felt like a memory instead of a plan. She would attack without mercy. The initial strike, quick and debilitating, would immobilize but not immediately kill. He would confess the conspiracy to murder her father, then little by little she would torture him until he begged for mercy and bled out. As she approached the target, her plan spinning repeatedly in her mind, his entourage raised their AK-47s in unison and aimed them at her.

"Let her through," Wachira ordered in a nonchalant tone, as if she were a fan seeking an autograph.

She continued toward him like an automaton, undaunted by the show of force, driven by her blinding need for revenge. She didn't care if she died in the process of avenging her father. She owed him that much after leaving him unprotected. The semicircle of men closed behind her as she entered Wachira's space, but still she advanced. She balled her fists and pounded the sides of her thighs as she walked, ready to execute her kamikaze mission.

"Madame Chambers, nice to see you again." His words dripped with insincerity. "I did not know you were helping with this project." He lied unconvincingly. Wachira pushed away from the front of the jeep and approached, circling her like a buzzard might a carcass. "You have become stronger, like a fighter. But we have no need to fight, do we?" He slapped her on the shoulder as if they were friends.

Pain shot down her back as his hand made contact with the tender thorn injuries. Her muscles tensed and she gritted her teeth to stifle a moan of anguish. She couldn't afford to appear injured in front of this man. He detected weakness like a bloodhound on a scent and pursued it as vigorously.

"What's going on here?" Zak heard Sara ask from what sounded like a great distance. The gentle yet authoritative tone of her voice flipped a switch inside Zak, as if her programming had been turned off. Her urge to attack Wachira dimmed in the presence of a more pressing directive, to protect Sara.

"Go back, Sara." Zak tried to sound matter-of-fact without being dismissive or overly concerned.

Wachira glanced from Zak to Sara and back, his dull eyes showing the first sign of interest. In a matter of seconds he had determined her Achilles' heel. "No, please join us, Madame Ambrosini. It is you I wish to speak with."

The guards parted and allowed Sara to join her and Wachira. "I'm afraid I'm at a disadvantage. Have we met?"

"Forgive me. I am Commander Titus Wachira of the Narok District." He took Sara's hand and cupped it in his. "You are even more beautiful than I'd been told."

Zak started toward them. Seeing Wachira touch Sara infuriated her. She imagined that even a second's contact with this vile man could potentially contaminate Sara's honest and compassionate nature. But Sara gave her that stare, the one that said, *Back off.*

"Commander, you flatter me. How can I help you this morning? I assume it's important to necessitate such an early visit by someone of your stature."

Wachira puffed out his chest and smiled. "You are very wise. There is a problem. It embarrasses me to tell you. Our County Development Office made a mistake. This land is not available for your school."

Zak's temper returned and she stepped between Wachira and Sara. "What do you mean it's not available? She's paid—twice—for the proper permits. What's the matter, Wachira, didn't get your cut?"

Sara lightly touched her shoulder and nudged Zak aside. "Please, let me handle this." Her voice was almost a pleading whisper.

Wachira watched the exchange and Zak's acquiescence. "Before your permissions were granted, others had already been approved but not yet reached the filing office. They are very slow with the filing. When I heard you had started to build, I wanted to personally give you the news. It saddens my heart. We need more schools for the children and you are most generous to help. Maybe I can assist with another location?"

Sara stepped closer to Wachira, her body language open and inviting. "Perhaps we can work out a mutually beneficial agreement."

"What did you have in mind, Madame Ambrosini?"

"Let me continue with the school, for a while, until this situation is resolved. I will of course compensate you for coming all the way out here and for any future efforts on my behalf. I'm sure a man of your influence will not rest until you get to the bottom of this and the correct paperwork is located. And if I eventually have to move, I'll write it off as a tax loss."

Wachira seemed to be considering Sara's offer. "What about your hot-headed friend?" He nodded toward Zak. "She causes difficulty."

"I can handle her. Don't worry, Commander. Do we have a deal?"

Zak watched in horror as Wachira and Sara shook hands. What had she done? It didn't make any sense. Didn't she know this man couldn't be trusted? Zak pulled her phone from her belt and pretended to dial but instead took several pictures as they chatted, shook again, and Sara finally handed him a huge wad of cash.

She guided Wachira around the school foundation, explaining her plans for the building and pointing out their progress. She treated him like a benefactor instead of the man intent on destroying her dream, walking and chatting until dawn. Zak lagged a few steps behind, refusing to allow Wachira an unguarded moment with Sara. As the sun rose, Wachira ordered his men to their vehicles and kissed Sara's hand before climbing into his jeep. Then he turned to Zak. "Madame Chambers, give your mother my regards."

Zak's violent thoughts returned and she wanted to hurl herself at Wachira like a missile. How dare he make reference to her mother, the woman he made a widow. She took only a couple of steps before Sara hooked her arm though Zak's and gently guided her to the mess tent as Ben appeared from around the back.

"He is a very bad man," Ben confirmed. "Trust nothing he says, miss."

"I won't," Sara replied.

Zak pulled loose from Sara's grasp and glared at her in disbelief. "Then you're sure one hell of an actress. It looked like you could eat him with a spoon."

"And you looked like you could kill him."

"Trust me, I could and probably would've tried if—"

"If what? If I hadn't been here? Is that why you agreed to continue with the job, so you could get a whack at Wachira?"

"What if it is?" Zak felt the exchange taking a dangerous turn but couldn't stop. She had often imagined eliminating Wachira but, faced with the possibility, doubted herself capable of such cruelty. And involving Sara in any way had never been an option. "Do you have a problem with a little justice for the man who killed my father?"

"I have a problem with killing, period, and with being used for any reason."

"Then maybe you do need another guide, because I can't promise not to do either." At this point she and Sara were standing almost nose to nose, their eyes locked in a staring battle. With her last statement, Sara reeled backward as if she'd been slapped.

The look on Sara's face was akin to fear. Her usually warm brown eyes were wide and filled with pain. Her full lips were pulled thinly around a mouth that pursed with disapproval. She stared at Zak like she was a stranger, a stranger to be dreaded and avoided. She'd never had a woman regard her with such alarm, and that it was Sara made it more unbearable.

Ben stepped between them and placed his hand on Zak's chest. His strong presence calmed her immediately. "Ebony, Miss Sara did a good thing." He waited for his words to reach through her haze of emotion. "It gives us time to find the truth without drawing Wachira's wrath."

"If you want to play her little game, go ahead, but count me out. I learned years ago not to put my hand in the fire. There are other ways to handle this." Zak turned and walked toward the river as the remnants of her rage seeped onto the parched African soil and the tenuous connection she'd experienced with Sara shattered into a million pieces.

❖

Zak had been gone since their visit from Wachira, running alone in the desert for hours. Sara was glad she wasn't around during breakfast so she could think without worrying about hiding her facial expressions. Her reality had suddenly taken a sinister shift. She knew Zak was intense and moody, but this morning she saw something else, a dark side capable of bloodshed. It surprised, frightened, and saddened her that Zak might intentionally hurt another human being. Sara was a consummate pacifist, and being involved in violence of any kind conflicted with her nature. The thought weighed heavily in her mind as she poked at her breakfast. Joey and the work crew pulled into camp as she and Ben finished cleaning the breakfast dishes.

"You had visitors?" Joey asked.

"How did you know?"

"Checkpoint just over the ridge, never there before. They stopped us."

"Are you okay?"

"Sure, they search everyone and let us go. Now we work."

"Actually, Joey, I was wondering if you'd take me into Talek. The other men can stay and work on the school. I'll pay for your matatu services, of course."

"Sure, miss."

She found Ben and told him she needed to go into town and get more supplies, blaming the shortage on feeding lunch to a group of hungry workmen every day. He was reluctant to let her leave without telling Zak, but acquiesced when she told him Joey would drive her. The two men conferred briefly in Swahili before Sara and Joey left.

"What were you talking to Ben about?"

"Ben says you don't need supplies, got enough for two weeks. So Ben says I must keep close eye on you. Don't let you make trouble." Joey smiled like he'd been entrusted with the family's prize cow.

She wondered how Ben had gotten to know her so well. And even though she lied about her reason for leaving camp, he gave her the time and space she needed to work through her concerns. Friendship like that was hard-won in the world she lived in but seemed so effortless from this kind man. She suddenly envied Ben's unassuming manner and his calming effect on Zak.

At the rise of the hill, Joey slowed the jeep as they approached the police checkpoint, and Sara recognized one of the men from their morning visit. He waved them through, staring intently at their license tag and speaking into his walkie-talkie.

While the lightweight van bumped along the washboard road, Sara wondered what had happened to Zak that morning. She had seemingly morphed into another person. Her entire body hummed with suppressed fury and the look in her eyes was pure hatred. Sara felt certain that if she hadn't intervened, Zak would've gone after Wachira in spite of the overwhelming odds. Her own safety didn't even appear to be a concern.

The only thing that stopped her was Sara's presence. Was she concerned about Sara being hurt, was she worried about another witness, or did she suddenly realize the lunacy of her actions?

Perhaps this was the reason for all the secrecy about her life and work. Maybe Zak Chambers was a professional assassin handling a very personal job and using her as a cover. She tried to reconcile this thought with her past interactions with Zak. Talking Sara through the thunderstorm on the plane, saving her from a crocodile attack, revealing such tenderness when she talked about her father's death. Zak's tears of pain didn't mesh with the behavior Sara had observed that morning. She just didn't want to believe Zak capable of something so distasteful.

"Joey, I need to go somewhere that has a land line and a fax machine." She needed to redirect her thoughts for a while, and the land situation was a good distraction. Randall had resources all over the globe, and property searches were a specialty of his.

"Not Talek for supplies?" Joey gave her a teasing grin. "I know a place."

Twenty more minutes of jaw-jarring travel brought them to a small strip of concrete buildings with tin roofs that looked like all the others she'd seen, only marginally habitable. "Here?"

"Yes, miss. This is library. Has phone and fax but you pay, right? I wait."

It took almost half an hour to get a connection through to Randall Burke, her attorney in New York. She directed him to conduct a thorough check of international corporations with interests in property in the Narok District of Kenya and to locate a map showing existing owners in the area. His timetable was immediately if not sooner. Then she waited while he faxed the PI's written report on Rikki's activities. The more pages that spewed out of the machine, the more depressed she became. When the final page came through, she was close to tears.

She folded the sheets and tucked them into her purse on the way back to the van. Joey gave her one look and averted his gaze. He seemed to know she didn't want to talk. "We make detour through the reserve. See animals, maybe." He drove away from the library in the opposite direction they'd come.

"I'd like that," she answered. Along the new route, Sara saw people planting in the right-of-way between the road and a large fenced farm. "What are they doing?"

"They plant gardens. These people have no land so they grow food here."

"How do they water the vegetables?"

"Tote water from the river at Talek, many miles a day."

Compared to these industrious people's fight for survival, Sara's girlfriend woes seemed petty and selfish. She tried to ignore the multipage report that screamed for her attention and focused on the sights around her. Ahead, Sara saw another checkpoint but this one looked different. The men who manned the station were dressed in camouflage uniforms instead of the police blue. Huge metal spikes crisscrossed the road in both directions, and warning signs indicated that all traffic must stop. They waved Joey over to the side with menacing-looking weapons. "Jeshi," Joey said, and his tone implied that wasn't good.

"What does that mean?"

"Military, worse than police."

Joey pulled into the directed spot and cut the engine. Officers encircled the vehicle. One read the license tag while another ordered them out and against the side of the van. The soldier closest to Sara grabbed her shoulders and slid his rough hands over her breasts, along her sides, between her thighs, and down her legs under the guise of searching her. His invasion felt personal and offensive.

She wanted to defend herself but decided it would only exacerbate the situation. What would Zak do? Strike that, she was better off handling it diplomatically. The combination of military, manhandling, and Zak would probably be deadly for someone.

"Is this really necessary? We haven't done anything wrong. What is this about?" The officer shrugged as if he didn't understand English and the groping continued. Next to her, Joey was being frisked by two men who shouted for silence each time he tried to address them in Swahili. "I'd like to talk with Commander Wachira."

The men laughed at her. "Wachira is nothing. We are jeshi," one of them answered.

"Mchuma, mchuma!" An officer yelled from inside the van and waved a handgun out the window.

Joey's horrified expression confirmed the weapon wasn't his. The panic on his face as he tried to explain was heart-wrenching. "It is not mine. I have no weapons." His voice cracked. "This is wrong."

The officer who was searching Sara jerked her arms behind her back and handcuffed her as she watched Joey being pushed to the ground. "Don't hurt him, please." The men hovering over Joey kicked his prone body, handcuffed him, and pulled him up by the cuffs.

"What are you doing? Where are we going?" Sara asked as they were led to a truck with a canvas-covered bed. She was shoved onto a long aluminum bench that ran the truck's length. Shackles snapped together around her ankles with a loud clank, emphasizing the severity of her situation. The heavy metals were cold and their jagged surface cut into the flesh around her feet.

An officer secured the shackles to the floor and closed the flap, leaving them alone. The enclosure smelled of urine and vomit, and it took all Sara's strength to control the churning in her stomach. When the truck started moving, Sara was unsure if her shaking was from the rough ride or her emotional state. She had to focus on something else.

"Are you okay, Joey? Did they hurt you?"

The young man forced a smile to replace the fear so clearly etched on his face. "I am good, miss. You?" His attempt to reassure her was touching.

"Fine, under the circumstances. What's going to happen to us?"

"They take us to Nairobi. Weapons are forbidden."

"That wasn't your gun, was it?"

"No, miss, and not my father's. Something bad is happening."

The ride to Nairobi seemed interminable inside the dark, unventilated truck bed. Sara tried to keep her breathing calm and steady despite the poor air circulation and oppressive heat. The space was like a furnace. And without visual references, Sara was unsure which direction they were traveling or how long they'd been on the road. The officers had confiscated her cell phone along with her purse, so contact was impossible. Once again she regretted leaving camp without telling Zak.

"Will they let us make a phone call when we reach Nairobi?" Sara wasn't sure who she would call first—Zak or her attorney. Since Randall was in New York, Zak seemed the most likely to get immediate results, though those results weren't guaranteed to be positive. Had Zak also had run-ins with the military in Kenya as well as local police? The thought did little to settle her anxiety.

❖

It was midafternoon when Zak and the crew stopped work for the day. There had been no word from Sara or Joey, and she was getting concerned. Ben stopped several times and looked toward the ridge, as if wishing would bring them back sooner. He apologized over and over for letting them leave without knowing their destination and possible return time. His repeated contrition gave Zak an uncomfortable feeling of foreboding.

Since Joey wasn't back with the van, Zak talked the crew into staying for dinner, after which she would drive them all home. But her phone rang just as she stepped from a cold shower. "Yeah."

"Zak?"

"Yeah." She recognized one of her contacts from Nairobi Police Headquarters.

"Jeshi just logged in Ms. Sara Ambrosini and a driver named Joey for possession of a handgun. They haven't been allowed a phone call yet."

"Thanks, I'm on my way. If anything changes, let me know."

Zak briefed Ben on the new plan as she threw a change of clothes in her rucksack for Sara. "I'll drop the men off in Talek with enough cash to get home. Can you mind the camp until we return?" When he nodded, she continued. "Get a couple of men from your village to come help out with security. We'll need them after I return as well. It's a six-hour drive each way to Nairobi, so we'll probably stay over, if I can even get her released tonight." She tossed the bag over her shoulder and started toward the truck, but Ben stopped her.

"This is not her fault, Ebony."

"A gun, Ben. Where in the hell did it come from?"

"Not Miss Sara, and I think not Joey. Be careful."

The drive into Nairobi seemed to take forever, and aggravating the situation was the memory of the distressed look on Sara's face earlier when she'd lashed out about Wachira. She'd grown closer to Sara as they'd worked and learned to respect each other's strengths. Their styles even seemed to complement each other temperamentally and with the men. But Zak's venomous outburst had obviously shocked Sara and left her at an uncharacteristic loss for words.

How could she have been so careless as to let Sara see her dark side? She'd kept it buried for three years while it festered and oozed around inside her, becoming angrier and uglier with each day. It never occurred to her that her desire for vengeance might hurt someone she cared for. The realization that she was beginning to care for Sara crept into her awareness. The adorably annoying redhead had effortlessly insinuated herself into her life. Her straightforward approach to life, her unabashed willingness to express her feelings, and the way she naturally interacted on a personal level with everyone she met whittled at Zak's defenses. What did Sara think of her now, and what else was she facing while a prisoner in a foreign jail?

The same worries looped continuously in Zak's head until she arrived at the Nairobi Police Department. She arranged for Joey's release first and, after a discussion of whether he wanted to spend the night or return home, provided money for the retrieval of his van. Sara's liberation was more complicated since she was not a resident of Africa, but Captain Stewart had made some calls on her behalf. Zak found the military surprisingly receptive to a large infusion of cash and a plausible excuse for the gun, with the assurance that no such problem would arise again.

When Sara walked outside the dingy walls of the station, Zak was waiting at the door. She looked scared and uncertain for the first time since they met. The desire to comfort and reassure her warred with her angry impulse to seek out her captors and exact retribution. But this morning's events made her cautious. "Are you all right?"

Sara looked around as if disoriented. "Where am I? Where's Joey?"

"Nairobi, and Joey is on his way back home." She took Sara's arm and led her toward the truck. "Did they hurt you?"

"No. What are you doing here? I didn't even get a phone call."

"I did. Let's go. I hope you don't mind, but I've booked rooms at the Stanley for the night. It's a six-hour drive back to camp and the roads are treacherous enough in daylight."

Sara's eyes were still wide and she looked around as Zak drove, taking in the city like she'd been incarcerated for years instead of hours. "I just want a hot shower and a change of clothes." The small detail seemed to register. "Clothes."

"I brought you something. I was in a hurry, so don't be upset if it doesn't match." Zak tried to snap Sara out of her shocked state with humor. It was unsettling to see her so quiet and obviously affected by the ordeal. Zak felt so inept in these delicate situations. If she was lucky, things would be ready at the hotel and Sara could relax and regain her composure.

When they arrived at the Stanley, Zak was relieved that Captain Stewart had fulfilled her request perfectly. In addition, the fax she'd been expecting was waiting at the desk in a sealed manila envelope. She signed them in and escorted Sara to her room.

"Why don't you have a shower and relax. If you feel up to it, call me and we'll order something to eat later. I'd like to know what happened today." She placed the clothes she'd hurriedly gathered for Sara on the bed and waited, unsure if she should leave her alone just yet. "Will you be okay or should I stay for a while?"

"I'll be fine once I'm clean again."

"Let me know if you need anything. I'm right next door."

Zak had a quick shower and scanned the fax Stewart sent. The land-development information was more convoluted than she'd expected, but she didn't have time to digest it all right now. Her first priority was Sara and her rattled mental condition. She sensed more was going on than just her arrest. When the shower stopped next door, Zak listened to the subtle noises of habitation as she imagined Sara drying herself and getting dressed. Then the room adjoining hers was silent. The stillness made Zak uncomfortable. She moved closer to the adjacent wall and listened.

"You stupid bitch," Sara screamed, then something slammed against the wall and shattered on the tile floor. She was pounding on Sara's door in seconds.

When it opened Sara didn't look like an angry woman but like an emotionally drained one. Her hair, still wet from the shower, hung down her back in loose amber ringlets, and her face was pale and drawn. The baggy pants and T-shirt made her look small and defenseless. Her bed and the floor were littered with sheets of paper that appeared to have been thrown in the air and left where they landed. Zak stepped lightly around shards of glass that used to be a drinking cup. "What happened?" Zak stopped at Sara's raised hand.

"Can't do this now."

"What? Sara, what's wrong?"

"Too much." Tears were streaming down her face and she seemed perfectly willing to let them come. "Too many feelings." She took a halting breath and tried to speak again, but nothing came out.

Zak inched closer. "Please let me help you. I don't understand what's happening."

Her statement seemed to drag Sara back to a semi-coherent state. Fire flashed in her dark brown eyes but the tears continued to fall. "Of course you don't understand." Her voice hitched as she spoke through sobs. "You don't understand anything emotional." She spread her arms wide and turned in a circle as she talked. "Imagine this. You're in a foreign country, your guide has a death wish and could be an axe murderer for all you know, your girlfriend is a lying, cheating slut who is spending your money to entertain her fuck buddies, and—" She paused for a breath and a fresh round of sobs. "And then you're arrested, thrown into a smelly, hot, scary vehicle with no windows or ventilation, driven for hours in the dark, tossed into a sweltering cell with human excrement, vermin, and unsanitary people who poke your body with their fingers, and allowed no phone call." She stared at Zak with eyes that alternated a look of challenge and pain. "Tell me, Zak, would you feel anything then? Would you?"

Zak was relieved that at least Sara was ranting again. This was normal, but the agony in her eyes was unnatural. It summoned Zak like a hypnotist calls his subject. She approached Sara slowly, gently hugged her, and guided her around the broken glass on the floor to the edge of the bed. Sara smelled of soap and a flowery shampoo, not her usual scents. She relaxed against Zak and the warmth of her body made Zak feel needed. Sweeping the papers onto the floor, she urged Sara to lie down and then sat beside her.

"I'm having a meltdown." Sara wiped tears from her eyes. "I usually let my feelings out, but I guess I've let things build up lately."

"It's okay." She stroked Sara's wet hair and fingered stray strands from her forehead. "Can I get you anything?" Zak felt so inadequate. How was she supposed to deal with an emotional unraveling? She'd always run away from her own. But she wanted to help Sara, to be whatever she needed, at least for a while.

"Would you lie down and just hold me for a few minutes?"

Zak hadn't expected such an honest and intimate request. Her body started moving before her mind formulated a response. "Um, okay."

"If it makes you uncomfortable, don't."

Zak's mind told her to stop, but she wanted to be near Sara more than she'd realized. She stretched out on the bed and pulled Sara into her arms. The action felt so normal, so instinctive that the tenderness of it surprised her. She sighed in relief and her body softened into Sara's curves.

Sara nuzzled her head onto Zak's shoulder. "Thank you." They lay in silence for so long that Zak thought Sara might have drifted off until she spoke again. "I feel like such a fool. Everybody told me about Rikki but I wouldn't believe them. Even after I saw the pictures, I still thought they could be wrong. She was always so attentive and affectionate. But this report." She waved her arms around the room. "It's worse than I imagined. She's been using my money to wine and dine her paramours. How stupid am I?"

Zak felt Sara's body stiffen against her. "You're not stupid. You just wanted to trust your lover."

"Yeah, and she just wanted my money. Is that my only redeeming quality?"

"Absolutely not." Zak looked her in the eye. "You're one of the most capable and principled people I've ever met. You constantly amaze me with your insight. You're compassionate to a fault. And that's just what I've seen so far."

Sara's face brightened a little and the spark returned to her eyes. "I knew you liked me."

"I can't help myself." Zak was surprised at the honesty of her reply. But the glimmer in Sara's eyes dimmed a bit and Zak's heart skipped a beat. "Did I say something wrong?"

"No, you said something very right." Sara touched the side of her face and heat scorched Zak's body like a brush fire during the dry season. "But you scared me today, Zak. I don't want to be afraid of you, but I can't handle violence. If it's part of who you are and what you do, I need to know now."

Sara's words were like a sudden African downpour, dowsing the heat in Zak's body. She'd always dreaded having a woman she cared about ask for something she couldn't give. She had nurtured her deadly intentions toward Wachira for years. She wasn't sure if she could let them go for a lover, even for Sara. Her job had never required that she kill anyone, but she might have to. How could she explain her conundrum to Sara without telling her the truth? Unfortunately, that wasn't an option in her profession.

Zak's conflicting feelings churned until she felt she might explode.

She was unaccustomed to such emotional intensity and had to do something with it. Cupping Sara's face between her hands, she held her gaze. "I would never hurt you. Please, believe me. I—"

Sara's mouth was on hers before Zak could say more. Wispy, tentative kisses teased her lips, and the tip of Sara's tongue traced the outline of her mouth, seeking entry. Zak answered with a hungry, demanding kiss. She buried her hands in the thick wet hair at the nape of Sara's neck and pulled her in so forcefully she was afraid their lips might bruise. With her tongue she probed the contrasting textures of Sara's tongue, teeth, and soft tissue, savoring each one and committing it to sensory memory. The delicate nerve endings in her tongue seemed directly connected to her clit as wave after wave of sensation swept through her. She had never been this physically present, as if her body was acting of its own accord while from above she mentally watched someone she didn't know doing something she'd always wanted to do—surrender to her feelings.

"Oh, Sara," she breathed, gulping for air. Sara raked her hands through Zak's hair and pressed their bodies closer. Her breath was moist against the side of Zak's neck. She bent from the waist, still maintaining contact with her lower body, and tugged at the buttons on Zak's shirt. "Please, Zak. I need you."

Her plea, like a double-edged sword, sliced through Zak and pulled her back to reality. She clung to Sara, not wanting to let go though mentally withdrawing from her. The physical connection was almost too overpowering to break. Her body craved it. She wanted it more than she could have imagined. But her traitorous mind replayed all the reasons this was not a good idea. She reluctantly withdrew from Sara's embrace.

"I'm sorry. I can't do this."

Sara stared at her with eyes full of pain. "You keep saying that. I believe you can do it. And I know you want to." As if another possibility suddenly came to mind, she pulled completely away from Zak. "You're not attracted to me? You just feel sorry for me?"

The idea horrified Zak and she froze, unable to articulate how absurd that option was. But the hesitation only fueled Sara's imagination.

"Get out. I don't need or want anyone's pity, especially not yours."

"Sara." Zak wanted to explain but Sara was in no mood to listen.

"Leave. Now."

Hoping to appeal to her on another level, Zak tried again. "I need to know about what happened today."

"By all means, let's keep this professional. Well, right now your needs don't matter much to me. I'm exhausted and I want to rest." She held the door open for Zak. "I'll be happy to brief you tomorrow on our drive back. At least we'll have something to talk about."

Zak stepped into the hallway and before she could protest further, the door slammed with a thud.

CHAPTER ELEVEN

The next morning Sara sipped coffee in the Stanley's Thorn Tree Café and distracted herself with her surroundings. When had the famous message tree downsized from a statuesque acacia to a tiny tree encircled by a felt tack board? However, it comforted her to think of all the people from decades before who had left notes stuck to its surface. How many family, friends, and lovers had the message tree reunited? It was sad that she wouldn't be so happily joined with her love.

She'd been up since three in the morning replaying her interaction with Zak, reviewing the private investigator's report, and rehearsing the conversation she was getting ready to have with Rikki. As the phone rang several times on the other end, she knew her performance had to be perfect because Rikki was always tuned in to her moods. Sara had assumed it was because she loved her. Now she knew it was a necessity of being an unfaithful partner.

"Hey, babe." The perky voice was a bit too high-pitched, an alcohol-induced condition Sara recognized from months of experience.

"Rikki, I've made arrangements for you to visit next weekend. You'll love the Stanley. It's one of the first and most luxurious hotels in Nairobi. It has quite a history and ambience. Say you'll come."

Sara struggled to keep the irritation and disappointment from her voice as she sold Rikki on the visit. While she hated the idea of spending one more dime on her philandering lover, she needed a face-to-face in order to end this farce of a relationship. Anything less would be a cop-out. She needed to take a stand on her own behalf, to prove she was worthy of being more than the holder of the purse strings.

"You know how I hate substandard. You sure? Will you have time for us to be together?"

Like that's ever going to happen again, Sara thought. "I've arranged everything. All you have to do is pack a bag and get yourself to the airport."

"Great, I'll be there. Can't wait to see you, babe. I've missed you so much."

The words almost made Sara gag. Was she really hearing Rikki for the first time or had her infidelity colored everything with a film of distrust and self-doubt? "See you next Saturday."

"Love you, Sara."

She knew the automatic response Rikki expected but couldn't force it from her mouth. "Good-bye, Rikki."

She felt as if a partial weight had lifted off her shoulders. The other half of the boulder would have to wait until Saturday. She stared into the cold cup of coffee in front of her and massaged her throbbing temples. Yesterday's arrest seemed like a bad dream turned nightmare when she'd asked Zak to hold her. She'd felt so emotionally distraught, but what made her think this woman would understand that well enough to offer solace? If she knew nothing else about Zak Chambers, she knew that she didn't do emotional.

But it had felt so right. When Zak cradled her in her arms, Sara knew nothing bad could touch her. Their bodies settled into a perfect fit. She felt completely safe, but beyond that it seemed as if Zak was comfortable with her as well. She hadn't imagined the release of tension from her body as they hugged. It was the ideal moment to kiss Zak.

As she traced the lines of Zak's mouth with her tongue and tasted the salty mint of her lips, shivers of arousal swept through her with such intensity she almost cried out. Zak was hungry and responsive, taking her tongue deep into her mouth. The heat between them flared and Sara wanted to be naked and sweaty with this woman who had intrigued her since the moment they met. Their kiss deepened and Sara clenched her lower abdominal muscles to stall an orgasm that threatened to overtake her. She loved kissing Zak so much she wondered if it was possible to climax from that alone. No other lover had affected her that way.

But when Sara had reached for the buttons of her shirt, Zak stopped her. Sara knew the look in Zak's eyes had been pure lust, but maybe she'd misread the extent of her interest. Zak disengaged emotionally, physically, and completely, as if they were strangers. That's when reality struck like a blast of arctic air. Zak felt sorry for her. She'd needed comfort and reached out to someone she thought cared for her, at least a little. But the expression on Zak's face had been both disturbingly arousing and terribly distant. She could take almost anything from Zak except that. If they ever had sex it would be because they both wanted it, not a pity fuck.

She chastised herself for being so open with Zak, then realized she had no choice. She couldn't hide her feelings, even if she appeared to be an emotional basket case. Her instincts told her that Zak cared for her but was unwilling or unable to express her feelings. The only way to reach her was to expose her own vulnerability, which was dangerous. Sara wasn't sure if she could take rejection from this woman who had so quickly insinuated herself into her life.

"Mind if I join you?"

Zak's deep voice vibrated through her like a low-volt shock, and she took a settling breath. The shirt buttons she'd pawed at the night before hung loosely through the button holes like they might fall off any moment. Sara imagined the firm breasts hidden behind the shirt as she watched the steady rise and fall of Zak's chest. Her body responded to their proximity and she couldn't force herself to make eye contact. She had to maintain composure or everyone in the restaurant would know what she was thinking.

"Actually, I'm finished and I need to get ready to leave. Meet you here later."

Zak touched her arm as she rose to leave. "Sara, I—"

"Enjoy your breakfast." Whatever Zak had to say, Sara couldn't hear it while surrounded by strangers whose presence made it mandatory that she appear unaffected.

Sara stopped at the front desk and made reservations for Rikki's visit the following weekend. When she turned to leave, the desk clerk handed her an envelope marked "confidential." She opened it and scanned the contents. Randall had worked quickly to retrieve the information she'd requested on land ownership in the Narok District. She wondered how he'd tracked her down to the Stanley and decided Zak must have contacted him when she was arrested. On the way back to her room, she scanned the pages and tried to make sense of the statistics and rough maps.

It was already after noon when she returned to the restaurant. She'd lost track of time reviewing the information Randall sent. Zak was seated in the same place Sara had left her, the table covered with several papers she was studying intently. "Light reading?"

Zak stuffed the pages back into an envelope like the one Sara received earlier. "Ready to go?"

Sara nodded and followed her to the truck. As Zak slowly traversed the congested Thika Highway out of Nairobi, Sara took in the sights she'd been unable to see on her way into the city. Nairobi could have been any other metropolitan area with its office buildings in the downtown area and people dressed for work moving quickly while talking on cell phones. But the farther from town they drove, the bleaker their surroundings became. Smog and exhaust fumes from the city permeated the outlying areas and mingled with the scents of wood smoke, rotting garbage, and sweat. Hundreds of people lined both sides of the road, either walking or selling goods. Bags of charcoal and vegetables were stacked along the right-of-way with signs and prices attached.

"Where do they get charcoal?" she asked Zak.

"They cut trees and burn them. Charcoal is used to do most cooking and for heat. It's cheaper and more reliable than electricity."

The makeshift markets continued for miles, then eventually gave way to lush green fields and greenhouses. "What do they grow here?"

"Coffee and tea in the fields and flowers in the greenhouses. Many of the coffee growers have converted to flowers because big business and the government don't control the industry, yet. The production of cut flowers is almost as lucrative as tea, coffee, and tourism." Zak sounded like a tour guide and Sara longed for a more personal connection. Her interest in and tolerance for small talk disappeared as the landscape provided less and less inspiration. She wouldn't be able to bear the silence between them for long. Sara needed to say some things, whether Zak wanted to hear them or not.

As if reading her mind, Zak asked, "Will you tell me what happened yesterday, please?"

Sara reiterated the stop and subsequent arrest in detail as Zak asked her to repeat things several times for clarification. "Knowing how I feel about violence, you can't think the gun was mine. And from the look on Joey's face, he'd never seen it either."

"He said they were stopped on the way to work yesterday right outside the camp and his van was searched." Zak's expression changed from concentration to recognition. "The police probably planted it then, called the jeshi with his vehicle description, and waited. It sounds like a Wachira plan."

"Why would he do that?"

"He wants us off this land and he'll do anything to make that happen."

Sara removed the envelope from her purse. "And I think I'm beginning to understand why. I asked Randall to dig into the property ownerships in the area. Two powerful companies are interested in developing land in the Narok District. The Kenyan Tourism Group, KTG, has just opened a large resort nearby, and Africa World Wide, AWW, wants this particular piece of property to do the same. Obviously KTG isn't excited about having competition so close to their operation. But I can't figure how Wachira fits in."

Zak's blue eyes were dark but her facial expression fluctuated between irritation and admiration. "I asked you not to get involved."

"I'm not involved. I just got some information. The more information we have, the better our chances of figuring this out."

Her answer seemed to satisfy Zak for the moment. "Okay, but let it end there. I'll take care of everything else."

"So, what does any of this have to do with Wachira?"

"It's financial and political. The KTG is associated with President Kibaki and his minister of tourism. KTG provides funding for financial institutions and infrastructure expansion, and focuses on health, education, culture, and rural and economic development. They've done a lot for the country and the affiliation works for both parties."

"That's all good, right?"

"Absolutely. But on the other hand, AWW purchases land near existing developments, taps into the infrastructure with low cost, strips the land, and puts nothing back into the community. The company is run by a group of corrupt men only interested in profits."

"Why doesn't President Kibaki just stop AWW from buying land in Kenya?" Sara asked.

"It's not that simple. AWW is affiliated with Vice President Musyoka and the minister of education. Kibaki and Musyoka have different political loyalties, but they are tasked with working together for the stability and development of Kenya. These land negotiations are very lucrative and very politically explosive. In order for Kibaki to take action, he would need irrefutable evidence that Musyoka is involved. And even then, the fallout would be minimal. He can't afford to alienate his vice president's supporters because of the country's volatility."

"Jeez, what a powder keg. Where did you get such detailed information about the political workings of this country?"

"I still have contacts that see the conflicts in government every day, and I have other sources as well." The last half of Zak's statement trailed off as if she hadn't intended to say it aloud. "Sounds like between us we've pieced together most of the puzzle."

"And Wachira?"

"He's the only missing link. I'm not sure what his connection is, but I'm sure there is one. And you can bet I intend to find it."

"Zak, please don't do anything crazy." Sara hoped her tone relayed her concern without having to mention Zak's earlier threats to Wachira. The thought that she might actually physically go after this man gave Sara chills.

An uncomfortable silence fell between them again as Sara reorganized once more what she wanted to say about last night and their kiss. Just as she started to launch into her carefully prepared speech, Zak's phone rang.

"Hello." Zak's face lit up like Times Square on New Year's Eve. Her eyes changed from a dark moody blue to sparkling, happy. Her lips parted in a half smile, revealing the tiny gap between her teeth. "It's good to hear from you. How've you been?"

Zak listened intently to the conversation that Sara couldn't hear. She raked a hand through her hair several times in a nervous manner and looked down at her clothes as if the person on the other end could see her and might disapprove. A wave of jealousy overtook Sara, similar to what she experienced when seeing Zak with Imani. Something about this conversation seemed personal and intimate, and Sara couldn't help being envious.

"I'd love to see you. Next weekend is perfect. Yes, I know it well. Love you, too."

Sara stared at Zak slack-jawed. *Love you?* Suddenly Zak's reluctance to get involved with her made sense. She already had a lover. Someone as attractive and sexually appealing as Zak would certainly have outlets for her physical needs. The thought constricted Sara's chest like a gigantic boulder, blocking breath and pressing the life from her. The weight of this revelation crushed the things she'd wanted to say to Zak. She'd practically thrown herself at a woman who was already in a relationship. And instead of using her partner as an excuse for her disinterest, Zak assumed responsibility and simply said she couldn't have sex with Sara. This information made the rejection even worse.

"Sara, about last night."

"It was my fault. I was emotionally overwrought. I shouldn't have asked you to hold me." The next statement hung in Sara's throat, refusing to move because it was a lie. "And I apologize for the kiss." The words tasted bitter on her tongue. She'd never experienced anything as right as that kiss. And the reason poked at her mind with its certainty—she was starting to care for Zak, and controlling those emotions would not be easy. "You've made it clear our relationship is strictly business. I should've listened. It won't happen again."

❖

The range of emotions that played across Sara's face knotted Zak's insides. She'd dreaded the kiss conversation because she had no idea what to say. She'd spent the night sorting through her feelings about Sara, her job, and the vendetta against Wachira and was no closer to an answer. How did she explain to Sara that she wanted her but couldn't have her? She couldn't trade the work and the narrowly focused emotions that had sustained her for years for something else. The cold, unaffected part of her bristled at the notion of love, tenderness, and belonging that had been missing for so long. Despite her mind's resistance, her body warmed at the thought.

As the memory of kissing Sara returned and brought its full complement of pleasurable feelings, Zak considered the possibility of changing her life. She liked the glimpses of her old self that Sara had evoked during their few days together. They had given her a glimmer of hope. And Sara seemed willing to express her feelings openly. Perhaps they had a chance. But what had Sara just said? "It won't happen again."

"What won't happen again?"

Sara stared at her like she'd asked the most asinine question imaginable. "I won't be throwing myself at you anymore. I'll even try to keep my feelings to myself, though that part could prove a bit harder. It makes you uncomfortable and that's the last thing I want to do."

"What's the first thing?" Zak couldn't stop herself from asking.

A look of surprise was replaced by defenselessness as Sara seemed to consider whether to answer honestly. "I want to—"

Zak's phone rang again and she cursed under her breath. Sara was evidently about to say something important, and Zak wanted to respond candidly for the first time. "Hello."

"Ebony, Wachira is back. Come quick," Ben whispered into the phone, and hung up.

"Damn." Zak snapped the phone shut and pressed the accelerator to the floorboard. "Hold on." The truck lurched and bounced along the dirt road while Sara clung to the door for support. They were close enough that Zak could see the high riverbank of the Talek near their camp. "Wachira again. He probably wants more money."

"Then I'll give it to him."

"No, you won't, Sara. I can't let this man bleed you dry. He'll keep coming back until you stop and then he'll turn on you anyway."

Sara placed her hand on Zak's arm and squeezed. "I don't care about the money, Zak. If I can't use it to help people, what good is it? Let me keep him appeased with cash while you figure out how he fits into the big picture."

"You're amazing, do you know that?" Zak wanted to stop the truck, take Sara in her arms, and kiss her until she forgot everything except the fire that burned between them. But that couldn't happen, not now, and perhaps never. The thought plucked at the tinsel-thin thread of hope Zak had spun earlier. She had to focus on the invisible danger that was beginning to take shape and on keeping Sara safe.

As Zak slid the truck to a stop and leapt out, Wachira moved toward Sara with outstretched arms like he was greeting a guest. His lone jeep and driver were an obvious contrast to the menacing entourage he'd brought on his last trip.

"Madame Ambrosini, I heard the jeshi accosted you. Are you all right?"

Zak watched in amazement as Sara's look of dislike changed to pleasantness and her tone oozed congeniality. "Commander, how nice of you to check on me. It was a distasteful experience, one I'm sure you would never have allowed."

"Of course not. The jeshi can be rigid and undisciplined, unlike my trained force. But you are here now and unharmed. This is what matters." Wachira nodded toward Zak and added, "She should have called for my assistance. I could have made things easier."

Zak started to lunge at Wachira but saw Sara tense. She remembered her last outburst and the anxiety it caused Sara. Checking her temper, she decided to let Sara handle Wachira for the time being.

"Thank you for that, Commander. I'll remember that should there be a need in the future. Is there any more news about the land issue?"

"Not yet, but soon I think the problem will be resolved. There are many people with their hands out. Everything costs." He shrugged his slouching shoulders in feigned apology.

"Well, that's certainly not a problem. Let me provide you with some financial incentive to pass along." Sara reached into her purse and handed him another roll of cash as Zak stepped behind the truck to snap a quick picture of the exchange on her cell phone.

"Madam, you are most generous. This will help." Wachira touched the bill of his cap in farewell and retreated to the jeep. "Please call if you require my assistance again."

As they watched his vehicle retreat over the embankment, Ben appeared from behind the mess tent. "You are well?" He clasped Sara's hands in his and shook them for several minutes. "I worried for you."

"Yes, Ben, I am well and very happy to be back. Who are the new men?" She nodded toward two Maasai who constantly walked the perimeter of the camp.

Zak answered, "We needed more security to help Ben while I was away, but I think I'll keep them on." She hoped her answer would appease Sara, but the skeptical look she got said otherwise.

They spent the rest of the afternoon sharing the information Sara and Zak had gathered about the land-development companies and surveying the school project. The men had consistently shown up for work, and the methodical stacking of concrete blocks had transformed the foundation into a reasonable facsimile of a square building. As Sara walked around the outside walls, a look of concern clouded her face.

"What's wrong?" Zak asked.

"I just wonder what will happen when Wachira decides he has enough money and shuts us down." Her tone was heavy with sadness and regret.

"I wouldn't worry about that just yet. We still have time to figure out what's really going on. Speaking of which, I have to go." Zak grabbed her rucksack and spoke to Ben but motioned toward Sara. "Take care of everything. I'll be back as soon as I can."

Zak took the flatbed supply truck, deciding that Wachira had seen her driving the pickup too many times. For this run, she needed as much anonymity as possible. There weren't many hiding places in the bush. When she was out of sight of the camp, she pulled over and rummaged through her bag. She always traveled with surveillance necessities, and returning to Africa had made her even more wary. She located the small night-vision camera, GPS tracking device, and monitoring screen in the bottom of her bag. After ensuring that each was sufficiently powered and working properly, she drove toward the Narok police station. If her hunch was correct, Wachira wouldn't be able to keep the news of Sara's arrest and her most recent payment to himself. His ego would demand that he share his brilliance with his partner/boss, and that was the person Zak wanted to identify.

When Zak pulled behind the tiny post office across the street from the police station, night had engulfed the sky. She was grateful for the semi-cover as she made her way toward the three jeeps parked in the police lot. Wachira's distinctively marked command vehicle was closest to the door and bathed in a shaft of yellow light from the building. Using the doorways of the closed shanty shops beside the station, she made her way to his vehicle and belly-crawled underneath. She pulled the GPS tracker from her pocket, attached it to the bed of the vehicle, and turned it on. When the green function light blinked, she started to crawl out, but the door of the police station opened, and Wachira and his driver emerged.

Zak slid back under the jeep and grabbed hold of the undercarriage, pulling herself up off the ground. Her muscles ached and the still-tender acacia pricks stung when the skin pulled tight across her back. The vehicle revved to life and backed toward the post office. She bent her neck and looked for a place to drop that would provide some cover. When the vehicle slowed close to the post office door, she let go and quickly rolled into the shadows, stifling a moan as her back slapped against the hard ground. Wachira's jeep disappeared in a veil of dust and the African night.

Within minutes Zak was in the truck following her target on the small monitoring screen that gave periodic latitude and longitude readings. She was grateful that Kenyan law allowed drivers to ride without headlights if there was sufficient lighting to see the roadway. Tonight, the moon offered just enough illumination. The fact that Wachira's driver chose to run his lights made her job easier. She was able to hang farther back and decrease the chances of being detected.

They had been traveling only an hour when the jeep in front of her made a quick right turn into a grassy area that seemed to lead into a forest of lush greenery. Zak slowed and watched the headlights through the vegetation until they came to a stop. When the vehicle's lights were turned off, she could see an area of illumination through the trees, obviously a house or compound of some kind. The GPS monitor indicated the latitude and longitude of the location and she pushed the Save button. The jeep started up a few minutes later and came into view again, but Wachira was not in it. She waited for it to leave the area, then drove back toward camp.

Whether that was Wachira's home, his partner's, or a girlfriend's, Zak didn't really care. He had some reason to be there, which gave her one more piece of information about her adversary. She dialed Captain Stewart and waited for the connection.

"Stewart here."

"It's me. I have a lat-long that I need an ID on."

"Ebony, do you have any idea what time it is?"

Zak felt her face flush with embarrassment. In her haste to get a step closer to Wachira's contact, she'd failed to calculate the time difference. "Not really. This is important."

"Okay, let me have it."

Zak read off the location and erased it from the monitor. "I need to know who lives there, or at least who owns the property, and I need it yesterday."

"Was the information I sent helpful?"

"Yes. Sorry, but I have to go. Get back with this ASAP. Just text it to me." Zak closed her phone before Stewart could reply. She knew her boss well enough to know that more questions were coming, and at the moment she didn't have any answers. She wasn't sure about anything except that Wachira had set his sights on Sara, and she couldn't let this evil man touch another person she cared about. Her personal vendetta would have to wait until Sara was safe and her project secure.

CHAPTER TWELVE

A fter the weekend break, the next four workdays were quiet, with steady progress on the school. Wachira didn't pay them any more unannounced visits, so the increased vigilance after her arrest calmed somewhat and Zak was more relaxed. Sara still had no idea where Zak had gone the night they returned from Nairobi, even though she'd asked twice. The answer had always been the same, "Out," which translated to "Don't ask again because I'm not going to tell you." It most likely had something to do with Titus Wachira and the school project.

Ben assured her they would be able to put the tin roof in place in another week and begin finishing touches on the inside. While the possibility of completion thrilled Sara, Wachira's warnings that they would demolish the building if the property dispute remained unsettled haunted her. But Zak assured her that she would get to the bottom of the situation and the school would open as planned. After lunch Zak called the crew together and spoke to them in Swahili. The men were excited about whatever news Zak shared, but instead of going back to work, they loaded into Joey's van and left, taking Ben with them.

"What's going on, Zak?"

"We're taking off early today for a celebration."

"Celebration of what?" Sara really didn't care, because the light she saw in Zak's eyes hadn't been there in days. If this concocted celebration made her happy, Sara was all for it.

"Our progress. We've completed most of the walls. The next big step is the roof sometime next week. I decided we should treat the men and their families to a cookout. They've done a good job for us and it'll encourage them to stay on."

"What a wonderful idea. I'll get to meet their wives and children. I'd love that."

Zak seemed genuinely pleased with her enthusiasm. "I have another great idea, I think."

"I can hardly wait," Sara teased.

"Would you like to go for a game drive in the reserve while we wait for the others to return? You haven't had any time to see the sights since we arrived, and believe me, the animals are the best."

In her excitement Sara threw her arms around Zak's neck and hugged her close. "That would be fantastic. I've been wondering how to get it in. What do I take? When can we leave? Is it safe? Who will drive us?" Zak's body had gone still. Sara tried to pretend she didn't feel the heat that flared between them as she backed away and willed her voice to remain calm. "Well, don't just stand there. I want to see Simba, Dumbo, Tigger, and Snagglepuss."

"Um—I'm not sure I can promise that, but you'll definitely see animals. Bring water. We can leave now. It's perfectly safe, and I'll drive." Zak's eyes never left hers and her voice had a heavy, sex-strained tone that made Sara's insides tremble.

"Right." Sara forced herself to move away from Zak and gather some bottles of water, a hat, notepad, and her camera. When she reached the truck, Zak was already waiting for her with the engine running. "Let's do this."

They had traveled only a short distance into the bush when Zak pointed across the savannah toward something Sara could hardly see. "There." Her voice was soft, barely a whisper, as if the creatures moving gracefully toward them could already hear her. "*Simbas*, Swahili for lions. A mother and three cubs."

Sara put her knees in the truck seat and stretched her upper body out the window to get a better look. She adjusted the camera to telescopic view and could scarcely distinguish the straw-colored creatures from the dry elephant grass. As the animals approached, the lioness sniffed the air and was apparently satisfied that the women posed no danger. Her speckled cubs followed close behind, their disproportionate ears almost comical perched atop small heads.

"They're so gorgeous, like kittens," Sara said as she snapped picture after picture.

"As long as you don't approach them, especially the cubs. Never forget they're predators."

"Ever the optimist," she mumbled as Zak drove farther into the bush.

Sara felt like she was in a *Wild Kingdom* episode as the dry grass stretched ahead of them for miles and dust plumes followed their every move. Huge termite mounds rose from the scorched earth like missiles pointed skyward. She stole a glance at Zak and was surprised by the look of utter peace and happiness on her face. This was truly her element—the open, untamed, challenging wilderness of Africa.

"Just ahead is an ostrich nest."

"How do you know?"

"I've seen it on my morning runs. The parents should be nearby. The females lay eggs in the same nest, and then one male and one female take turns incubating and guarding it until they hatch. We could learn a few things about family from these birds."

Zak turned the truck off a few yards from a shallow hole in the ground that held between ten and fifteen large dull yellow eggs. In a few minutes the male appeared, looking gallant in his black-and-white tuxedo outfit, bare neck and legs. He watched them for a while before settling gingerly onto his charges.

"Wow, those must be some tough eggs."

Zak waited patiently while she finished snapping pictures. "Ready?"

"What's next? This is so great. I can't believe I've never been on safari. We always stayed on the island and stuck to water sports. Thank you."

"I love your excitement." The look Zak was giving her made Sara's pulse accelerate. "It's like watching a child who's seeing things for the first time."

"Thanks, I think."

"We've probably got time to make it to the watering hole to see the elephants. We'll have to go back then. It's not safe after dark."

While she drove, Zak pointed out some of the birds that populated the area. Sara scribbled names and descriptions of the white-capped weaver, superb starling, and secretary bird as she looked, took pictures, and asked questions at the same time. When Zak edged the truck through a stand of umbrella acacias, Sara saw four elephants standing in the edge of the water, two large and two smaller. She pulled on Zak's sleeve and whispered, "Look."

"Two cows and two babies. These guys can grow to ten feet tall and weigh six tons. They're herbivores and eat up to five hundred pounds of vegetation a day and drink forty gallons of water at a time. The females are head of the herds while males live solitary lives."

Sara couldn't suppress a smile. "You sound like Animal Planet. How do you know all this stuff?"

"When you live as Maasai you learn everything about the land and animals. It's part of your survival." One of the baby elephants waded farther into the pond and sprayed itself with water. "The elephant's trunk is probably the most versatile appendage on the planet. They can use it as a nose, an arm, a hand, a voice, a straw, or a hose." One of the cows suddenly rapped her trunk on the ground, producing a resonating rumble, and the watering hole was alive with activity. "Sara, get in the truck."

Before Sara could sit down completely, Zak was driving away from the pond. "What's happening?"

"It's almost dark and the predators are coming to drink. We need to leave."

"Thank you for doing this. It was amazing." She touched Zak's arm and the muscle under her hand twitched. "Sorry. For someone who tries to be so distant and untouchable, you do the nicest things sometimes. I just don't understand you."

"Why, because I don't want anything from you?"

The question surprised Sara, but when she thought about it, that was one of the many things that perplexed her about Zak. "Probably." She considered the ramifications of her answer as Zak drove them back to camp.

The men still hadn't returned when they arrived. While they waited, Sara helped Zak pick up wood for the fire and stack it nearby. They worked in silence, unspoken words and ambiguous comments hanging between them like spider webs. She glanced at Zak's muscled arms and legs as she stooped and gathered, remembering their feel against her body when they lay together at the Stanley. Her resolve weakened as the memory of their interrupted kiss returned. She hadn't been able to tell Zak how she really felt about that night, and they hadn't spoken of it again.

What could she say? Zak had a lover and that was the end of it. Nothing Sara could do would alter that fact. Though common sense told her to back off, her body was instinctively drawn to Zak's like an animal in season. The slightest whiff of her scrambled Sara's senses and started a fantasy that ended with unfulfilling masturbation in the cocoon of her sleeping bag.

"Is something wrong?" Zak stood with her arms full of firewood, a shy grin on her face.

"You make me so hot." Sara clasped a hand over her mouth but it was too late. The flush on Zak's face confirmed that the curse had struck again. "I'm sorry. I promised I wouldn't do that. It's unfair."

Zak dropped the wood she held and came to her. "We have to talk." The desire in her eyes was so intense it pulled Sara in and she swayed forward. Zak encircled her waist and brought their bodies closer. How could someone with a lover look at her that way, like she was the only woman on earth? At that moment Sara believed she was and that the passion she saw was for her alone. Their lips were so close she could taste the heat of Zak's breath.

"Ebony!" A familiar woman's voice pierced the twilight stillness as three trucks full of people rolled into camp.

"Imani," Zak said, and backed away from Sara, her eyes full of apology. Sara cursed the gods of timing for yet another inopportune interruption of a poignant moment with Zak. The odds seemed to be against them having a heartfelt conversation. Maybe the universe was trying to tell her something. She brushed the unpleasant thought aside as the trucks stopped and people disembarked. Joey ran toward Sara with a plump, very pregnant woman and three children in tow.

"Miss Sara, my wife, Lola, and my children." The woman and kids gave shy smiles and quickly rejoined the group.

"They are lovely, Joey. Introduce me to everyone." Sara contented herself with meeting the men's families and making small talk while periodically glancing at Zak as she welcomed their guests. When Zak slid her arm around Imani's waist in greeting, Sara couldn't help but wonder if this was the lover who'd called her yesterday, the woman she was planning to meet in a few days for a rendezvous. Their level of intimacy hadn't diminished since their last time together, Sara noted with a twinge of discomfort.

Imani wore a bright yellow shuka that clung to her striking figure like a form-fitted garment. Her generous breasts were firm and perky, her waist narrow, and her thighs curvy and inviting. Looking at her own body, Sara felt frumpy and ill-proportioned. A feeling of inadequacy gripped her and she looked away from the couple. There was something so wrong about this. Perhaps she was having a delayed reaction to the disintegration of her own relationship and couldn't bear to see others happy. But that wasn't her style. She rejoiced in the happiness of her friends, so what made this different?

Maybe her uneasiness was simple jealousy, but it wasn't entirely about Zak and Imani being together sexually, though that thought certainly prickled her skin. The depth of their connection and the ease Zak displayed in Imani's presence made Sara profoundly sad. The two moved with an economy of motion that came from years of close interaction and mutual respect. Their conversations seemed supportive, encouraging, even humorous, never the kind of taxing exchanges she and Zak often had. While she appreciated the fact that someone could help Zak relax and enjoy life, it stung that it wasn't her. She reined in her emotions as Zak and Imani approached.

"Sara, you remember Imani, Ben's sister?"

"Of course." Sara offered her hand but the woman pulled her into a warm embrace.

"It is good to see you again, Sara." She stepped back and gave Sara a discerning gaze that felt almost too familiar. "You are adjusting to our climate. Your delicate skin now browns instead of burns, unlike Ebony, who never tans. Beautiful." Sara wasn't sure if her last reference was meant for her or Zak, but they both blushed.

Zak stepped between Sara and Imani, hooked their arms together, and led them toward the fire. "Ben's got the fire going, so we should be eating soon. I've got something special for you to try," she said to Sara.

"Not more of that blood stuff, I hope." Sara's stomach did a nasty flip.

"Oh, no, this is a time-honored tradition in Kenya. It's called muratina, basically a weak beer made from muratina, the sausage-tree fruit, and sugar cane. It can be a little sour but won't hurt you unless you drink too much of it."

"You will like it," Imani said as they joined the others.

Several women squatted by the fire, stirring and turning food as it cooked over the open flame. The workmen boasted about their building skills and pointed to the school as evidence of their prowess. While Ben supervised the food preparation, Joey poured the drink into plastic cups and passed them out.

Sara looked at the liquid in her cup and sniffed before deciding whether to drink it. Cow's blood and milk had cured her of downing anything without a careful inspection. The smell was definitely fermentation-inspired and the look was muddy, at best. She took a tiny sip and the taste was similar to bitter citrus fruit, though not entirely unpleasant.

Zak had been watching and when Sara finally drank, she raised her cup in a toast. "To our fantastic work crew and the progress they've made."

Everyone joined in the toast and after several more Sara forgot all about the bitter taste of muratina. The mystery-meat stew, corn mash, and vegetables provided the most delicious meal she'd had in days. They all sat on the ground surrounding the fire eating, telling stories, and laughing until the children fell asleep and the adults spoke in whispers. One by one the mothers gathered their sleeping toddlers and placed them in the truck beds, covering them with light wraps against the cool night air.

"Now we dance." Ben rose and started clapping his hands together in a rhythmic beat. The other men joined in humming and chanting as the women danced beside them. Sara, Zak, and Imani were still seated but swayed from side to side with the pulse. The men's deep chants and the women's softer replies vibrated with a sensual quality that made the dance seem more like foreplay. One of the men tried to pull Imani into the revelry. She stood but, instead of going with him, grabbed Zak's hands and dragged her into the circle. Zak offered no resistance as Imani pressed their bodies together in a slow sway. They moved as if they'd danced together hundreds of times. Sara watched their provocative movements and the subtle touches that passed between them.

She'd never seen this side of Zak—physically loose, totally

relaxed, and seemingly sexually available. The memory of their kiss returned and Sara took another gulp of beer. It cooled her throat but did nothing to quench the fire that raged inside her. She couldn't watch another woman caressing Zak. More to the point, she couldn't bear that Zak was allowing it when she'd told Sara no.

She poured another cup of bush beer and walked toward the camp's perimeter. If it was going to happen, she didn't have to watch. That was too masochistic for her taste. She chugged the beer quickly and the flush of intoxication raced through her. The starlit sky was too beautiful, the music too arousing, and the image of Zak and Imani too disturbing to face sober. The dregs of her muratina went down as easily as the tears rolled off her cheeks. Watching the stars, letting her tears fall, Sara didn't notice when the music stopped behind her.

"You shouldn't be out here alone." Imani had approached silently and stood close to Sara's back. "Ebony is concerned for you."

Sara wiped the tears from her face and turned too quickly, her balance faltering. Imani's hands on her waist steadied her. The touch was soft and gentle, but Sara's mind boiled with questions whose time had come. "Why do you call her Ebony?"

If her inquiry surprised Imani, it didn't register on her flawless face. Her golden eyes locked on Sara's as if measuring her intentions. "As children we three played together. When Ben was old enough to herd, she followed, learning the ways of men. I did not understand."

Sadness shadowed Imani's bright eyes as she spoke, the memory obviously painful. "Her body was like mine but the men accepted her as equal. She was light on the outside but rich and black inside like my people, like the ebony tree. So I called her as Ebony."

The story touched Sara and she asked, "Why did it make you sad?"

"She did things I was not allowed with my people, men's work." Imani paused as though trying to decide if she should say more. "But then she came to me as a man."

"As a man?"

"She wanted me as men do."

Sara heard the soft gasp escape her lips. The star-laden sky seemed to spin above her as Imani's words registered. The connection she'd sensed between them was real. All the beer she'd consumed soured in her stomach and her head pounded with the new information. Too much information, but she couldn't stop.

"Are you in love with Zak?"

"For years." The answer was immediate and definitive. "But—"

"I can't hear any more, please." Sara ran toward her tent, almost charging into Zak on her way past the campfire.

Zak had been watching Sara and Imani as they chatted near the thorn perimeter, and her anxiety grew. They seemed intense, and she wanted to know what the conversation was about. When Sara ran past, Zak tried to grab her but she shook off the hold. "Sara. What's wrong?" Her eyes were wet with tears and dark with pain. She couldn't imagine what Imani said to elicit such a response. She stood outside the tent and called in, "Sara, will you talk to me?"

"Not now. Go away, Zak."

"I don't understand."

"Please, Zak, leave me alone."

Zak was tempted to rip open the flap and go inside, to confront Sara and clear up whatever misconception had occurred, but her voice had turned hard and cold. Like a cornered animal that sends out warning signals, Sara was clearly not in the mood to be approached.

"Okay, we'll talk tomorrow. Good night."

Zak found Imani still standing beside the barricade. "What happened with Sara? She's pretty upset."

"She cares for you deeply, Ebony."

Zak kicked a clump of dry earth and the dust exploded across the toe of her shoe. "I'm afraid you're right, but there's nothing I can do about it."

"Do you care for her?"

"It doesn't matter how I feel. Nothing can happen. She has no idea who I really am or what I do for a living."

"Maybe it is time to tell her."

"Nice thought, but no. Now stop avoiding my question. What upset her?"

"She asked questions she did not want answered."

"Imani, I love you but sometimes you can be very frustrating. What did you say to her?"

"She asked if I am in love with you and I said yes."

Zak's toe-tapping ended. "You said what?" Her heart seemed to have stopped. She remembered their childhood together and the bonds of trust they developed through play. The teenage phase had been more difficult as she gravitated toward men's work and Imani learned the tribal ways of women. And then the year Imani pointed out that Zak's feelings for her were more than mere friendship. The most difficult revelation had been that Imani couldn't return her love. "But you're not in love with me. You've been very clear about that."

"My feelings for you were very powerful, but I could not go against the teachings of my people. It was forbidden."

"Why didn't you tell me?" Zak held Imani's hands and gazed into the cat-like eyes. "Rejection like that is pretty tough when you're as young as I was and just coming out."

"If I told you of my feelings, you would have stayed, tried to convince me to go away with you. I had to remain here, to help my tribe. Your parents taught me that."

"But *you* left. You ran from me." Zak was trying to understand what happened.

"I went to university, to learn and teach the children. I did not run from you. I learned that I have choices."

"And now?"

"And now I am too late. The fire in your eyes is not for me."

Zak started to object, to deny Imani's assumption, but the words died on the tip of her tongue. She had grieved the loss of this beautiful woman for years before allowing herself to move on. What she felt for her now was the love of a best friend or a sister.

She opened her mouth to speak, but Imani covered her lips with her fingers. "Do not dishonor our bond with false words. The truth lives in your eyes as you look at Sara. But now she thinks we are lovers. She did not let me finish."

"That would explain a lot."

"Do one thing for me, Ebony?"

"Anything."

"Do not wait too long as I have done and lose the one you love."

As Zak watched Imani walk back toward camp, she wondered if she was right. Was she in love with Sara? The thought created shards of excitement and fear fighting for dominance throughout her body.

CHAPTER THIRTEEN

After the party crowd dispersed, Zak nestled into her sleeping bag outside the door of Sara's tent. She heard soft sobs from inside and toyed with trying to talk to Sara again, but the memory of her dismissive tone changed her mind. Was it possible that Sara cared for her as Imani said? Their kiss had certainly been intense and Sara wanted more, but that could've merely been a way of getting back at Rikki for her infidelity. A loud guttural growl pierced the night silence and Sara whimpered inside the tent.

The sound of big cats taking down prey was very close to the perimeter of camp, too close. Zak tossed the sleeping bag aside and located the two night guards. They walked the fence together, checking for possible breaches in the line. Satisfied they were as secure as possible, she headed back to bed. She shook her sleeping bag to dislodge any creeping invaders and prepared to step into it.

"Zak?" Sara's voice was small and scared, even though she stood very near at the opening of the tent. "What's going on out there?"

"Nocturnal hunters, go back to sleep." The red puffy eyes that shone in the moonlight indicated that she probably hadn't been sleeping at all.

"I can't." She stood tentatively in the doorway with the sleeping bag clutched around her waist. Her V-neck sleeping shirt plunged between her breasts, revealing the inviting cleavage Zak had admired so often. "Would you sleep in here, just for tonight? I'd feel better. Those noises were too close."

Zak hesitated, looking from her sleeping bag to Sara and back.

"Bring your bed."

"Okay." Zak obediently lifted her bed roll and rearranged it just inside the door.

"Over here by me. I won't bite, at least not as hard as whatever's out there."

She spread her sleeping bag a couple of feet away from Sara's and climbed in. The fragrance of Sara's sweet perfume wafted her way, causing an involuntary spasm low in her abdomen. She had turned on her side to face the opposite direction when an animal's death wail and the ripping of flesh disrupted the quiet. Sara moved closer and stretched along her backside.

"Talk to me or something. I can't bear to hear that."

"What do you want to talk about?" Once the question was out, Zak was afraid of the answer. But the fear in Sara's voice made her willing to do anything necessary to erase it.

"I don't care. I just need to hear your voice."

"We're safe. The fact that the lions have actually found prey makes us less likely to be a target." She didn't reveal that the lions should not have been hunting this close to camp since the game reserve was a few miles away. "Besides, the guards are well equipped to protect us. Animals in the wild prefer—"

"Zak, look at me."

She turned and did as Sara asked. The faint moon glow that permeated the tent reflected in the sad brown of her eyes.

"Are you and Imani lovers?"

"What?" She hadn't expected such a direct question, but this was Sara Ambrosini. If nothing else, she'd learned that Sara asked questions when she wanted answers, etiquette and protocol be damned.

"She said she's in love with you. Are you in love with her?"

"I love Imani very deeply."

Sara started to turn away. "That's all I need to know."

"No, it isn't. You didn't let me or Imani finish."

"I also have a lover, such as she is, so I have no right to even ask the question. You just make me so unbelievably crazy. I've never been around a woman who pisses me off and turns me on at the same time. And I can't seem to stop it."

Sara's words infused Zak with desire and discomfiture. Her willingness to put herself so totally on the line made Zak want to reassure her. But she was in no position to promise Sara anything, regardless of how she felt. She wasn't free to love her and she certainly didn't intend to place her in danger by involving her in the feud with Wachira and the Company's clandestine life she was forced to live. "Sara, I—"

"You don't have to say anything. It's my problem."

"Please, let me explain at least?" When Sara nodded, she continued. "I was in love with Imani years ago, when she helped me realize I was a lesbian, but she couldn't return my love. The lifestyle is taboo here. I never knew she shared my feelings until tonight."

"So what happens now? She's obviously still in love with you."

"It's too late. Too much has happened, and we're different people. I have nothing to offer her or…"

"Or anyone else?"

"Yeah, that's pretty much it."

Sara stroked the side of Zak's face and she craved more. "Do you think so little of yourself, Zak?"

"It's not about that."

"Then you're not attracted to me? You feel nothing when I touch you?"

The inside of Zak's sleeping bag suddenly felt like the relentless heat of a day in the desert. Her temperature rose with each touch of Sara's hand, her pulse quickened, and her crotch ached and dripped with the evidence of her arousal. "That's definitely not it."

"What's the problem then?"

Sara's mouth was close to hers and she wanted to kiss her so badly her insides tensed. "I told you, I don't have anything to offer."

"Offer me sex. Surely that won't be too unpleasant. That's all I ask, just once. I have to get you out of my system or I'll explode. Please."

Her words were like an accelerant on fire. The more she talked, the more they fanned the flames in Zak's body. Sex she could do. She'd done it often enough with marks. She'd just close her eyes and imagine it as another job. Besides, that's what Sara was, a job. A pang of something akin to conscience urged her to reconsider, but Sara was too compelling.

Her mouth was on Sara's before the thought fully formed. Their tongues sought each other in a hungry battle, their lips pressed almost painfully together. She pulled their lunging bodies closer and they joined in a rhythmic coupling, the sleeping bags between them irritatingly restrictive. Sara stripped Zak's T-shirt over her head and cupped her breasts. Her breath was hot against tender flesh as she hovered, admiring. "God, you are gorgeous. They feel better than I remember." She lowered her mouth and sucked a hard nipple inside her hot lips.

Zak arched toward her, the pain shooting straight to her clit. Her hips thrust to each eager pull of Sara's mouth. She needed more contact. The bedding between them was too thick.

"Oh, Zak, I need you so much. Get out of these things."

"I need you so much." Gwen's pleading words reverberated over and over in Zak's mind. She'd hurt Gwen and every other woman she'd ever bedded because she couldn't or wouldn't commit to them. Now it was Sara's turn. The thought was like a cold shower, shocking and exhilarating. *I can't do this to her. She's different. I can't use her this way.*

"Sara, stop." Her breast popped loudly from Sara's pursed lips as she pulled away. "Stop, please. This isn't right."

"No, Zak." The pumping of Sara's hips intensified as Zak tried to move from under her. "Please don't do this. I know you want it." Her eyes, heavy with desire, bored into Zak's. Her lips sought Zak's mouth again. "I won't ask anything more of you. It's only sex."

"No, it's not." With one forceful heave, Zak pushed Sara off her and onto the floor. "I won't do this to you."

Sara lay on her back, staring at her with hungry eyes, her hands clamped between her legs. "I really wish you would. I'm so close. Do you know how much that hurts?"

Zak had been so preoccupied with her nightmarish thoughts that she'd momentarily disconnected from her physical body. The question revived the sexual tension that ravaged her body and she flinched.

"See, you need it too. What's so damn important that you'd deny both of us a little pleasure? It's not like I'm asking for a lifetime commitment."

Zak started to answer but couldn't find any words. Nothing made sense anymore. She turned away but Sara snuggled tight against her. Their body heat seeped through their sleeping bags. "What are you doing?"

"If you won't relieve my suffering, I'll have to do it myself. Can I at least touch you?"

Zak didn't respond as Sara placed one arm around her and stroked steadily between her legs with the other. Their bodies were so close that each time Sara's hand came up from her crotch, it rubbed against Zak's ass. The motion made her clit twitch in her hand where she cupped it for control. She eased her ass backward, tighter against Sara's pumping hand, tweezed her clit between two fingers, and pulled to Sara's rhythm. She tried to keep her body still so Sara wouldn't know how badly she needed relief.

"That's it, baby," Sara whispered into her neck, "that's my hand teasing you, making you rock hard. You want to come. I can smell your need. It's okay."

Her pretense having failed, she pulled Sara's free hand across her breast and clamped it down hard. She plunged a finger into the wet folds of her sex and rubbed it across her painfully swollen clit, imagining Sara's mouth on her. Pinching the head of her clit between her fingernails, she fantasized Sara's teeth scraping across the tip. She pulled the engorged flesh between her fingers faster and harder until a spasm exploded in her crotch.

Sara's voice was strained and pleading. "I'm coming with you. Please don't stop." The tremors racked Zak's body forward and back. She shoved her ass against Sara's hand and heard her soft cry of release. As the ripples of pleasure flowed through her body, Zak tried to remember the last time she'd climaxed so quickly or so hard with anyone. When the last wave of orgasm subsided, she knew the answer: never. And Sara had done it while barely touching her.

"Now you don't have to feel guilty, right?"

Zak thought about Sara's statement and wondered if that was what she needed, plausible deniability. If they didn't actually have sex, she was off the hook, emotionally. But the nagging voice in the back of her mind suggested that was semantics, just splitting hairs. Sara nuzzled closer to Zak, her hand still covering a breast. "Thank you. I needed that."

"Me too," Zak murmured, as sadness tainted her pleasure. Did Sara only want sex? The question hovered while she drifted into a deep slumber.

Sara lay awake until Zak's breathing settled into the regular cadence of sleep. It was the first time she'd seen Zak really sleep, not just rest her eyes while listening. The fact that she was sleeping while wrapped in her arms made Sara feel special.

Zak's right arm was crossed over her chest and her hand rested on her shoulder. Sara wiggled closer and inhaled the musky fragrance of sex on her fingers. Another ripple of desire surged through her. Sara was tempted to lick the nectar from her fingers but was afraid she might disturb Zak. How could just a smell excite her again? Because it was Zak's smell, her very essence.

She hugged Zak and tried to dispel the romantic thoughts and the tantalizing effects they had on her body. Zak had maintained distance by not actually having sex with her, but then indicated that it wasn't just sex. What had she meant? Their nonverbal agreement for mutual masturbation required some level of trust. Perhaps Sara was breaking through to her after all. But to what end? The answer was immediately sobering. *Because I'm in love with her.*

Sara rolled away from Zak and covered her eyes with her arm. That was impossible. The pain over Rikki's deception had simply made her more susceptible than normal. She didn't even know Zak Chambers beyond the secrecy that surrounded her like a protective shield, the angry vendetta she nurtured as a life goal, and the rabid aversion to feelings. But Sara had never denied her gut instincts, and love was simply not rational. She was in love with Zak, but that was only half the journey.

She snuggled up to Zak's back again, draped her arm over her waist, and whispered, "Please come with me on this journey, my love. I can't take it without you."

❖

"Ebony, you in there? Come out," Ben whispered loudly outside Sara's tent.

Zak awoke feeling completely rested. Sara was still spooning her backside, her arm draped over Zak's waist. The position and the fact that it was Sara next to her made Zak want to stay exactly where she was. Their activities the night before came back full force and Zak felt a jumble of emotions. Something about Sara touched her intimately, touched her heart. Sara made her want things she'd never imagined she could have. She was tempted to kiss her before she left but wasn't sure she'd be able to stop with that.

She moved slowly, trying not to disturb the amber-haired angel next to her. As she slid from her sleeping bag and dressed, the smell of sex floated from inside, reminding her that last night had not been a dream. She wanted Sara again, but this time completely. If they kissed once more, she wouldn't be able to settle for a hand job unless it was Sara's hand.

She tiptoed to the flap, quietly unzipped it, and stepped outside. The sun was already high in the morning sky and the day's heat had started to build. Ben had walked to the riverbank and was standing with his hands on his hips looking into the murky water. "What's up?"

"It is late. You never sleep late." He stopped as if giving her a chance to explain. She didn't. "The men will not come today."

"Why?"

"Walk with me." Ben led her toward the perimeter of the camp. On the outside of the thorn bush fence the ground was sprayed with blood and the remnants of a recent kill. "This was last night."

"I heard the lions. We checked the fence before I went to bed. It was secure."

"The animals should not be so close to camp. The reserve is farther north. Look." He pointed to a stripped skin half buried in the sand.

Zak grabbed a stick from the ground and poked in the remains. She turned the hide of the animal over and suddenly understood Ben's concern. "This was a cow."

"This is why the men will not come. Joey says a lion has escaped the reserve and is hunting cattle. They will stay with the herds."

Zak understood all too well the ramifications of this news. Cattle were the measure of wealth and position in pastoral tribes. Protecting their herds was the main priority. Until the lion was captured and returned to the reserve, the men would not work on the school.

"Zak, Ben?" Sara's voice still carried the soft, dreamy timbre of sleep.

"Go to her," Ben said. "I will cover this. No need to worry her."

As Zak walked back toward the tents, she wished she'd gotten carcass-covering duty. She wasn't looking forward to facing Sara after their night of non-sex, sort of sex, whatever they had. What could she say? Nothing had changed except her feelings. She felt rawer, more exposed than yesterday. But her life was still a mess of secrecy and lies, not something she could offer anyone as a gift, especially not Sara.

"Good morning, where is everybody?" She looked around the

camp and back the way Zak had come. "Did I miss breakfast? I'm starved." Sara acted as if nothing had happened between them. Her eyes didn't linger suggestively over Zak's body. She made no attempt to touch her. Her voice was not heavy with innuendo. Maybe Zak had overreacted, placed too much emphasis on their liaison. Perhaps Sara truly only wanted sex, to purge the passion. She'd even said, "Just once. I have to get you out of my system or I'll explode." The possibility left Zak inexplicably unsettled.

"The men are taking a few days off, trouble with their herds. We haven't had breakfast yet. Everybody slept late."

Ben walked up proudly displaying a handful of bird eggs. "Fresh. Anybody hungry?"

"Starved," Sara repeated, and started helping Ben with preparations. "I guess it's just as well we're taking a break. I have to be in Nairobi tomorrow. Rikki is coming." She paused for a moment as if reshuffling ideas in her mind. "Does this mean we can leave today? I could use an extra day in the city. You know, shopping or whatever I do," she teased Zak.

Zak felt a stitch of something foreign in her gut and opened her mouth to speak, but changed her mind. What could she say? Rikki was still Sara's lover, in name, and she had no right to express an opinion about it. Then she remembered her own plans in Nairobi. "I have to meet someone as well." Sara's expression shifted. For a moment Zak thought she saw a flash of anger, but just as quickly it was gone. "Ben, why don't you take the weekend off? Find a couple more guys to guard the camp and go home for a few days."

"Maybe, or maybe I have the family come here. Like a vacation for them."

They ate their late breakfast in relative silence. Ben kept looking back and forth from Zak to Sara with a shy smile but never commented. Afterward, they policed the camp and secured everything that wasn't going with them.

Zak grabbed her rucksack and crammed it full of clothes, fresh and dirty. There would be time to have laundry done in the city now that they had an extra day. River water just didn't clean as well as she liked. She helped Sara put her bags in the back of the truck as they said their good-byes to Ben.

"Take good care, Miss Sara. Drive safe, Ebony, the rains come soon." He looked toward the sky and pointed to a gathering of fluffy white clouds in the distance.

As the two trucks departed in separate directions, light sprinkles of rain dotted the dust-coated windshield. "This should be fun," Zak said.

"What do you mean?" Sara looked at her like she was trying to decide if Zak's comment was serious or sarcastic and whether it referred to an extra day in Nairobi alone with her or the weather.

"You're in for a treat. You've never been in an African downpour in the bush. It makes the roads thick, slick, and sticky as porridge."

"Sounds yummy. It'll be a change from the breath-sucking heat." They both laughed and some of the tension between them dissipated.

They'd been driving for almost an hour, chatting amicably about the scenery and an occasional animal, when Zak's phone rang. "Hello."

"Stewart here. I've got the information you requested but didn't want to send it by text. There should probably not be a written record to trace. The residential coordinates you gave me belong to the Kenyan minister of education. Whatever you're into over there, drop it."

"Thanks for the info. I'll have to get back to you."

"Ambrosini is with you. Just as well, because I need you to listen for a change. I don't like how this is adding up. First you want information about landholders in the district, now you're following people to the homes of government officials. Do not pursue this, whatever it is. If it affects the school project, that's not your concern. Walk away and do it now. Your job is over. You were hired to get that woman safely to the district. She's there. Come home. Do you understand what I'm saying, Ebony?"

"Yes, but I can't do that."

"You bloody well can. She can sort out her own building problems, probably better without your help. You're just using her to camouflage your vendetta against Wachira. If you want to help her, get out."

Stewart's words stabbed at Zak's heart like only the truth could. He was mostly right. Sara could probably handle the project just as well without her, and Zak's feud was putting her in unnecessary danger. But it was too late to back out. She was no longer certain why. It was either her driving hatred of Wachira or her developing feelings for Sara or both.

"Did you hear me, Ebony? Come home, now."

"I can't." She ended the call to a string of Stewart's expletives.

Sara looked at her questioningly. "That didn't sound very friendly."

"Just business, and it's seldom friendly."

"Tell me about it. I can be a good listener." When Zak gave her a teasing look, Sara continued. "I'm quite capable of keeping my mouth shut long enough to listen to a friend's problems. It sometimes helps to bounce things off an uninvolved party. Just the other day when I called home, the housekeeper was going on about her family's— I'm doing it again, babbling, aren't I? Not a very good recommendation for a listener, but try me anyway."

"I can't talk to you about my work."

A glimmer of understanding flashed across Sara's face. "Is that what all the secrecy is about, your job? Is that why you're so guarded and unwilling to share yourself?"

"Partly, and that's all I can say."

"It's not, really. Here's how it works. I share something with you and then it's your turn." Sara's joking tone became more serious as her attempts to convince Zak were shot down one by one. "I can be the epitome of discretion, and you can trust me."

"No." Zak purposely sounded gruff and inflexible. She wanted to relay that no matter how discreet or trustworthy Sara was, it wasn't safe to share her life with her. But how could she say that without saying it?

"Of course you can trust me, unless you're a hired assassin or maybe a corporate spy."

The look on Zak's face must have revealed more than she intended because Sara's mouth dropped open but nothing came out. The shock and pain in her eyes was disturbing.

"Sara, please don't jump to conclusions. I'm not confirming or denying anything, but if either of those were true, can't you see why I couldn't tell you? It could be dangerous for you to know anything about me."

Zak hoped her last statement would deter any further speculation about her work. She needed to think about the information Stewart had given her. Wachira was friends with the minister of education, who was close allies with the vice president, who was aligned with Africa

World Wide. President Kibaki and the tourism minister worked with Kenya Tourism Group. The picture was becoming clearer. Both of these wealthy and politically connected organizations wanted the land on which Sara's school was being built, but for entirely different reasons.

Wachira's group wanted to build a resort adjacent to the game reserve, tap into the accessible infrastructure, and make money. KTG had established the existing resort bordering the reserve and it was already quite profitable. Having another facility so close to theirs would cut into their earnings. But they were funneling some of their proceeds back into the neighborhood. Sara's plan for the school fit into their overall development ideas nicely. Now all Zak needed was concrete proof of her suspicions and to keep Sara from digging deeper into her personal or professional life.

Sara sat quietly staring out the window at the endless landscape that never seemed to change and trying to make sense of her conversation with Zak. What had she just heard? Did Zak admit, without doing so, that she was an assassin or a spy? Suddenly her obsession with Wachira took on a whole new meaning. Perhaps the story of her father's death was just a cover for her job, to kill the man. Or maybe the story was true and she was being paid to exact her revenge. Sara didn't want to believe any of it, not of the woman she nearly had sex with last night, not of the woman she had just discovered she was in love with.

Zak drove in silence, her eyes constantly searching forward. Soon the rain started to come down in solid gray sheets, perfectly matching Sara's mood. She replayed the exchange in her mind again but couldn't accept the worst about Zak. The windows fogged over from the inside and droplets of condensation made trails down the glass. A cold shiver shot up her spine in spite of the heat inside the vehicle. She crossed her arms over her chest to stave off the apprehension that threatened to consume her. Suddenly the truck slid sideways on the slimy road, and Sara was thrown against her door, then horizontally toward Zak.

Zak took her hands off the steering wheel to catch Sara and the vehicle skidded off the roadway. When they settled into the slight drop-off, she was sitting in Zak's lap and they were both pressed against the driver's door. Zak's arms encircled her, protecting her from the steering column and the metal console divider.

"Are you okay?" Zak asked.

Sara turned and gazed into the azure blue eyes that were filled with concern and something she'd seen last night. Desire? "I think so. What about you?"

"I'm good."

They didn't move for several minutes, locked in a visual embrace neither seemed willing to break. Heat built between them and the windows became steamier. Sara moved closer, targeting Zak's luscious, slightly parted lips. She wanted to kiss Zak again, long and hard. In spite of what she might have heard earlier, her body refused to distinguish between the Zak of last night and today. God help her, she still wanted Zak.

Another vehicle came alongside theirs and honked. Sara moved reluctantly back to her side of the truck and rolled down the window. "Need a hand?" a smiling young man asked.

"That would be great," Zak answered, and opened her door. "Move over here and when I tell you, give it the gas, slow and steady, not too fast."

Zak slid out of the truck and into the thick, ankle-sucking mud. She pulled two boards from the bed and shoved them under the back tires. When she and the young man got behind the vehicle, she called to Sara, "Try it now."

Sara inched down on the gas but the tires merely spun. "Hold on," Zak yelled. She repositioned the boards and told her to try again. Slowly the tires caught hold and the truck eased back onto the road. Zak handed the young man a few dollars, waved good-bye, and walked back to the driver's door. She looked like a gorgeous mud wrestler, covered from head to foot with the gooey gray sludge. Her ninja T-shirt clung to her chest and accentuated erect nipples. The cargo shorts hung low on her hips and were plastered against the V of her thighs. Sara thought she was absolutely edible, minus the gritty covering. As she stood at the door in the pouring rain, some of the mud slid from her face and arms.

"Look the other way," Zak instructed.

"Why?"

"Because I'm going to strip and take a rain shower. It's the best option. We don't have enough bottled water to hose me down, and I'm not driving four more hours like this."

"What if somebody comes by?"

"We can see them for miles. I'll just dive into the truck bed." She'd already started peeling off the sticky clothes.

Sara turned away from Zak but positioned the rearview mirror so she could watch. Zak shucked the T-shirt off first, and Sara gasped at the sight of the compact breasts she'd sucked last night. The reminder discharged a liquid flow onto her panties. The cargo shorts were next and Zak was completely nude, standing ankle deep in mud. Sara grabbed at the ache between her legs as she did a slow visual inspection of Zak's long, toned body. Her ass was firm and perfectly rounded with just the right amount of lift. Her legs were slender but ripped with definition. When Zak turned, Sara saw the neatly trimmed crop of dark hair at the apex of her thighs and wanted to be there. How could anyone this gorgeous be capable of anything nefarious?

She watched Zak turn in the drenching rain and rub mud from her body like a kid playing in a sprinkler. She stretched backward, exposing her breasts to the sky, and scrubbed her fingers through her short muck-caked hair. The gray waves soon turned black and she finger-combed them into place. When her gorgeous body once again glowed with its normal ivory sheen, she bent over, pulled her shoes from the clinging mire, and threw them into the back of the truck. Sara stared at her upturned ass and imagined all the things she could do to it and places she would like to put it.

Zak rifled through her rucksack in the covered portion of the truck bed and pulled out a clean T-shirt and pair of shorts. She wiggled them onto her wet body and climbed back into the driver's seat. "Now, isn't that better?" she asked. "It certainly feels better." Sara was still visualizing Zak's nude body and merely nodded in agreement. Zak started the truck and maneuvered back into the rutted roadway. She adjusted the rearview mirror and gave Sara a teasing look. "Did you enjoy the show?"

Sara knew her blush was a dead giveaway. Denial at this point was futile. "I—of course I did. I enjoy all the wildlife. Besides, there are so few opportunities for entertainment out here."

Zak spent the rest of their trip telling generic stories about some of her adventures in Africa, clearly avoiding anything that might reveal information about her personal life or profession. Sara listened closely, trying to tease those very tidbits from the untold story or the nuance of Zak's voice and expressions. When they arrived at the Stanley Hotel, Zak insisted on securing their registration while Sara made arrangements for Rikki's arrival the next morning. As they followed the porter to their rooms, Sara realized why Zak had been so adamant about making the bookings.

Their rooms were on the same floor but several doors apart and across the hall instead of side by side, as on their previous stay. Sara hadn't thought about Zak's lover since last night. After they settled the issue of Imani, Zak hadn't really denied that there was someone else. She'd simply changed the subject, as usual. Now Sara wondered if the mystery lover was a screamer, thus the need for so much distance. The thought rankled and Sara grabbed her suitcase from the porter, handed him a tip, and opened the door to her room. When the attendant was out of earshot, she turned to Zak. "I hope you have a nice visit with your friend. Don't look for me to resurface until Sunday afternoon. I'll meet you in the lobby to head back to the site. Is that agreeable?"

For the first time since they'd met, Sara saw a flicker of surprise in Zak's eyes. "If that's what you want. But please be careful. It isn't safe on the streets alone."

"I don't plan to be alone." She closed the door and immediately felt guilty. She'd never tried on jealousy and obviously didn't wear it well. It made her say and do things she didn't mean, things that couldn't be further from the truth. But she needed time to think about what really was true. The things Zak had said about her job required reconsideration and investigation. If she lived some sort of secret life, there was no chance for them. Sara Ambrosini lived out loud and would suffocate in any other context. Her parents had taught her to be proud of who and what she was, to revere life, and to help others. She couldn't do that in a cloak-and-dagger existence hiding from shadows.

She pulled out her cell phone and dialed Randall Burke's number. It was time for her attorney to earn his exorbitant salary. "Randall, I need a complete background check, the works, on my guide, Zakaria Chambers."

"I checked her out before we hired her."

"I'm aware of that, but you went through an old friend, as I recall, someone from your military days. I want a separate check from the ground up: parents, date of birth, driver's license, social security number, education, employment history, financial status, everything.

Don't go through your friends. I want to dig deep on this. And get back to me ASAP." She hung up before Randall could question her motives or she lost her nerve.

It felt sleazy to poke around in someone else's life without their permission. Her reformed-Catholic guilt resurfaced. She hadn't recovered from the first bout when she had Rikki investigated. Prying into Zak's background was not something she wanted to do, she had to. Like Rikki, Zak withheld vital information that could adversely affect her future. She had to look out for herself because so far the women in her life had consistently failed her. Sara opened the minibar, unsealed a shot bottle of vodka, and downed it in two gulps. Then she collapsed on the bed and prayed that alcohol would numb the feeling that she had betrayed Zak. A woman as private as Zak wouldn't easily tolerate this terribly invasive process.

Chapter Fourteen

Zak stared out her hotel-room window, sipped a cup of weak coffee, and watched the sun rise over smoggy downtown Nairobi. She compared last night's restless tossing and turning with the night before when she fell deeply and peacefully asleep in Sara's arms. The possible reasons for the difference could be exciting if she chose to accept them. She was comfortable with Sara, perhaps even trusted her to some extent. But the cynical part of her chose the more practical answer: she'd had an orgasm and sleep was a natural by-product. The fact that Sara acted as if nothing happened between them and chose to spend the weekend with Rikki was all the reinforcement she needed. The more distance between them the better. This weekend wasn't about a romantic getaway, at least not for her. The sun had just topped the jagged skyline when a light tap sounded at her hotel room door. Estelle was early, as usual. She opened the door and quickly pulled her into a huge hug. "It's been a while, Mother."

"A year, three months, two weeks, four days, and—"

"I get the picture. Too long." Zak squeezed her mother for several minutes then held her at arm's length to scrutinize the woman most dear to her heart. Estelle Chambers was four inches shorter than she was, but had the same lean build, ivory skin, and wavy black hair. Instead of being close-cropped, Estelle's hair shot out in three-inch spikes, giving her more height and the appearance of a classy punk rocker. As a child Zak found lying to her mother difficult because it was like staring into her own slate blue eyes and denying the truth.

"You're too thin." Zak wondered if any mother thought her children ate enough. "And you haven't been sleeping." She waited for the clothing critique. "This is actually quite striking on you, cheri.

What is it, parachute fabric?" She fingered the black pants and camp-style shirt, rubbing the fabric between forefinger and thumb. "Black always was your color."

"Oh, Mother, don't treat me like a child." Her pale blue suit and white silk blouse were obviously expensive and the latest Paris design. Estelle wasn't pretentious, but she'd always dressed the part of the cutting-edge artist. She said it helped sell paintings if people thought she knew not only art but fashion. Zak wondered how she'd survived so many years of following her father to the African bush.

"You will always be my child, and don't forget it. Therefore, I reserve the right to treat you as such at any time. But in public I'd prefer you let people consider me an older suitor. Now tell me what's going on in your life."

Another of Estelle's motherly talents, reading her too well and cutting directly to the chase. "How about some breakfast? The Thorn Tree Café has a great buffet."

"You know me, I'm always starving. But you're not getting away with that lame diversion attempt. We'll talk over breakfast."

Zak opened the door and led the way to the restaurant, engaging in idle chitchat to further distract her mother from the subject of her. But it would be nice to catch up. Estelle was more like a best friend than her mother. "You've acquired a bit of the French accent. I didn't think it would take so quickly."

"I'm trying to assimilate."

"It's definitely working." Zak secured a table in the corner of the restaurant near an exit so she could watch all points of entry and egress. They helped themselves to the buffet and settled for what she hoped would be an enjoyable meal.

"I have to be honest with you, cheri. I'm not here just to see you, although that was the deciding factor."

Zak dangled a piece of bacon between her fingers and lowered it back onto her plate. Sometimes she wished her mother wasn't quite so candid. A few minutes of make-believe would've been nice. "Yes?"

"It's been forty-two months today since your father's—"

"I know. Do you really think I could forget?"

"I can only hope," Estelle mumbled just loud enough for Zak to hear.

"What?"

Estelle's hand covered Zak's on the table and gave it a light squeeze. "I only meant that I wish you could let go of the guilt you carry about that day. It was not your fault. Your father wouldn't want you to live your life under this cloud. It was an unfortunate accident."

"An accident? An *accident*? Is that how you live with it so easily?" Zak felt like a pair of unwelcome fists compressed her chest. The ache was almost unbearable as her temper roiled and spread like a tumbleweed.

Estelle withdrew her hand, her face ashen. "Easily? I still miss your father every day. We were together since grade school, best friends and then lovers. That is a connection not easily broken."

The deep hurt in her mother's eyes cut through Zak's annoyance. She took her hand and brought it to her lips. "I'm so sorry, Mother. That was unkind."

As Zak held her mother's hand to her lips, Sara walked into the restaurant. Their eyes locked and Sara stopped, taking in the scene. Her auburn hair was pulled back in a French braid that hung down her back, like the first time Zak had seen her. She was dressed in tight blue jeans and a copper-colored blouse that hinted at her cleavage. Blond bimbo Rikki followed closely on her heels and, when she saw Zak, encircled Sara's waist with her arm. The freckled skin of Sara's face flushed as she broke eye contact, turned, and left the restaurant.

"Yes, it was very unkind. I don't like what this job has done to you. I hardly know you anymore, how you think, how you will react. The greatest change has come over the last three years. That temper does not belong to the daughter I remember."

"My job has given me access to information that will allow me to avenge my father's death. Without it, that wouldn't be possible. And just so we're clear, his death was not an accident, Mother."

"I know you believe that, Zakaria. But I'm afraid you have been seriously misled. I have had his death investigated three times in three years by different people, all reputable with connections that run deep into clandestine affairs. Each one concludes the same thing. I brought the reports for you to read." She pulled a heavy envelope from her oversized bag and handed it to Zak. "You need to let this go."

"Is that why you're here?" Zak rearranged food on her plate so her mother would think she had eaten some of it. Her appetite had disappeared at the mention of her father's death.

"One of several reasons. Most importantly, I wanted to see you. You have to read this information. And the local hospital is dedicating a new children's ward in your father's memory this afternoon. I would like you to accompany me."

"I can't."

"Of course you can. Many people in this country still remember the work he did here. They want to honor him and you cannot deny them."

She saw her mother so seldom. She didn't want their time together filled with tension and disagreements. "I'll consider it." Zak motioned for more coffee and tried to lighten the mood. "I didn't know you and dad were friends in grade school."

"Your father was the only man I have ever loved. There's been no one before him or since, though I am considering women as an alternative."

Zak nearly sprayed her mouthful of coffee across the table. "Mother!"

"If it's good enough for my daughter, it's good enough for me. Now who was that curvy redhead you just locked eyes with?"

"No one" came to mind, but Estelle was too astute to let that pass. "She's why I'm in Kenya. It's just another job."

Estelle relaxed in her chair and appraised her briefly. "She might very well be a job, but she's not *just* a job. I've never seen that particular look in your eyes. It's a cross between passion and something else—fear, I think."

Zak finished her coffee and motioned for the check. "Mother, you've spent too much time in Paris. The romantic in you is showing."

"It always has, darling. But I know my daughter. What's her name?"

"Sara Ambrosini."

"Of Ambrosini Philanthropic? That Ambrosini?"

"You've heard of her, I take it."

"I'd have to live in a cave not to have heard of the great work that organization does around the world. Her parents were amazing people. I met them at a function in Saint-Denis just outside Paris a few years ago. They were charming, intelligent, gregarious, socially conscious, and devoutly nonviolent, to say nothing of charitable. If she is anything like her parents, she is quite the young lady."

Zak thought about her first impression of Sara and how it had changed since they met. "She is very much like that, rather amazing."

"We should invite her to the dedication, and perhaps she could join us for dinner."

"She has other plans this weekend, Mother. Maybe another time." The last thing Zak needed was to have her mother and Sara Ambrosini at the same table for a meal. Estelle would have them engaged before the entrée and married before dessert. And if Rikki tagged along, the entire restaurant would be in for an X-rated show. Fortunately, Sara had made it clear that she would be busy all weekend.

Zak signed for breakfast, agreed to attend the ceremony with Estelle, and pointed her in the direction of the masseuse and manicurist. She looked at the bulging envelope her mother had given her and decided against reading the reports immediately. Information was too easily manipulated to give credence to the idea that her father's death was an accident. The Company had conducted a thorough investigation on her behalf, and the results were clearly different from what her mother believed. But now was not the time to be at odds with Estelle. Today was too important to her and to her father's memory.

Sara met Rikki in the lobby when she arrived early in the morning and decided to feed her breakfast before blasting her with the private investigator's report about her infidelity. But when they walked into the Thorn Tree Café, Zak was there with a strikingly attractive older woman, kissing her hand and looking way too cozy for Sara's taste.

"Isn't that Miss Tall Dark and Ninja over there with a sexy cougar?" Rikki asked when she saw the direction of Sara's gaze.

"Yeah, let's go somewhere else."

"I like it here." Rikki put her arm around Sara's waist and pulled her closer. "Romance is definitely in the air if even your uptight guide has snagged a date."

Sara didn't want to think about Zak with that woman or anyone else, much less sit across the room and watch them gaze lovingly into each other's eyes while she tried to eat breakfast. "We'll order room service and have a quiet meal in the suite."

"Well, all right." Rikki wiggled her eyebrows and gave Sara a look that usually meant sex was in her immediate future.

In your dreams, Sara thought. Since she'd arrived, Rikki had been the epitome of the devoted and attentive lover. But the constant touching and consideration made her cringe. All she could think about was how many other women Rikki had touched, kissed, and fucked since she'd left the country. When room service delivered the order, Sara watched while Rikki devoured her meal like she hadn't eaten in days. She barely contained her temper until the utensils clanked against the plate with finality.

"That was great. Plane food sucks." Rikki got up and retrieved her suitcase from beside the door and threw it onto the king-sized bed. "Guess I'll unpack."

"Maybe you should wait." When Rikki gave her a curious look, Sara continued. "We need to talk—about us." Rikki sat on the edge of the bed and watched as Sara paced back and forth in front of her. She'd never actually broken up with anyone and wasn't sure if she wanted to do it gently or just throw the damn pictures at her and be done with it.

Rikki seemed to have her own idea of the topic. "It's been hard being apart, but I've managed okay. You were worried that I wouldn't handle it well."

"This isn't working, Rikki." She decided to take the high road because hurting Rikki would do nothing but assuage her anger. And she wasn't a spiteful or vindictive person.

"What?"

"Us. I've been doing a lot of thinking since I've been here. We just want different things." Was that ever true. Rikki wanted to screw every woman that looked her way and use Sara's money to finance her escapades. Sara wanted a real relationship that included fidelity, commitment, and equality.

"Are you crazy? We're perfect together. We have a great time. We look like the ideal couple. Sex is fan-fucking-tastic. What more could we want?"

"I simply need something different. I'm sorry to do it this way, but you deserved a face-to-face explanation, not a phone call from halfway around the world."

Rikki's normally pale complexion turned bright pink, and her eyes became saucers of disbelief. "You can't be serious. Babe, we just need a few days to get back to where we were." She moved to embrace her but Sara stepped back. "Don't be like that." She tried again and Sara dodged her.

"It's over, Rikki."

Her now-ex put her hands on her hips and her face contorted into an angry mask. "Is this some kind of joke? Have I done something to piss you off? It's your friends, isn't it? They've been telling lies about me. Whatever it is, I can explain." She rushed Sara, grabbed her, and kissed her roughly. "I know this is a joke or I wouldn't be here for the weekend."

"About that—you're not. You have a return flight that leaves in three hours. That's just enough time to get back to the airport and check in."

"Yeah, right, like you'd spend all that money to fly me over here just to break up."

"It's never been about money, Rikki. If you understood me at all, you'd know that. Unlike some people, I believe in honesty and facing problems head-on. It's worth the money to do things the right way. This couldn't wait until I returned. That wouldn't be fair to either of us."

Rikki's ire turned to shock and the tears started. "Please, Sara, don't do this. I love you. There has never been anyone but you. I'll stay the weekend and we'll work things out."

"You can stay if you'd like, but it'll be on your own dime and it won't be with me. If you miss this flight, you'll have to pay your own way home."

"Sara, how can I prove that I love you?"

She'd had enough. Rikki wasn't about to let go without undeniable evidence. "I have all the proof I need. You've been followed since I left. Would you like to see the pictures?"

Rikki's face went completely blank, but her eyes shifted from side to side like her mind was spinning in search of some plausible explanation for her deception. She started to speak twice, seemed to reconsider, then gave up. That pretty much said it all. She had no defense.

"I can't believe you had me followed."

"I can't believe you made it necessary." Sara opened the door and waited. "I think you better leave or you'll miss the plane."

Rikki pulled her suitcase off the bed and dragged it toward the door. "It's that guide person, isn't it? You're fucking her. That's why you're breaking up with me."

"Even if I was, it's none of your business. You gave up the right to question me when you stuck your tongue down another woman's throat. Good-bye, Rikki." She slammed the door in her face and smothered an urge to cheer aloud.

Sara walked to the balcony and watched the street activity below, trying to decide if she was angry, happy, sad, or unaffected by her sudden singleness. She concluded that her fury had come and gone when she received the private investigator's report and saw the photos. The happiness hadn't kicked in yet but she was sure it would. She'd finally ended a bad relationship instead of waiting for the other person to do it. It was both empowering and gratifying to stand up for herself. She deserved better and had taken the first step to getting it.

She grabbed a sweater and threw it over her shoulders. It was a beautiful day and she wanted to be outside, to celebrate her freedom with a walk. When she reached the lobby, she snagged an area map from the concierge, stood on the front stoop of the hotel, and looked both ways. More people were going right, so she followed the stream of foot traffic.

The car exhausts, smog, and decaying garbage permeated the air, making Sara long for the racy smells of wild game and their droppings in the bush. But like the indigenous people she'd encountered, the pedestrians along her route were friendly and accommodating. She adjusted her pace to keep up with the flow and enjoyed the simple architecture of the buildings as she strolled.

It seemed she'd been walking for hours when the midday heat finally began to affect her. She pulled off her sweater and tied it around her waist, then consulted her map to get her bearings. Suddenly everyone around her seemed to have stopped. She bumped into the woman in front of her and the map fluttered to the ground. As she stooped to pick it up, people crowded closer and pushed her forward toward a building where some sort of event was occurring. Banners announcing the dedication of a special children's ward hung across the entrance of the Nairobi Hospital.

Police and military personnel surrounded the area. Sara pushed her way through the crowd to get closer. She couldn't understand why an event like this would necessitate such a heavy law-enforcement presence. The front steps of the hospital served as the dais for the ceremonies and were lined with people dressed in hospital and military uniforms. A tall, distinguished soldier was speaking to the crowd, but Sara was too far away to hear what he was saying.

"Who is that?" she asked a woman standing beside her.

"That is President Kibaki. He is a great man."

Sara worked her way around the perimeter of the gathering until she could hear Kibaki as he made the final dedication. "It is with great pride that I dedicate this unit to a man of foreign descent who did so much for the youth of Kenya. He was a humanitarian and a powerful healer. That his life was cut short is a great disservice to us all. Dr. Franklin Chambers."

Sara stumbled off the raised curb on which she was standing. Dr. Franklin Chambers? Was it possible that this man and Zak were related? She knew Zak's father had been a doctor and spent the summers working in Africa. This was too similar to be a coincidence. She scanned the crowd as it started to thin.

President Kibaki walked down the hospital steps and shook hands with several people inside the police barricades. He worked his way along the line in Sara's direction and stopped in front of two women, one very tall and dark-haired. Zak. She'd know that statuesque frame anywhere—the set of her shoulders and the tilt of her head. Kibaki spent several minutes with Zak and the woman Sara had seen her with earlier.

When the president left the area, Sara started toward Zak. She wanted to acknowledge the honor bestowed on her father. But before she could work her way through the milling groups of people, Titus Wachira approached Zak's companion. Zak stepped protectively between them but Wachira reached out to the woman. In a blink, Wachira was on the ground and Zak stood over him, her arm cocked for another punch. The commander's detail scrambled, but Zak landed two more blows before they could stop her.

Sara elbowed her way past people, apologizing as she ran, her eyes riveted on the scene in front of her. Zak disappeared in a sea of blue uniforms, hands and feet flailing her as she fell. "Stop," she yelled. "Let her go." But the beating continued. Wachira rose slowly, put his hat back on, and ordered his men to stand down. They complied, pulling Zak from the ground as they stood. Sara was now close enough to hear

VK POWELL

but still not close enough to reach out or intervene. The commander approached Zak's friend again, took her hand, and kissed it. He turned to his men. "Let her go. This is a sad day for us all."

The officers holding Zak shoved her roughly away and followed Wachira. Her friend ran to Zak, her eyes conducting a visual examination for injuries. Then she grabbed Zak, hugged her, and lovingly kissed the red splotches on her face and knuckles. Sara turned from the tender scene and hailed a taxi back to the hotel. It was probably just as well. She couldn't handle Zak's angry, violent tendencies or seeing her with another woman.

❖

Zak spent the rest of the afternoon alternating ice and heat on the areas of her body destined to swell and bruise. When she stepped from her preparatory dinner shower, her mother was standing in the bathroom staring at her. "Let me see you."

"Mother."

"Oh, Zakaria, really, I need to make sure they haven't hurt you any further." She remained obediently still while her mother examined her. "You'll have a few nasty bruises, but otherwise, you're perfect." Once satisfied, she stepped back and handed her a towel. "You should spend some time in France. You're way too uptight for a young woman. Nudity is a thing of beauty, especially feminine nudity."

"Not with your mother." Zak wrapped the towel around her and fluffed her hair to deflect some of the discomfort.

"I'll be in the other room when you've recovered your composure and your clothing."

Zak slid into the black tuxedo slacks, long-sleeved pale lavender shirt, and black sequined vest her mother had purchased for her dinner attire. The ensemble molded to her body like it was tailor-made. Her mother's taste was impeccable and her visual ability to gauge Zak's size had been a source of amazement since childhood. She stepped into the classic black flats, gave her hair one final finger raking, and joined her mother in the sitting area.

"Gorgeous, cheri, simply gorgeous." Estelle patted the sofa cushion beside her. "Join me for a cocktail. I've ordered that terribly sweet Riesling you like so well." She handed Zak a glass and raised her Manhattan in a toast. "To beautiful women."

"Hear, hear." Zak sipped her wine and regarded the woman beside her. Estelle wore a wrap resembling a traditional shuka, but the colors were the blues and greens that flattered her complexion and it was customized to hug her slender body. She sported red open-toed stiletto heels that added at least two inches to her height. She was certainly a beautiful woman, and Zak was proud to call her "Mother."

"Did you read those reports yet?"

"No, I've been a little busy."

"You might have avoided this unpleasant business if you had." Estelle finished her Manhattan with an uncustomary gulp that Zak recognized as nerves.

"What unpleasant business is that, Mother? The part where Titus Wachira had the crap beaten out of me or the part where you actually let him kiss your hand? Please clarify."

Estelle rose from her seat and moved toward the door. "Let's go to dinner. This discussion is pointless. I'd like to enjoy my final meal in civility. We have reservations at the Thai Chi here in the hotel. I don't have time to go out before my plane leaves."

Zak met her mother at the door and snuggled against her chest like a child. "I'm sorry. I don't want our day to end badly. Seeing him touch you infuriated me. After what he did to my father, he has no right to even speak to you. He just makes me crazy."

Estelle stroked her hair, then kissed her cheek as she pulled the door closed behind them. "I know, my darling. I know. Forget him for a while and let's have a nice dinner."

They had been sitting in the restaurant long enough to order their second cocktail when Sara walked in. Zak spotted her immediately and couldn't look away. The knee-length sheath dress had fringed lace over the bodice that cupped and accentuated Sara's generous breasts. Her creamy shoulders were bisected by tiny spaghetti straps that Zak imagined would snap with the slightest tug. The sheer fabric gently draped across her midriff and gave it a gloved fit. The color, emerald green, was the perfect choice to emphasize her auburn hair that was twisted into a fashionable knot high on her head.

"Cheri, did you hear me?"

Zak took a quick drink of wine and forced herself to look at her mother. "Sorry?"

"I said, why don't you ask the young lady to join us? I'd love to meet her."

She struggled for an answer that would both appease Estelle and get her out of inviting Sara to dinner. Failing, she rose and motioned Sara to their table. "Would you like to join us?" *Please say no. I don't think I can sit here and look at you without touching you.*

Sara's eyes roamed over Zak and sparked with heat. Then she turned to Estelle and the fire cooled to a simmer. "I don't want to intrude." She turned toward another table.

Zak started to sit back down, but her mother nodded vigorously in Sara's direction. She placed her hand on Sara's arm and stopped her. "Excuse my manners. Sara, I'd like to introduce Estelle Chambers, my mother. Estelle, this is Sara Ambrosini."

Sara's jaw went momentarily slack, then a huge smile emerged. "Your mother?"

The two women shook hands as Zak pulled out the chair beside her. "Won't you join us for dinner, please? You look amazing, by the way."

As Sara sat, she slid her hand over Zak's where it rested on the back of the chair. "If you're sure it's okay and I won't be interrupting a long-awaited mother-daughter reunion."

Estelle answered, "It is and you aren't. Cheri, I love your dress. Eyelash lace is so chic and feminine. And the cut and flow of that piece suits your figure exquisitely."

Zak moaned and took another sip of wine. "Good grief."

Sara and Estelle looked at her simultaneously, then back at each other, and broke into a laugh that sounded like they'd been friends for years. The next three hours passed with Estelle recounting stories of her painting, her travels, and of meeting Sara's parents. Zak listened to their friendly exchanges to distract herself from the nearness of Sara and the realization that their time together was disappearing too quickly. She had her favorite women beside her and she didn't want to give either of them up. The thought disturbed her.

When Estelle folded her napkin and placed it delicately beside her plate, Zak rose and pulled out her chair. She did the same for Sara, and they exchanged prolonged hugs and whispered good-byes. It was a somber parting, as if they were all unsure when or if they'd meet again.

"I'll drive you to the airport, Mother." Zak started to make her apologies to Sara.

"You'll do no such thing. I already have a cab waiting and my bags are loaded. Stay and entertain your guest."

Sara gave Estelle a parting kiss on both cheeks and said to Zak, "Walk your mother to her car. I'll wait for you in the lounge."

As they strolled through the lobby arm in arm, Zak was comforted by her mother's presence and the calm perspective she brought to her life. She missed the consistent influence of Estelle's wisdom and wondered if her job had totally erased the values her parents instilled in her.

"Take care of yourself, cheri. And hold on to that one." She nodded back toward the restaurant. "She's a keeper." Estelle gave her one final hug and got into the cab. Before Zak closed the door she added, "And for God's sake, read those reports. I love you."

When Zak walked into the Exchange Bar, Sara was at a corner table in the back with a drink and a glass of wine in front of her. "I took the liberty of ordering you another Riesling. I hope that's okay."

Zak smiled and sat down next to her, missing her mother but glad to finally be alone with Sara. "I probably shouldn't," she said before taking a hefty sip.

"Estelle says it makes you horny."

Wine shot up Zak's nose as she grabbed a napkin and tried to keep it from flying out in all directions. "She said what?" Sara was obviously enjoying her discomfort. To emphasize the point, she rubbed her bare foot down Zak's thigh and up under her pants leg.

"She said Riesling mellows you out and puts you in a loving mood. I'm all for that."

Zak took a smaller sip while searching for a safer topic of conversation. "Did you know that the Nairobi Stock Exchange started in this place in 1954 and operated here for thirty-seven years? You can't beat the nineteenth-century décor for ambience. This is still considered the premier networking location in the city."

Sara's foot continued its distracting work on her leg. "Fascinating. Anything else I just can't live without?"

Pressure was building in Zak's crotch and the dampness had

already soiled her new tuxedo pants. "Over there," she pointed to the opposite side of the bar, "is the Wall of Fame. There are photos of the chairmen of the current top twenty companies on the Nairobi Stock Exchange."

Sara finished her vodka tonic and stood. "Are you planning to drink that?" She motioned toward Zak's wine.

"No."

"Then come with me." She offered her hand and Zak took it.

"Where are we going?"

She looped her arm through Zak's and brought their bodies closer together. Stretching up on tiptoes, she whispered in her ear, "To my room."

CHAPTER FIFTEEN

Sara closed her room door behind them, leaving the lights off, and led Zak to the small sofa adjacent to the balcony. She opened the door, allowing the cool breeze and street noises to rush in, then sat beside her. Touching the side of Zak's face, she examined the darker patches that had formed on her jaw and cheek. "Do these hurt?" The memory of the officers kicking and hitting Zak as she lay on the ground tugged at Sara's heart.

"Not really. I just had a—"

"I was at the hospital for the dedication." Zak surveyed the room, refusing to make eye contact.

"I'm sorry you had to see that. He touched my mother. He had no right."

"You're a complicated woman, Zakaria Chambers, and I want so much to understand you. But I'm having a hard time reconciling your secrecy and temper with the kindness I see. It just doesn't fit. Have you always been so reclusive and hot-headed or have circumstances changed you?" Zak picked at the cuff of her shirt but offered no immediate response. "Please, Zak, talk to me."

"I don't know what you want me to say." Her blue-gray eyes were pleading orbs of pain and confusion. "I can't give you whatever it is you want."

"You don't even know what that is. How do you know you can't give it to me?" Sara knew she was pushing, but her time with Zak was limited and her desire to be closer wasn't.

"Then why don't you tell me and I'll be more specific about my deficiencies."

Sara took Zak's hand and held it between hers, forcing her to meet her gaze. "I want you to tell me something about yourself. I don't need your entire life story, yet."

"I'm just not very good at small talk."

Zak's words and tone were as unconvincing as her shifting stare. "No, you're just very good at concealing things. And Estelle seems to be trained as well. I've never sat through an entire meal with a parent without hearing at least one bragging story about her child. She is obviously very proud of you and wanted to share some of your successes, but knew it wouldn't be acceptable. She talked about herself, which appeared to be a struggle for Estelle. Whatever your secret life has become, you've dragged your mother unwillingly into it."

Zak shifted uncomfortably on the sofa. "You don't know me or my mother well enough to psychoanalyze us."

"No, but I do know people and the nuances of behavior."

"In a few days we'll part company for good and I'll be just another entry in your collection of sob stories. Trust me, you're better off not knowing. I'm doing you a favor."

"Do you file that under deception or hypocrisy?"

"Why is this so important to you anyway?"

Sara rose from the couch and slid the spaghetti straps from her shoulders. She mentally recited a list of adages to bolster her courage. If only those who risk are truly free and anxiety is the dizziness of freedom, she had reached a new level of enlightenment. Why else would she subject herself to almost certain rejection?

"What are you doing?" Zak asked.

"Telling you why this is so important to me. I'm sure that in your world actions speak much louder than words." She folded the laced bodice of her dress over her breasts and let the sheath slide down her body to the floor. It pooled around her feet and she stepped from it and her shoes simultaneously. She stood there naked. "I'm baring my body and my heart to you, Zak. I have all these feelings for a woman I know nothing about. Do you feel anything for me? Please, just tell me if I'm crazy."

Time seemed to stall, locked in a freeze-frame of Zak's steel gray stare, void of action. Sara felt raw and too exposed to endure the stillness and uncertainty. Her choices were few: retreat and give up on Zak entirely, or keep pushing until she hit a wall or rejection. Again, she chose the direct approach. She might never know more about Zak than she did at this moment, but it wouldn't be for lack of trying. Regrets were not something she suffered well.

Zak stared at Sara's body, silhouetted against the dim light from the street below, and struggled not to go to her at once. She'd never had a woman offer herself this completely with such unselfish abandon. Sara's breasts were lusciously full, nipples already tight and extended. The curve of her waist and hips outlined the feminine beauty of her shape and called to Zak in a language as old as time.

"Oh, Sara." The words Sara needed to hear threatened to choke Zak as she fought to keep them from coming out. Her body was already on fire and her mind spun with too many things she wanted to say but couldn't justify.

Zak watched Sara step closer to where she sat on the sofa and her insides coiled with a hunger she'd forgotten she possessed. Sara reached for her hands and pulled her up so they faced each other. She shucked the vest off Zak's shoulders and fingered loose the buttons of her shirt, lightly skimming her skin underneath. Tugging the shirttail from her trousers, she left the garment open down her chest. The night breeze ruffled the fabric back and forth against her body. Bolts of arousal shot through Zak and her nipples hardened into painful points against the cool cotton. Her pulse quickened and her breath escaped in short, needy gasps.

Partially unzipping Zak's pants, Sara let them hang loosely on her hips. She slid her hand inside as if checking for more clothing but dipped deeper into the slick heat between her legs. Zak bucked against her hand, then pulled back, afraid of the level of her desire. Sara raised her moist fingers to her lips and licked Zak's juices from them, moaning as she sucked each digit clean. She reached up and removed the jeweled hair comb that held her hair atop her head. The coppery waves fell across her shoulders and spilled onto her breasts. Grabbing handfuls of hair, she rubbed it over her own nipples. Still squeezing one breast, she trailed a hand down her abdomen and Zak watched it disappear between her thighs. "Animals judge people by their smells and body language. What are mine telling you, Zak?"

Sara closed her eyes and arched her back as she rhythmically stroked above the waist and below. Her breaths were coming in broken pants as her fingers slid easily back and forth over her glistening bush.

Zak couldn't take her eyes from the lithe movements that edged Sara closer to orgasm. Another throaty moan and Zak's desire consumed her like heat scorching the desert.

"Don't." Zak's vision blurred as she descended on Sara. She didn't remember undressing as she moved toward her, but when she threw Sara onto the king-sized bed and came to rest on top of her, they were both naked. Pain stabbed between her legs and propelled her pelvis against Sara's in voracious thrusts. Grabbing Sara's ass, Zak forced her to meet her driving hips. She clamped her mouth over Sara's breast and sucked, feeling as if she could drain life itself from the malleable flesh. She desperately clawed and humped, wanting only to release the spiraling energy that threatened to render her mad.

"Zak."

Her body ached and no amount of pounding eased the pressure. She needed more from their bodies. Lowering her hand to Sara's thighs, Zak forced her legs apart with her knees and shoved her fingers inside. Her thrusts were powerful and unyielding, her intent to satisfy Sara's passion without being consumed by her own savage demands.

"Zak, please stop."

The power of being in control of Sara's body fanned Zak's lust. This stage of desire was foreign to her and frightening in a way she refused to acknowledge. Years of stifled emotions flooded her body, insistent on liberation, and sex was the only acceptable release. She had to manage Sara's response and still contain her own, but the more she tried, the more uncontrollable her reactions became.

"Stop, Zak!"

Zak froze in mid-stroke, hovering over Sara like an animal crouching over its prey. Sara's expression was clouded with questions and fear. Tears trickled from the corners of her eyes. Zak rolled away from her, clutching the ache between her legs as if it could distract her from the shame she felt. Her body quivered like she'd been disconnected from life support. "I'm sorry. I don't know what happened." She swung her legs off the side of the bed and buried her face in her hands.

"Things were getting a little too forceful for me. It felt like you weren't really here."

"I knew this was a bad idea."

Sara scooted beside her. "This wasn't a bad idea."

"How can you say that? If I haven't hurt you yet, I probably would have."

"Would you? Hurt me?" Sara's voice sounded scared, whispery and unsure.

Tears stung Zak's eyes as Sara's words stabbed at her heart. "No, never. At least not intentionally."

Sara stroked Zak's back in a calming manner. "Darling, tell me what happened just now." She wiped the tears from Zak's cheeks and placed a soft, reassuring kiss on her lips before easing her back down on the bed.

"I'm not sure." Zak rested her head on Sara's chest, ashamed to look her in the eyes as she tried to explain her emotional defects. "I couldn't control what I was feeling. It was like a drug rush that I wanted to ride but knew I had to contain. It wasn't even entirely sexual. It was more like…"

"Rage?"

The lump in Zak's throat confirmed that Sara's guess was on the mark. Years of suppressed resentment and revenge were finally beginning to take their toll, demanding release in some form. She raised her head to look in Sara's eyes as she spoke, knowing that what she was about to say was important. "Yes, but not at you. Do you believe me?"

Sara held her stare, the reassurance in her eyes answering before she spoke. "Yes, I do. From what I've seen, you work very hard at emotional restraint. And when you do let it out, it's usually as hostility. Years of that can stifle intimacy and sexual enjoyment."

Zak wanted to object because she'd never had problems with sex. But it had only been sex without an emotional or intimate component. Being with Sara was different. She wanted to feel more with her, to express more, to let herself go, but giving those feelings free rein made her uncontrollable and dangerous. Was there no middle ground between her cold, calculated life and the passion that flared inside? "I should probably go." But Sara hugged her tighter, refusing to be separated. "Sara, please. It's best."

"Don't you want me?"

"Of course I do, but I can't risk hurting you. And I can't promise that won't happen."

"Let me try something."

Sara's fingers trailed lightly up Zak's body and felt like sparks landing on her flesh. "What?" Zak breathed, barely able to speak.

"I don't want you to do anything but feel and tell me what you're feeling. Let me make you come. Can you do that?"

Before she could answer, Sara delicately traced the outline of her lips with the tip of her tongue. When Zak opened her mouth to take her in, Sara continued a teasing play across her lips and up to her eyelids. Her tongue and breath were hot on Zak's skin and felt so light as to be almost imperceptible.

"What do you feel?"

"Tension. Hunger. Pain. Fear."

"Kiss me." Zak grabbed Sara's face between her hands and claimed her mouth. She thrust her tongue inside, probing deeply, sucking her, wanting more. Sara gently released Zak's grip, guided her hands back to the bed, and withdrew from the kiss. "Kiss me slowly, with your eyes open."

Zak watched Sara's mouth as she lowered herself for the kiss. Her lips were red and swollen, wet and inviting. When they were about to touch, Sara licked Zak's lips, then breathed on them. Cool replaced the heat and Zak's body shivered.

"What did you feel?"

"Fire and ice, more hunger, lots of pain."

When their lips met, Zak held Sara's liquid brown gaze as a series of emotions flashed as if on a screen. Surprise accompanied their initial contact, followed by joy as the kiss deepened. Subsequently desire took over, and finally raw hunger before she withdrew. Zak felt a connection she'd never experienced as the kiss flowed through her like a shot of hundred-proof liquor, powerfully strong and slowly spreading its warmth. "So hot. Like I'm melting inside."

Sara kissed her way to Zak's ear, tongued the rim, and probed inside. "I'm going to make you come harder than you ever have," she whispered. "You want that, don't you?"

"God, yes. Do it now."

"Not yet, baby. Just feel it, slow and easy." She left a tongue trail of wet and chilly kisses on Zak's skin as she worked her way over to her breasts. Sucking a nipple into her mouth, Sara ground it gently back and forth between her teeth.

"Harder," Zak pleaded.

"What does this feel like?" Sara asked, her mouth still around Zak's breast.

"Teasing my clit. Not hard enough." Zak tried to control the labored pace of her breathing, but Sara's ministrations were making concentration impossible.

"Easy does it, love. Pleasure doesn't have to hurt to feel good."

"I need to feel it." Zak grabbed her other breast and squeezed the soft flesh up to the tip like a Popsicle. When she reached the nipple, she pinched it between her thumb and forefinger and her pelvis pumped the air in response.

"Zak, please. Let me." Sara released Zak's grip on her breast and replaced it with gentle, circular tongue strokes. "Tell me how this feels."

Zak tried not to allow Sara's tender touch to alter her sexual routine. Sex for her had always been hard, fast, and satisfying, and she'd always been in control. Slowing down meant actually taking time to experience the sensations leading up to orgasm. It meant feeling more than the physical. Neither gentleness nor mere emotion had ever aroused her. But Sara's hands and mouth were warm on her skin, their effects soothing yet stimulating beyond corporeal reason. Tears clouded her eyes and she blinked to keep them from falling.

"Too—tender." Her voice cracked. "Too gentle. I need more—"

"I know, darling. It's exactly what you need. More tenderness. Just relax." Sara settled between Zak's legs and rested her cheek against her thigh. She continued to slowly massage Zak's breasts as she blew a steady stream over her wet sex.

"It's good." Zak's craving reignited. "Touch me, please."

"Soon, very soon." Sara buried the fingers of one hand in Zak's curly bush and tugged tenderly. Zak's clit twitched and she got wetter. She wanted to shove Sara's hand into her opening but took a deep breath and concentrated on Sara's actions.

She pulled again, then trailed a finger across Zak's clit with a feathery touch. "You like that, don't you? Tell me."

"So horny. Need you inside me." She tried to grab the aching spot at the join of her thighs, but Sara pushed her hand aside.

"You're so wet. I want to taste you so badly."

"Do it, please, Sara." Zak's sexual pain was easy to identify. It hung hard and insistent between her legs. But her emotional need for Sara transcended understanding. It seemed to permeate her body and mind with a yearning more overpowering than any physical desire. When had this connection become so imperative and how had it happened?

She lay suspended between bodily heaven and hell, and yet the sweetest anticipation was wondering what she would feel for Sara next. Where would she touch her and what sentiment would it elicit? Sara handled her with delicate precision, as if she might disintegrate. If Sara suddenly withdrew all physical contact, their link would remain, an almost tangible thread tying them together.

Sara dipped her head between Zak's legs and licked her clit with a slow, tantalizing stroke. Zak's hips thrust upward in response, but she forced herself to still and let Sara's lovemaking bring her closer to the abyss. Sara's hair cascaded over her legs like silk and heightened her awareness of the lightness of her touches. Another series of licks and her control was strained to the limit. Fire burned in her belly and spread down her legs like a menacing subcutaneous itch. Sara continued slow, methodical tongue swipes over the head of her clit, alternately flicking just inside her opening.

"How does this feel, baby?" Her eyes seemed to gauge Zak's reactions and she adjusted her workings accordingly.

"It feels like you're inside me, everywhere." The words stunned Zak and she tried to figure out what they meant, but Sara's actions distracted her.

"That's good, very good. Are you ready to come for me?"

Zak heard a sound emanate from inside herself that she'd only heard from other women when she had sex with them, a cross between a plea for mercy and an animalistic growl for release. She spread her legs wider and encouraged Sara to take her. But instead of the fast, forceful finish she expected, Sara entered her slowly with one finger, then pulled it out with the same excruciating lack of speed. She flattened her tongue against Zak's clit and dragged it back and forth in time with the agonizing finger pace. The tempo took hold somewhere deep inside of her and she relaxed into the flow. "Oh, Sara."

"Faster, harder?"

"No—perfect, don't stop." A sharp spear of arousal stabbed at the base of Zak's clit and quivered up the shaft. Unlike orgasms of the past, this one didn't gush from her in a frenzy of hip thrusts and pinched breasts. It oozed through her system, satisfying and relaxing until it seeped out her toes. It moved with the surety of the African sun, slowly warming to a burning crescendo. Wave after wave of release washed away emotional poisons, left her sated and connected to Sara in an inexplicable way. It was like this woman had exorcised something wretched and unmanageable inside her and made her feel alive again. She trembled and shivered with the final ripples of orgasm as Sara slid up her body and rested on top of her.

"Are you okay?" Sara kissed her face. "You're crying."

"I am?" Zak swiped her hand across her eyes, surprised at the moisture there. "It feels like I'm leaking everywhere. I'm totally drained. How'd you do that?"

"It's that gentle touch. You like?"

"I've never had an orgasm like that. It was amazing."

Sara slid a leg between Zak's and snugged her thigh against the tender flesh of her crotch. "Now will you do something for me? It'll only take a minute and not much energy."

"Anything." Zak held Sara's gaze so she'd know that she was serious.

"I want you so much. I'm going to slide along this muscular thigh of yours a couple of times, and when I tell you, I want you to go inside me with this finger." She took Zak's right hand and sucked her middle finger into her mouth, licked it, and let go. "Can you do that for me?"

"Uh, yeah." Sara was already rubbing herself along Zak's leg, the hot juices slick between them. "What if I come again? You're so damn hot."

"Please do. Oh—yes. That's it." Zak could see the passion rising in her eyes, the painful pleasure on her face. "Now, Zak, now. Slow and easy."

Desire pounded between Zak's legs again and she wanted to bring Sara with her quickly to climax. Instead, she remembered the exquisite release Sara had given her minutes before and entered her slowly, letting her set the rhythm. She rode up and down Zak's finger with a pace designed to milk nectar from the gods.

"Yes, so close. Do you feel it?"

Zak felt the walls of Sara's vagina tightening around her finger. She tilted her pelvis for greater friction with Sara's pumping thigh. The realization that Sara was only seconds from orgasm started her own tremors.

"Now. I'm coming now."

When Sara's body sucked her finger with strong orgasmic spasms, Zak came as well. She cupped her hand over Sara's sex and Sara's fluids filled her hand. They clung to each other until the last of their climaxes subsided. Zak marveled at the sexual proficiency and emotional openness of this amazing woman. She pulled her closer and wrapped her arms tightly around her, wishing they never had to part.

She'd never had an experience like this one and doubted she ever would again. Sara had not only given herself completely, risking rejection, but she'd also shown Zak another way to love. She was relaxed mentally and physically in a way she hadn't been in years. Sara calmed a violent place inside her that not even she could quiet. But Zak had been selfish, accepting her kindness without sharing anything. And that wouldn't be good enough for Sara in the long run. "Leaving so soon?" Sara raised her head from Zak's chest and stared into her eyes.

"I'm not going anywhere."

"You're already gone, wondering how you got here, what I've done to you, how you're going to make a graceful exit without hurting my feelings. And most importantly, if you mumbled anything of a personal nature during orgasm that might give me a hint of who you really are. Am I right?"

"I don't know how you do that. It's like you know me better than I know myself."

Sara smiled at her. "That wouldn't be hard, darling. You don't seem to know much about your real self."

"What does that mean?"

"You've been taught or trained to disregard your feelings. And when we ignore or discount them, most feelings turn into anger. You've got that one down pat."

Zak still held Sara in a tight embrace and didn't want to let go even though the conversation was making her slightly uncomfortable. "Then why did you have sex with me?"

"I didn't have sex with you, Zak. I made love with you. And I did it because I wanted to show you that there are other ways to express feelings. It doesn't have to wild and animalistic to be good. It can be, but soft and sensual works too."

Zak had never felt so much a part of another person. She wanted to curl around Sara and sleep the sleep of the completely contented. "You've done something to me, Sara Ambrosini. And I like it."

"Good." Sara pulled the covers around them and snuggled into Zak's shoulder. "Tomorrow I have questions about the woman I love." Her breathing quickly leveled off into a peaceful slumber.

"The woman I love?" Zak's initial response to the statement was to run, but her body was too comfortable, her feelings for Sara too new and undefined. Instead she relaxed into the moment, letting the words sink into her mind, finding a safe place to settle and grow. She fell asleep holding on to Sara and the words no other lover had ever spoken.

CHAPTER SIXTEEN

Sara woke several times during the night, anxious that Zak might have slipped out while she slept, but each time, warmth from the body next to hers reassured her. It amazed her how peacefully Zak rested, how her face and body assumed an almost naïve innocence. This was the woman she loved, in spite of the shell she assumed during the day to protect herself and her feelings. The calm that surrounded her now was so different from the almost inimical energy that consumed her as they started to make love.

She'd finally aroused a response in Zak. The fire in her eyes filled Sara with excitement and apprehension. She'd seen that look before, once when they kissed and once when she threatened to kill Titus Wachira. It was an almost blind stare, hazy with a mixture of uncontrolled emotions. For a second Sara considered stopping, unsure of what to expect. But her gut and libido urged her on.

When Zak's ardor became progressively more demanding, Sara tried to shift her body to alleviate the rough pistoning between her legs and realized too late that she'd misread Zak. The passion she'd seen was a thin overlay covering a deeper more explosive fury. If she allowed this intensity to continue, neither of them would ever get past it. Zak had to know another way to express feelings that didn't involve aggression. And she had to know Zak was capable of it.

It had taken every ounce of her love and courage to ask Zak to stop. The look on her face had been devastating. But Zak respected her boundaries and was receptive to her guidance as she slowed the pace. Their lovemaking took on the duality of passion and intimacy that Sara craved. It had been everything she hoped. Now, more than ever, she wanted to know more about Zak, not to invade her privacy or her life but because she loved her. She'd opened herself out of love and knew Zak would see that. Maybe now she could do the same.

Daybreak brought a chill to the air and an empty space at her back. She rolled over just as Zak reached for the doorknob. "Do you have to go?"

She scuffed her shoes into the plush carpet and shrugged like a self-conscious morning-after lover caught sneaking out. Sara went to her, naked and shivering, and stood in front of her. "Do whatever you need to, but remember one thing. I love you and I was willing to make a complete fool of myself last night to prove it."

"Are you sorry?"

"Never. I'd do it again if I thought it would make a difference. Maybe I'm not meant to satisfy, just to draw you to the desire. Only you know the answer. The decision is yours. I've given you everything I have."

Zak embraced her and kissed her with such hunger that Sara felt giddy. She curved into her body and surrendered to the kiss until heat threatened to consume her. *She loves me. I feel it.* When she stepped back, Sara's lips still burned. Zak's eyes were a deep passionate blue but her face was a veil of conflict and confusion.

"I need time to think. And we need to get back to camp. Meet me out front in an hour." With that, she was gone. Sara's emotional heart stiffened in a progression that if unchecked could harden into stone. Stop it, she told herself. Zak didn't say no. She didn't reject her. But somehow it felt like the first step toward a strategic retreat. As she showered and packed for the return trip, she wondered how to fight such a well-entrenched army of defenses.

When Sara checked out, the clerk handed her a sealed envelope. She handled it like it might be toxic and stuffed it into her oversized handbag. If the ride back to Talek was too awkward, at least she'd have something to distract her.

Three hours into the drive, Zak was still regaling her with tour-guide recitations about giant termite mounds, habits of the long-necked gerenuk, and how the Ewaso Ng'iro River was being drained by farmers to the detriment of wildlife in the plains. An occasional glance in her direction and her nervous prattle were the only indications that Zak even realized she was in the vehicle. Her expression remained unchanged, and her tone and words never hinted at their intimacy from the night before.

"Zak, you don't need to entertain me. I promise not to ask questions or reminisce about last night if you're quiet. I told you, no pressure." Sara heard Zak's sigh of relief over the constant rattling of the truck, and her grip on the steering wheel relaxed. It saddened Sara that being in her presence made Zak so tense, especially after their lovemaking.

Last night Zak had relinquished physical control and allowed Sara to soothe her frazzled emotions. That was huge. It required a level of trust she hadn't demonstrated before. She'd seen a new side of Zak, a softer, more expressive aspect that confirmed her belief that she was capable of deep love. Sara felt she'd been given a gift and wanted desperately to keep it.

She looked at the envelope sticking from the corner of her purse and wondered if the news contained in it would be helpful or damaging. If it shed some light on her understanding of Zak, it would be worth the intrusion. But if Zak knew she'd had her investigated, it would certainly destroy any tentative trust she'd earned. Maybe she'd never have to know. Sara could file the information for future reference and not mention it. As she tore open the small flap, she knew she'd never be able to keep this secret, no matter how detrimental to their relationship. She withdrew a single sheet of paper with her attorney's bold handwriting across it.

> *This person does not exist in any database accessible to law enforcement or government agencies up to the level of top secret. I'm not sure what I've gotten you into, but please call and let me know you're okay. Randall*

Sara tried to fold the paper and put it back into the envelope but her hands were shaking too badly. Instead, she stuffed it inside her purse and dropped it on the floorboard. What did it mean and what was she involved in? Suddenly her joking reference to Zak about being a spy or an assassin wasn't so funny. In this context the purposeful distancing and mystery made too much sense. Sara had been brought up in a family that shared everything, but her relationships had certainly tested that practice. Rikki had proved to be less than reliable and honest. Now the possibilities of what Zak might have done in her life and the things

Sara would never know overwhelmed her. And she couldn't simply ask. She wasn't supposed to know any of this, but what did she really know? Nothing. At this point she could only speculate, imagine, and agonize. She refused to believe Zak was capable of anything evil. Her body was still too tender from last night's lovemaking and her mind was regurgitating at warp speed.

"Stop the truck." Sara slapped her hand over her mouth, holding down the bile that crept up her throat. She had the door open before the truck came to a complete halt. She fell into the sand on her hands and knees clawing, needing to feel something real, something tangible. When she raised her head, Zak was standing beside her offering a wet towel, a worried look on her face. "What happened?"

Sara took the towel and motioned for her to back off. She wiped her face and held the cool cloth to her forehead. "Too much African massage on an empty stomach."

"Let me help you." Zak offered her hand.

"I can manage." She got unsteadily to her feet and backed up against the side of the truck for balance. She couldn't force herself to look at Zak, torn between wanting to throw herself into her arms and beg the truth out of her. Instead she looked out across the savannah at a herd of elephants and thought, *How apropos. Big-picture life continues undisturbed. It's the unseen minutiae that cripples and devastates: the lies told, the responsibilities shunned, the feelings withheld, and the words not spoken.* These were the silent killers that robbed people of their lives little by little. She couldn't be one of those people.

"Who are you, Zak? There's no record of you anywhere."

Zak's heat-tinted cheeks paled as she removed her sunglasses and drilled Sara with a stare that was, at best, unfriendly. "You had someone check me out?"

"Yes, and I'm—"

"Who? How long ago?"

"What?" Based on Zak's past behavior, Sara expected an angry response, but she seemed more concerned than a simple background check justified. "Zak, I'm sorry, but I'm in serious trouble here."

"You have no idea. Who did the search?"

"My attorney, Randall Burke, a couple of days ago. What difference does it make? I'm talking about us, you and me, if there can ever be an us."

"That's the last thing you should be worried about. Get in the truck." Zak spoke as she dialed her sat phone.

"It's Ebony. I may have been compromised. An attorney named Randall Burke attempted a background search. He didn't find anything but they could know by now. It's been two, maybe three days." She listened for a few minutes. "Yes, let me know if I need to do anything. Thanks."

When Zak hung up, Sara crossed her arms like a petulant child. Still resting against the side of the truck, she announced, "I'm not going anywhere with you until you answer some questions. I could be in the hands of an assassin."

Zak stepped into her body space, her legs on either side of Sara's, and pulled her into an embrace. "You know that's not the case. Now, please, get in the truck. I'll talk while I drive." Sara gave her a skeptical look. "I promise."

When they were on their way again, Zak kept her word. "Ask your questions, Sara."

For a moment Sara was so overwhelmed with the consent that she had trouble choosing the first one. Her heart won. "Do you have any feelings for me at all?"

"What?"

The disbelieving look on Zak's face said she'd been expecting another question, any other question. "Do you?"

"That's it? That's what concerns you most?"

Sara placed her hand on Zak's thigh. "After what I told you last night, that answer determines whether I have any more questions at all."

Zak's hand covered hers and she gave her a quick glance. "Yes, Sara, I have feelings for you. And quite honestly, they scare me more than anything."

Sara slid her hand up the tight thigh to Zak's crotch and squeezed. "Don't worry. I won't hurt you, much." She kissed her on the side of the face and steeled herself for the rest of Zak's revelation. "Okay, so now tell me about your secret life—whatever you can."

"First, you have to swear that what I tell you goes no further, not even a hint of it, not while drunk at a party or while making love with your life partner fifty years from now."

"I so solemnly swear. Get on with it. All this cloak-and-dagger stuff is tedious." Sara hated the biting tone in her voice, but she also hated prying tidbits out of Zak like she was a suspect.

"Let's assume, hypothetically, that there is an individual or a country that wants certain information and can't obtain it through normal channels. I could be employed to retrieve it for them and leave no trace that it ever existed."

Sara waited for the part where Zak murdered the original document holders and shredded their bodies into tiny pieces. "And?"

"And that's basically what I do. Gather intelligence, conduct research, locate, retrieve, and return things of great financial or global consequence. Often these items involve terrorists or other underground factions whose retaliation efforts can span decades."

"You're a spy."

"Loosely interpreted, yes."

"Do you kill people?"

"Only once, in self-defense. I draw the line at wetworks."

"And what about Wachira? Are you making an exception to the I-shall-not-kill policy?" Zak stared out the side window and Sara was relieved. She was afraid of what she might see in her eyes. And she really wasn't sure she wanted to know the answer to that particular question. She chose to remember the woman she made love to as a passionate, caring individual incapable of murder. Her mind felt bombarded by the things Zak told her and the possible ramifications. "So a background check could alert these people that you're in Africa, put you in danger, and, by extension, your mother, Ben, Imani, and anyone else close to you."

"And you. It's not possible to have a normal life or ordinary relationships with a job like mine. Now do you see why I don't want you involved? I don't know what I'd do if anything happened to you because of me. These people make Wachira look like a priest."

"It's too late. I'm already involved—in Africa, in the school, with you, Ben, Imani, and Estelle. And, in case you forgot, I'm in love with you, Zak. If that's your real name."

"It is, but my original birth records were pulled from the system. There is no publicly available verification that my mother ever had a child, no school transcripts to document my attendance, no traceable social security number, driver's license, or credit cards."

Cupping Sara's hand where it rested on the seat between them,

Zak said, "So, you should probably reconsider the love thing after all I've told you."

"It's not that simple. You don't turn love on and off at will. I'm just not sure how it fits into a life of violence, clandestine operations, and an absentee lover."

Zak released Sara's hand. It felt as if the temperature inside the truck grew suddenly cooler and her tentative connection with Sara more elusive. She'd never considered sharing part of her life. Now even this limited revelation seemed to pull Sara farther away from her. She had just violated the Company's number-one rule against disclosure of information, and she'd done it for a woman.

Sara looked pensive. "But you're right. I need time to think about all this."

The admission filled Zak with an urge to shout at the top of her lungs in equal parts exhilaration and terror. Sara had touched something inside her that made further avoidance and denial seem sordid and painful. She wanted to share everything with her, as they'd given their bodies last night. But the more Sara knew about her past assignments, her connections with the underworld, and any future projects, the more danger she'd be in. And what about the hatred she carried for Wachira? Was there room enough for two passions of such strength to exist without destroying each other? Could the diametrically opposed forces survive in the same heart? And if not, which would be stronger in the end? The thought chilled Zak.

Distance and secrecy were the best weapons for protecting her mother, and now Sara. Love, if that's what it was, had proved itself to be not only blind but a cruel jokester. She'd been offered the most precious gift but knew she couldn't accept it. Her feelings for Sara would remain locked in her heart where they would both be safe. She didn't have the right to claim happiness when it placed others at risk. Zak vowed to free Sara and any hope she had of a future with her when they reached camp. She deserved to hear the words, not just be subjected to another round of rude, dismissive behavior.

Ben ran to meet them as they approached the mostly deserted site. It was obvious the men had not returned to work on the school. It stood as it had before they left, and the look on Ben's face said he had more bad news. After the greetings and unloading, Sara read by the river and Ben briefed Zak.

"The lion still roams at night whereby the men will not return. They fear for the herds."

"Has there been any trouble here?"

"No, but I make big fire and much noise at night."

"Good, let's keep this quiet. Sara doesn't need to know. Tomorrow we'll go out and find ourselves a lion."

The late afternoon and early evening passed with no distractions. They sat by the fire while Ben told stories of his family's visit. When Sara excused herself and started toward her tent, she asked Zak to walk with her.

"Will you be joining me inside tonight?" Her tone wasn't challenging or sarcastic, but the soft inquiry of a woman who wanted her lover beside her.

"I thought you needed to think."

"My mind works quite nicely without my body's participation. And the body wants what the body wants, and I want you so much."

Zak was torn between her desire to give Sara what they both wanted and her responsibility. "I need to relieve Ben on watch. He deserves a break."

Sara pulled her into the shadows on the opposite side of the tent and kissed her long and hard. "I'll be here all night, and I believe we both think more clearly when we're touching."

"See you in the morning, Sara." She stole another quick kiss and took the long way back to fireside. She retrieved the GPS monitor from her bag and, after a short explanation to Ben, drove away from camp with her lights out. Tomorrow she and Ben would track big game, tonight was for Wachira watching.

❖

As Zak approached the Narok Police Station, the flashing indicator was barely visible on her screen. She realized that the vehicle was in motion away from her and hurried to catch up. It was headed in the same direction that she'd followed before, toward the minister of education's home. Praying that she was right, Zak drove off the road and cut cross-country toward the stand of trees surrounding the residence.

She had barely made it into position behind a rock close to the house when Wachira's vehicle arrived. The minister met him on the front porch and they sat, apparently comfortable that they were secure in the remote setting. Cool night breezes swept through the trees, and the men's voices, along with the strong smell of alcohol, carried easily to Zak's location.

Removing a voice-activated recorder from her pocket, she attached a small amplifier antenna. She hoped she was close enough to capture the conversation and that they felt free to discuss their dealings openly. Fortunately, Wachira was both arrogant and boastful.

"Mr. Minister, I have fulfilled my part of the bargain. The wealthy American woman's stay has not been an easy one. The guide sent to replace Chambers worked for me. Too bad that he was threatened and ran like a scared dog, spineless man. They had water problems at the camp. She was arrested for possessing a weapon, a grand plan, if I must say. Now there is talk of a lion terrorizing the area." Wachira's laugh confirmed that he was somehow responsible for this latest obstacle as well. "The land dispute is still unresolved. Her original paperwork is lost and her claim cannot be proven. These things have cost her much money. The Ambrosini woman will soon leave Kenya with her school unfinished and much less wealthy."

"You have done well, my friend. Soon the land will be ours and the new resort will make us very rich. The vice president will reward us handsomely. What about the Chambers woman? She will not go quietly, especially with her dislike of you."

"I will see to her. Do not worry."

"Very well." The minister stood, obviously dismissing Wachira. "We will talk again soon."

Wachira shook his hand and returned to his vehicle. Zak maintained her position, waiting for the headlights to disappear. Another man approached the minister and stood beside him. She pointed the small night-vision camera in their direction and snapped several quick pictures. He could be inconsequential, but documentation obtained and not needed was always better than the reverse.

"You have a job for me, sir?"

"Soon, I think we can solve two problems at once, very soon."

Zak waited until the two men were inside the residence and left. On the way back to camp she retrieved the tracking unit from Wachira's vehicle and gave the device, monitor, camera, and recorder to Ben for safekeeping. Then she took guard duty and alternated her watch with reading the reports Estelle had left for her.

The three documents were typed on letterhead of the FBI's Criminal Justice Information Services Division, the most prestigious and effective investigative branch of the United States government. The fact that Estelle had gotten not one but three separate reviews of her father's case from an agency so overwhelmed with terrorism and crimes on its own soil was no small accomplishment.

A cover memorandum accompanying the reports indicated that the officer who conducted each probe was unaware that others were directing parallel cases. This was done, the memo stated, to assure the integrity of the individual outcomes. The letter was signed by the director of the FBI with a handwritten postscript.

> *Estelle, I sincerely hope this puts your mind to rest. If I can be of further help, please let me know.*

Zak finished the first report and threw it to the ground, unwilling to accept what she'd read. Wachira gave the command to physically subdue the crowd of workers the day her father died. His order did not include the use of deadly force. The officer who fired the shot was a new hire only on the job for two weeks. His weapon's safety was not engaged, and when the crowd rushed the officers, it went off. In conclusion, her father's death was the result of an accidental discharge, not the intention of Titus Wachira or his officer. The young man was so distraught over the incident that he resigned from the police the next week.

She stared into the fire until it was almost extinguished, trying to reconcile this information with what she'd believed. She added more wood and stomped around the perimeter of the camp in a mindless security sweep. Disbelief and confusion swirled in her head until she was running the exterior of the barricade at a trot. Perhaps if she ran far and fast enough, the words wouldn't fully register. Maybe if she just kept going the lies would be swallowed up by her mood and the deep African night. Heat and exhaustion finally persuaded her to sit and read the other two reports. Maybe the first one got it wrong and the others would clarify the events and make everything right again.

Without Wachira's culpability she couldn't hold onto the feelings that had sustained and driven her.

But the other two accounts were identical, including interviews with the young officer and his deep remorse about the incident. She reread all the documents, looking for gaps or inconsistencies in the facts, but found none. This wasn't possible. She'd believed another version of the story for years. First thing tomorrow she would call Stewart and check her facts. She had dedicated so much of her life to making Titus Wachira pay for her father's death. Now it seemed he wasn't responsible, at least not directly. What would she do with that information? How could she disengage the fury and vengeance that coursed through her veins like a virulent contagion?

Zak tossed the reports onto the fire, watching them disintegrate into a cloud of ash. She started toward the acacia-thorn fence to make another round when she heard it, a low, guttural rumble from the shadows just beyond the firelight's reach. She recognized the sound from many years of bush hunting with Ben and the others of his tribe, the wounded growl of a lion.

Clutching the staff in her right hand, she pounded the ground as she strode toward the sound. Eyes glowed like lighted candles and fixed on her from a clump of dry elephant grass. She was about to rush the lion, yelling and flapping her arms as distraction, when Ben came alongside her, a rifle in one hand and a fire stick in the other.

"We must lure him from the tents." They sidestepped into position as they'd done many times while hunting, arm's length apart and advancing. Ben waved the fiery bush wand in front of the lion as they began a methodical dance away from their site. Slowly the illumination from the camp fire dimmed and disappeared into the dusty light of dawn behind them. They led the restless lion farther westward into the murky savannah. The animal seemed anxious as they herded him back into the darkness. His growls of pain and discontent increased along with lunges at his tormenters.

CHAPTER SEVENTEEN

Sara awoke to the sound of a lion's powerful roar, gunfire, and an ensuing silence so deep it felt ominous. She dressed as she stumbled to the tent opening and flung it back. A quick scan of the outside confirmed that something was definitely wrong. The fire, which usually burned all night and into the morning, was completely cold. Both vehicles were parked in their usual spots, although one had been moved from the position it was in when she went to bed. There was no sign of Zak or Ben. She was never left unattended, even for short periods.

She ran to the trucks and checked inside—nothing. Tiny hairs at the nape of her neck stood on end. Grabbing a pointed stick from the ground as if it could protect her from the growing discomfort, she turned 360 degrees and scanned the plains as far as she could see in the dim morning light. Still nothing. She headed back to the mess hall calling for Zak and Ben, with no response. A quick look in the tent verified that she was truly and frighteningly alone.

What could have happened while she slept? It was possible that Zak and Ben were hunting, reminiscing about childhood adventures. Maybe they'd taken a morning stroll and lost track of time. Perhaps Wachira's men had returned and arrested them, leaving Sara to fend for herself. As the possibilities quickly came to her, she dismissed each one as unlikely. It was not like Ben and Zak to deviate from their established pattern of behavior for recreational purposes, especially when they were responsible for her safety. And a visit from the police would have raised enough confusion and resistance to awaken her. So where were they?

Sara's skin grew clammy as panic rose in her chest. She reached for her cell phone, thinking she should probably call the police, but didn't have a number. Did they use 911? How about Imani? Maybe she'd have a suggestion. Again, no way to contact her. Randall Burke came to mind, but he was thousands of miles away. As panic started to give way to full-blown fear, she remembered that she had Zak's cell number programmed into her phone. She started to dial but stopped as a noise in the distance captured her attention.

Heavy pounding. Slow, even strokes. Drumming, possibly. No, it sounded more like labored steps or the hard footfalls of an animal in distress. She turned in the direction of the sounds and strained to hear more clearly. Not a four-footed gallop, only two. A person. Zak and Ben. She ran toward the methodical thumping, hoping her instincts were right. She'd traveled only a few hundred feet when she saw them emerging from the gray night sky to the west. The sight stopped her, fear bunching in her muscles like a storm cloud. Ben ran like a burdened but very determined pack animal. Across his shoulders Zak was draped like a heavy blanket, her limbs swinging limply, her midsection wrapped in Ben's colorful shuka. Ben's bare chest and legs were shiny with dark, wet liquid—blood. It seemed to flow from around his neck—from somewhere on Zak's body. Sara's knees almost buckled but she forced herself to keep moving. "Ben, let me help."

"No," he panted heavily, "can't stop. Make bed. Hurry."

Zak looked helpless and pale flung across Ben's back, and Sara didn't want to leave her. But he could get Zak to camp, and maybe by then she'd be together enough to render some real assistance. How, she wasn't quite sure. She ran ahead and threw a sleeping bag and blankets on top of the picnic bench that served as a dining table inside the mess tent. Emptying four bottles of water into a pot, she set it on the stove and started the gas burner. She put unsoiled towels and the first-aid kit on the table just as they arrived.

Ben eased Zak onto the table on her back with the tenderness of a loved one. The multicolored fabric bound tightly around her waist was soaked with blood. "What happened, Ben?"

"Lion."

"She's bleeding so much. Is that why she's unconscious?" The sickly metallic odor of blood was overpowering and Sara suppressed an urge to gag.

"Hit her head. Ebony will wake." He spoke as if it were a statement of fact.

"Shouldn't we try to stop the bleeding?" Sara felt helpless as Zak lay so still, her body slowly draining of color and life.

"I called Imani. Told her to come quick. She is a nurse. We leave the cloth on until she comes. It stops some of the bleeding."

"How could this happen?" She looked at Ben, desperate for answers but not really expecting any. "Didn't either of you have a gun?" This was one time when violence seemed completely justified. The thought was sobering. Zak had been injured by a wild animal, not another person with evil intentions. Suddenly the idea of doing bodily harm to someone who hurt a loved one didn't seem so far-fetched.

"Ebony would only let me scare it away." Ben opened the first-aid kit and looked from Zak to the items inside. He seemed confused about what to do next. The rattle of an approaching vehicle drew their attention to a stream of dust moving toward the camp. "Imani." The relief on his face was obvious.

A few minutes later Imani was at Zak's side with a knapsack full of medical supplies. She took one look at Zak and spoke to Ben in Swahili in a tone laced with irritation. They would probably both be distraught if it hadn't been for Imani's professional training. Fortunately, she shifted into automatic pilot and started assessing the injuries.

"How long has she been unconscious?" she asked while checking Zak's pupils with a small penlight.

"Ten, fifteen minutes maybe," Ben answered. In response to another scathing look from his sister, he continued. "I carried her from the bush." His answer seemed to satisfy her.

Imani felt Zak's head and checked for external trauma. "No blood from the head. This is good." She unwound the garment from Zak's waist and Sara gasped. Her T-shirt was ripped on both sides and plastered to her body. At Imani's nod, Ben pulled his knife from its sheath, sliced the shirt up the middle, and peeled it away from her injuries. Two distinct sets of claw marks raked Zak's sides along her rib cage just below her breasts. Torn skin hung loose and revealed irritated red flesh underneath. Imani swabbed the wounds with an antiseptic that elicited a low moan from Zak. "No damage to the muscle. This is also good," Imani announced.

The stingy antiseptic smell, blood-soaked materials, and Imani's skilled hands transformed the natural African environment into a third-world triage center. Sara tried to detach from the fact that Imani was treating Zak but couldn't. The clean gashes were even more frightening, deeper toward her back and tapering at the front as if she'd been clawed while pulling away. Sara's eyes stung with tears. No human body should be exposed to such trauma, especially not this one, not the smooth, alabaster skin of the woman she loved. Sara grabbed her stomach as it lurched in objection to the sight.

"Sara, would you wait outside?" Imani asked. She continued to flush the wounds and Zak stirred with obvious discomfort. "The suturing will take a while."

"I'd rather be with her. Maybe I can help." She didn't want to leave Zak's side for an instant, afraid she'd wake up but more terrified she might not. What if the time they'd spent together was all they had? The thought sent shivers down her spine and she clung to the table for support.

"You look pale. I cannot handle two patients at once. Please."

Sara touched Zak's moist forehead. "Call me the minute she wakes up." When she turned to leave, Imani was aiming a syringe at Zak's side. She flinched and stepped outside into the cool morning air. Pacing back and forth, Sara felt the minutes crawl in direct opposition to her wishes. She wanted Zak awake, healthy, and in her arms, but none of that would happen soon, if at all. Their conversation yesterday about Zak's job seemed inconsequential. She'd gladly make a deal with any devil to have her safe and unharmed again. Even sharing a life of secrets and absence was more appealing than a life without Zak.

Morning turned to midmorning and early afternoon before Imani and Ben emerged from the canvas hut turned emergency room. "How is she? Is she awake?"

Imani looked exhausted and slouched into a chair beside the fire pit. "She woke briefly. I had to sedate her to finish the suturing. She did not like it."

"What do you mean? Doesn't she need the pain medicine?" Sara wanted to make sense of what she was being told but it wasn't registering.

"She has a head injury and should stay awake. I can not tell the extent of any damage if she remains medicated. She knows this and resists the drugs which make her sleep. She will be in much pain. Perhaps you can talk to her when she wakes."

Sara started toward the tent but heard Imani ask Ben, "Tell me what happened." She stood by the entrance and waited for the answer.

"Ebony was on watch. The lion came toward camp. He was dazed, injured on his side from a spear or prod. We herded him back toward the reserve, following his blood trail until we lost it in the rocks. We found pieces of fresh meat along the way. Ebony used one to lure the lion but he lunged. She dodged but he struck her. If not for his injury, she would be—" Ben hung his head and dropped into a chair beside his sister.

"You had a rifle," Imani accused.

"She would not let me kill him."

Sara's heart ached for Ben. He had to watch his friend being mauled by a lion and blamed himself for not doing more. She walked into the tent and stood beside Zak. Her body was wrapped in gauze dressing from just below her breasts to her waistline. The pallor of her skin, the result of too much blood loss, matched the stark white bandages. She took Zak's hand and raised it to her lips. "Why do you have to be such a damn hero?"

"My job."

Zak's answer sounded dry and brittle as it swished softly across parched lips.

"You're awake. Oh, my God, how do you feel? Don't talk. I'm so glad to see you—" She almost said *alive*. Zak's normally blue-gray eyes were the color of old cement, and in their depths she saw only pain and fatigue. She looked around as if trying to decide where she was and how she got here. Ben and Imani rushed in and hovered at her side like concerned parents.

"Do not talk or move," Imani ordered. "You need to go to hospital for fluids and observation for the head injury."

Zak shook her head vigorously but stopped as her chest heaved. "No hospital."

"I can not give you an IV, and you need fluids. You lost a lot of blood. This is why you feel nauseous and dehydrated. Let us take you, Ebony."

"No. Water and rest. For a while."

Ben looked at Zak with wide eyes. "No, Ebony. You cannot go after him again. It is too dangerous. Even injured, he is stronger. We must wait for help."

"What are you talking about?" Sara wanted to know.

"She is thinking of going after the lion, trying to find out why he left the reserve."

"Absolutely not!" Sara stared at Zak, unable to believe she was considering such an insane idea. "You were almost killed. You'll rest even if I have to knock you out myself."

A smile tugged at the corners of Zak's mouth. "Yes, ma'am."

❖

Zak opened her eyes and squinted in the dull morning light filtering through the sides of the woven enclosure. She tried to move, but her spine felt fused and her midsection ached with every breath. A lion. The confrontation flashed through her mind but not much after that, beyond an occasional glimpse of Sara standing nearby offering water and soft words of encouragement. She raised her head to look around and a dull ache throbbed behind her eyes. "Jesus."

Sara was immediately at her side. "Zak, lie still. You shouldn't move so quickly."

"How long have I been out?"

"Two days, more or less."

"I have to get up." She slowly rose and propped herself up on her elbows.

"Where do you think you're going?"

"Things to do. Get Ben."

"I'm here." Ben stepped inside the tent, followed by Imani. "You should rest, Ebony."

"It's been too long. The trail may already be covered. We have to find out if the lion was purposely led to our campsite."

"You're the most stubborn, single-minded woman I've ever known," Sara said. "In case your memory has been affected, you're injured and shouldn't go anywhere for a few more days. Tell her, Imani."

Placing a hand on Zak's chest, Imani eased her back down on the makeshift bed. "Let me look at you." She checked her pupils, vision, and reflexes, then helped her sit up. "Do you feel sick? How bad is your headache?"

"No, I don't feel sick and the headache is bearable. My sides hurt like a bitch but I can move. Please, I need to go back out there. It's important."

Sara moved closer and stroked the side of her face with a lingering touch. "Nothing is more important than your life. Please don't do this."

Imani gave Sara a look of resignation that Zak recognized from years of experience and turned back to her. "If you can walk without head pain, I will not stop you. But you must promise only short treks, no day-long hunts."

Sara turned away from them. "If the injuries don't kill you, this country certainly will." She walked out shaking her head.

"Sara, wait," Zak called, but she closed the flap behind her. With Ben and Imani's help, Zak rose from the bench and walked a few steps, the pain in her sides reminding her to move slowly. Her head ached mildly but the stabbing jolts of the past two days were absent. "I'll be fine," she said to Imani. Then she turned to Ben. "Can we leave now before it gets too hot?"

Imani said, "Sara has been at your side for days. She would not sleep or eat until she knew you would live. If you must do this thing, promise to use great care and come back soon. If you do not, Sara and I will come for you."

"Agreed." Zak stepped outside. Sara was by the river staring off into the desert like she might find a more agreeable solution there. She approached Sara and touched her arm. "Thank you for taking care of me." They stood in silence for several minutes before Zak found the courage to speak again. "I have to do this, but I'll be careful."

Sara turned and looked at her, and the pain in her deep brown eyes was almost too much to bear. "I almost lost you, Zak. It made me realize that nothing else really matters. Your job, whatever it is, will never keep me from you, if you want me. I've made my decision. You need to make yours."

"Sara, I—"

"Just go. Do whatever it is you have to, but get back here safely."

Zak hugged Sara gingerly, inhaling the freshly washed fragrance of her hair and skin. Sara's love, in spite of the uncertainty surrounding her profession, touched her deeply. She wanted to tell Sara how much it meant to her, how much she cared, but something stopped her. "Thank you." She released her and walked toward Ben, who waited at the edge of the camp.

Soon she and Ben picked up the trail of the wounded lion. Bloody remnants of butchered game led them in a circuitous path from their site toward the reserve. A dark patch of earth beside a badly mangled guinea fowl marked the spot where the lion had been injured. His blood trail led back to the starting point just outside their barricade. It appeared as if someone had deliberately baited a track directly to them. Ben confirmed her suspicions.

"No animal hunts in a pattern and leaves its prey. Only man kills for no purpose."

"There was a reason, Ben. Someone wanted to lead the lion to our camp. And they injured him to make sure he was angry when he found us."

"Who would do such a thing?"

"Someone who wants to scare us off."

By the time they reached the edge of the game reserve, Zak's sides ached with each step. Heat waves bounced off the savannah like spear-toting warriors, and her stomach churned from the pain, temperature, and lack of food. She kept her head soaked with water so the pounding was minor, but she was ready to be horizontal again. They'd seen no signs of the injured lion so she suggested they head back to camp.

As they walked, Zak considered her suspects for this latest scare tactic. Wachira, as usual, topped the list. He'd even referred to it in his clandestine meeting with the minister of education. Their plot to reclaim the school property and build a new resort was certainly motivation enough. She had audio and photographic evidence of that scheme, and now was the time to put it to use. Even if her mother's reports were accurate, all they showed was that Wachira wasn't a cold-blooded killer. Her facts proved he was still a lying, corrupt cop who disgraced his uniform and his people.

Her hatred for Wachira still burned in her chest, but it had begun to seem more manageable. It no longer required a piece of her soul to be quenched. She didn't have to abandon her values by killing him and try to justify it for the rest of her life. Making him pay for his crimes was a simple matter of presenting the evidence to the right person: President

Kibaki. At the least, Wachira would be disgraced and kicked out of public service. The best-case scenario, he would be imprisoned for malfeasance. She took a deep breath that shot stabbing pains through her injured sides while simultaneously relieving a huge weight that had rested in her chest for years.

Her thoughts shifted to Sara and their conversation before she left camp. Sara had once again professed her love for Zak, exposed her heart, and let her walk away. And Zak had once again been a coward. She wanted to talk to her, to say out loud what she'd known for days—that she loved Sara. Instead, she'd chosen to track an injured lion rather than admit the feelings that could potentially change her life.

In the past several days with Sara, Zak had learned a very important fact about herself. She wanted to love and be loved by someone. Her job offered only limited satisfaction and no opportunity to share her frustrations or successes. Shutting down her feelings for the sake of work suddenly seemed too high a price to pay. And it had taken Sara to bring her to that realization. Sara's willingness to be intimate and emotionally available had initially been a source of irritation, a constant reminder of what Zak had given up. As they spent more time together, Zak craved their connection and the revitalization of emotions buried under a façade of distance and bravado. She wanted Sara more than she'd ever wanted anything or anyone. But would she be able to let go of life as she knew it for love? The question tormented Zak, as did each step she took back to camp.

"Ebony, look." Ben pointed to the circling vultures ahead of them.

As they got closer, Zak saw the carcass of the injured lion. His throat had been slit so he would bleed out and attract the scavengers more quickly. "Compliments of the most evolved species," she muttered under her breath. Titus Wachira would pay for his crimes. It was time to put her plan into motion.

"Ben, if anything happens to me, promise you'll deliver the items I gave you last night to the president. No one but him."

"President Kibaki?"

"I know it'll be hard to get to him, but you must do it. Trust no one else."

Ben nodded. "I will do this. Now you rest. You do not look good."

Zak was starting to feel weak and unstable. She could see the tents ahead and tried to walk faster but stumbled. Sara and Imani ran toward her, draping her arms around their shoulders and practically carrying her back to the improvised hospital bed in the mess tent. "You are too pale," Imani said. "Bring water," she instructed Sara.

Zak drank and poured the remainder over her head and face. "I have more to do."

"No." The volume and force of Sara's tone drew everyone's attention. "You are not going anywhere else, at least until you rest for a while."

Ben and Imani voiced their agreement and Zak finally acquiesced. "I'll rest for now." Imani checked her stitches and replaced the dressings that were soiled from the leakage caused by so much activity. When Imani and Ben left, Zak took Sara's hand and pulled her nearer the bed. "We need to talk, or I guess I need to talk. There are things I have to say to you."

"It can wait." Sara kissed her with a tenderness that promised more, and Zak drifted into restful sleep full of images of their future together.

The sun was setting when Zak opened her eyes again. Sara sat beside her reading a book, and Ben and Imani whispered outside as they prepared the evening meal. She started to get up and Sara rushed to her. Together they swung her legs off the side of the bed and Zak stood. She felt stronger than she had in days and hungry for the first time. She inhaled the aroma of meat and vegetables, and a loud growl sounded from her stomach.

As they stepped outside, Imani was filling bowls with stew. "You look much better. It is my excellent nursing skills. Come and eat."

Zak said to Sara, "I forgot to tell you that Imani is not only a highly sought-after nurse in the district but a licensed teacher as well."

"Impressive," Sara replied. "And thank you for being here. I'm not sure what would have happened if you hadn't come."

"That's behind us now." Zak wanted to change the subject and erase the concern in Sara's eyes. "Let's talk about something more productive."

They sat by the fire and discussed the next week and plans for continuing the school construction. Ben would be responsible for contacting Joey and the other men and informing them that the lion was no longer a threat. Imani would stay until the end of the week to make sure Zak's injuries didn't become infected, to administer antibiotics, and to periodically change the bandages. Sara was to revisit the Land Development Office and check on the status of her original permits.

"And I need to run an errand tonight." Zak finished her second bowl of stew and started toward the truck. "I have to talk with Wachira." The looks on the faces of her friends made it clear they didn't think this was a good idea, tonight or any other time. Sara seemed to be the only one willing to voice her concerns.

"Can't it wait until you're feeling stronger, or at least until tomorrow?"

"I really want to get it over with. I've put it off for too long. He has questions to answer."

Sara moved closer and lowered her voice. "Please, don't do this. He's not worth it."

"Don't worry. I won't do anything stupid. I have too much to live for now."

"At least let Ben go with you." Sara kept trying for compromise.

"This is my fight. I need to do it alone."

As Zak drove away, she regretted not having the talk with Sara that she had promised her. And she wondered if going after Wachira was even more dangerous than tracking the lion.

❖

Titus Wachira's men searched her, poking her bandages in a few strategic places, before they allowed her to enter his inner sanctum. He sat behind a huge mahogany desk inside the otherwise sparse police-headquarters building. The desk dwarfed the man and made him seem physically insignificant. A heavy odor of stale cigar smoke clung to the room and made Zak's visit more unpleasant.

"Ah, Madame Chambers, come in and have a seat." He dismissed his men for the evening and ordered his driver home, assuring them that she would be no threat to his safety. "I have long waited for this visit. You have read your FBI's reports?"

Zak stood in front of Wachira's desk, maintaining the advantage. "Yes."

"And have you come to kill me still or to apologize?"

The thought of either filled Zak with revulsion. "Neither. I have come to end your campaign against the Ambrosini Foundation's school. Release the property and allow the facility to be completed, for the children. Surely you won't deny them a proper education."

"Why do you think I can do this? I am a mere policeman, not a politician."

"But you're working with one, a very powerful one. And if you persist, I'll have no choice but to expose your moneymaking alliance."

"You know nothing which can hurt me."

"I know you were responsible for Roger Kamau being sent to replace me. I know you paid someone to damage our water system, to plant a gun in Joey's truck and have him and Sara Ambrosini arrested. I also know that someone under your orders lured a lion from the game reserve toward our camp with the intent of scaring us away from the land."

"You have proof of these things?"

"I have your confession, in your own words. Is that good enough?" If a black man's face could pale, Wachira blanched. His lips quivered slightly and perspiration popped out on his forehead. "Now I know you are bluffing. Leave my office."

"And I also know that you and the minister of education are working to reclaim that parcel of land to build a resort to line your own pockets. The press would be very interested in that story, I think."

"Get out." Wachira's eyes bulged with disbelief and fear.

Zak turned to go, her heart light with the knowledge that she had read Wachira correctly. He was responsible for everything, and the information she had on tape and in her photos would be enough to expose him. "You have until tomorrow afternoon to give me your answer."

"You have my answer now. Go to hell."

CHAPTER EIGHTEEN

When Sara heard the old truck pull back into camp, she turned up the lantern in her tent so Zak would know she was awake. She'd been gone for hours and Sara had started to worry that she might not return.

"Sara?" Zak whispered from outside.

"Yes, come in."

Zak stepped inside and zipped the flap closed behind her. "Can we talk?"

"Never thought I'd hear you ask *that* question." Sara moved into her arms and kissed her lightly on the mouth. "We can do anything you want. But talking sounds good considering your physical limitations. How do you feel?"

"A little tired but okay."

Sara moved two folding chairs closer to the lantern. "It'll be more comfortable than sitting on the ground." When they were seated, she asked, "How was your meeting with Wachira? Did you find out what you needed to know?"

"Not really. He refused to admit the truth, so I had to take other measures. But I don't want to talk about him right now."

The evasive answer made Sara uneasy, wondering what had happened between them. The possibilities were many and all unpleasant. But prodding would not provide an answer any sooner. "Okay."

Zak raked her fingers through her short black hair and finally made eye contact with Sara. "I told you a little about my work, but there's more you need to know."

Sara waited for Zak to continue, certain that whatever she had to say would not be easy. Whether she planned to disclose something about the nature of her job or about her feelings, the honesty and vulnerability required would be a challenge.

"I've already told you the work is dangerous, for me and anyone close to me. That's why I avoid personal involvements. I don't even see my mother on a regular basis because of the risks to her. We meet in random places on the spur of the moment. That's no way to treat someone you love."

The look on Zak's face told Sara this part of her life caused her great unhappiness. After seeing them together, she knew that Zak loved her mother deeply and being separated from her, especially after her father's death, had to be particularly difficult.

"Jesus, Sara, I don't even have a home, a physical place to lay my head. When I'm not working, which is seldom, I live in hotels and flophouses around the globe. The few possessions I value are in a sixteen-by twenty-four-inch rucksack that I carry everywhere."

Tears formed in the corners of Zak's eyes as she spoke, and Sara wanted to brush them away, to ease her pain and reassure her that life could be different. But she sensed that if she touched her, Zak would recoil or break down, either of which could stop her verbal flow. She chose to let her continue at her own pace. Comfort would come later.

"You have such a great network of friends and family. I haven't had that in years. I'm not even sure I know how anymore. Attachments have become a liability I can't afford."

"Is that still how you want to live your life?" Sara touched the side of Zak's face and forced her to look at her. "Honestly, is it what you want now?"

"I'm not sure I deserve anything else." The words were barely a whisper. "I was on assignment when my father died. I should have been there to protect him. But I failed him, just like I've failed you. They threw you in a godforsaken jail and I couldn't stop them."

Sara knelt between Zak's legs and hugged her gently against her chest. "My darling, you are not to blame for your father's death. If you had known he was in danger, you would have been there, just as you've been there for me since the day we met. Your father wouldn't want you to carry this guilt. Being alive and happy is the way to honor his memory. You have a choice. Is this life you've been living what you really want?"

"It was until I met you." Zak's gaze burned a path to her soul down which the words glided, settling into the empty space and filling it with possibility.

"What are you saying, Zak?" Sara's heart pounded so loudly it drowned out the chorus of crickets outside.

"I'm trying to say that I'm in—"

The camp was suddenly ablaze with bright beams of directed light. A man's voice, magnified by a bullhorn, bellowed, "Zak Chambers, come out."

"What the hell?" Zak jumped to her feet too quickly and grabbed her sides as the pain struck.

Sara was so stunned she looked from Zak to the ominous shadows of men with long weapons projected on the sides of the tent. Circumstance once again had buried the words she imagined Zak was going to say, the words she wanted to hear more than any other. "What's going on?"

"I don't know. Wait here." She wiped the tears from her face, opened the flap, and stepped out with Sara behind her. "Please, Sara, wait here."

"I'm sorry, but I can't let you go out there alone. I have to be with you."

Ben and Imani were already standing beside the fire pit, a combination of police and military personnel searching them. As Zak approached, several weapons were leveled at her.

"On the ground. Get down," an officer shouted.

She raised her hands in the air but continued toward them. One of the men fired a burst of rounds in her direction. She shielded Sara with her body. "Are you crazy? Stop shooting."

"On the ground, Madame Chambers," he commanded again. This time Zak knelt with her hands on top of her head. Four officers approached and one kicked her in the back, sending her face-first into the dirt.

Sara rushed toward the men screaming, "Stop. She's hurt. You'll tear loose the stitches."

Two military men grabbed her and dragged her beside Ben and Imani. "Watch your friend or she will go to jail too."

The police officers who surrounded Zak kicked her arms and legs wide apart and roughly searched her for weapons. When they pulled her up to shackle and handcuff her, scarlet stains formed on the sides of her khaki shirt. "You bastards, you've popped her sutures. She's bleeding again." Sara started toward Zak but Ben restrained her. "What are you doing? Where are you taking her?"

"Madame Chambers is under arrest for the killing of Police Commander Titus Wachira."

"What?" Sara's question squeaked out in a combination of fear and uncertainty. Zak looked at her but said nothing as the officers shoved her toward a small paddy wagon.

"Stop. Wait." Sara's commands went unheeded. "Where are you taking her? How can I get her released?" Sara called after the receding entourage.

Several of the officers laughed in response and she heard one say, "No release and no visitors for a very long time."

Sara stood by helplessly as the officers locked Zak in a windowless van that looked like a tin can. She struggled to free herself from Ben's grasp, to do something, anything to change the course of these horrific events. The spotlights were extinguished, plunging the camp into eerie darkness as the police caravan disappeared over the river embankment. Minutes ago she and Zak were safe in her tent having a conversation that might have changed their lives. She felt certain Zak was about to declare her love. And then her world turned upside down.

Was it even remotely possible that Zak killed Wachira? Her hatred for the man and her quest for vengeance were no secret. She'd threatened him in Sara's presence on at least two occasions. Numerous police and military personnel had witnessed her attack on him at the hospital dedication. That day Sara had seen for herself the uncontrollable violence that Wachira evoked in her. And tonight when Zak returned from her meeting with him, she had been very evasive about their encounter. She'd said, "He refused to admit the truth, so I had to take other measures." Did those measures include murder? Could she have done such a thing and then returned, unfazed, to talk of love? The possibility rattled around in Sara's mind, but she refused to accept it.

"Let me go, Ben." Sara's voice was so soft she wasn't sure she'd spoken out loud. "Ben, let go of me," she repeated, and shook his hands from her arms. She looked toward the retreating line of police vehicles and then ran toward the truck.

"Miss Sara, where you going?"

"I'm going to follow them, to find out where they're taking her."

Imani followed Sara and pinned her against the side of the truck with her body. "Sara, stop. You cannot do this thing. Ebony would not wish it."

Tears stung Sara's eyes and she cursed her emotionality. It was not the time for tears. She needed courage and strength, and after witnessing Zak's mistreatment, she had an abundance of both. "Don't try to stop me, Imani. You saw what they did to her. She's bleeding again and will get infected. They can kill her without doing anything."

Ben joined them and tried to explain. "If the jeshi know you are following, they will ride all night to confuse you and conceal their destination. You do not know the country."

"Then you do something. You know she didn't kill him."

Their expressions confirmed Sara's greatest fear. They were also conflicted. They knew Zak was entirely capable of this crime and the most likely suspect for the police. But like her, they wanted to believe their friend was too principled and too compassionate to go to those extremes.

Sara collapsed against Imani, crying and clinging to her. "What can we do? We have to help her. The confinement alone is enough to drive her mad."

Ben answered. "Ebony has friends here. Tomorrow we will find her and prove she did not do this thing. But tonight, we must rest. Day comes soon."

"Our Ebony will not be lost," Imani assured her. "It cannot happen. Come." She guided Sara back to her sleeping quarters and lay beside her until restlessness exhausted her enough to sleep.

❖

Zak spat out a mouthful of sand and tried to get her bearings inside the cramped paddy wagon. Her legs were shackled together, the chain running through a large eyebolt on the floor. She was handcuffed with old bracelet cuffs connected to her shackles by another length of chain, limiting her movements. The bench she sat on was metal, bolted firmly in place. Other than a half-full bottle of water that rolled and bounced with the motion of the vehicle, the space was empty. She didn't see anything she could use to loosen her restraints or as a possible weapon. No windows, just small holes around the roof line barely large enough for the hot, choking air to enter. She had no idea where they were taking her or what would happen when she arrived.

The assessment of her confinement completed, Zak focused on her physical condition. With no possibility of immediate escape, she needed to preserve her energy for future opportunities. Her sides ached and warm stickiness matted her shirt to her body. Some of her stitches had come loose and she was bleeding again. Definitely not good. That meant she would continue to lose strength, speed, and mobility. *Block the pain and check for other limitations*, she told herself. Her eyes burned from fine granules of sand that scratched and irritated them each time she blinked. She waited for the water bottle to roll toward her and grabbed it. Lying down on the floor, she irrigated her eyes and felt some relief. At least she could see more clearly. She shifted to find a comfortable position on the hard surface. Rest would help her heal, but the constant jolting of the vehicle made it impractical. Planning was futile, escape unlikely, and sleep impossible. The only other option was mental diversion to keep her occupied and sane.

She thought of Sara and the few minutes they'd shared before her arrest. Her business with Wachira completed, she'd intended to tell Sara that she loved her and ask if she could accept the unattractive restrictions of her world. She had never felt this way about anyone, and the possibility of a future with Sara had given her hope. But separated from her now, it felt like all the tenderness they shared had turned evil. Just thinking of Sara dispatched a twisting, tormented ache more devastating than any other. Maybe this interruption was an omen, a sign that her life would never be simple or uncomplicated. Perhaps love was not to be a part of her existence.

The idea summoned a wave of despair and sadness. She could still hear Sara's shouts, demanding the officers release her, the love and concern so evident in her voice. Zak's heart ached when she considered the anguish and uncertainty Sara must be going through. Even if they were eventually allowed limited contact, Zak didn't know if she could comfort her. Sara was too perceptive to be easily deceived by reassuring platitudes, and Zak knew too much about Africa to lie convincingly.

African justice came in many forms and depended on countless variables. The officers who arrested her could kill her before she was ever booked into the sluggish judicial system. Escape attempts, staged suicides, and animal attacks were the jeshi's favorite methods of human disposal. Or they might simply allow her to die a slow, agonizing death from her preexisting wounds. Zak shivered, her body suddenly cold and weak. As her thoughts drifted, another possibility surfaced. Perhaps Ben would get the photos and tapes to President Kibaki. Wachira's corruption would be exposed. But even so, she would still be the suspect in his death. She'd been foolish enough to meet him without electronic backup, so there was nothing to substantiate that she left him alive. And the evidence she'd acquired before wasn't likely to clear her of his murder. As the gravity of her situation registered, a deep chill soaked into her bones and Zak slipped into unconsciousness.

"Get up." The vehicle had stopped and a soldier jabbed the bottoms of Zak's shoes with his assault rifle, motioning her toward the door. Another officer waited with a black hood in his hand. When she moved, her body ached and sharp pains ripped through her sides. She scooted slowly toward the two men, hoping to mitigate some of her discomfort and glimpse her surroundings. But before her feet touched the ground, her head was covered with the dark fabric and any chance of visual observation extinguished.

Two men flanked her, leading her across a dusty expanse of ground and into a building. It smelled of stale food, soiled linens, and unhygienic bodies. She surmised they were in one of the austere block structures that the military used to temporarily house prisoners. The men talked in Swahili, unaware that she understood the language. One was irritated that she'd bled in the back of the van and they would have to clean it. The other spoke of having a girlfriend in Mwingi that he hoped to visit during the layover. They also exchanged guesses about how long she'd last once they dropped her in Liboi in three days' time. Mwingi was hours from the Narok District where she'd been arrested. The police, with assistance from the military, were obviously putting distance between Zak and any support or efforts to intervene. Liboi was in the northeastern province of Kenya closest to the Somali border. The area contained a high refugee population and the prisons were the worst in the country. If they were taking her to a Liboi detention facility, she would be buried in a sea of forgotten humanity.

"She is bleeding," a gruff male voice announced in broken English. "Take off the hood."

The soldiers complied and Zak's head cover was removed. She had no difficulty adjusting to the light because the room was almost dark. A short, pudgy man wearing baggy jeans and a worn flannel shirt stood beside her.

"Leave us," he ordered as he unbuttoned Zak's shirt and slid it as far down her arms as the handcuffs would allow. The soldiers stared at Zak's breasts and commented in Swahili about what they'd like to do with them. "I said leave."

"She is a prisoner, Doctor. She killed Wachira. We must remain."

"Outside the door. She can go nowhere."

When the guards left, the doctor mumbled under his breath, "Wachira was a pig." He turned to Zak. "Now, your wounds." He gingerly removed the gauze wrapping and bandages that Imani had applied and examined her sides. "Lion?"

Zak nodded.

"You are a very brave or very crazy woman."

"Probably both."

"I have to staple this. It will hurt. No pain medicine." He handed her a wooden tongue depressor and she clenched it between her teeth. She thought of Sara for distraction as he worked his way up her sides clamping the open skin back together.

"There." The stapler's metal teeth dug into her flesh one final time and she flinched. "I will give you strong antibiotics. You see me only this time."

"Thank you, Doctor. Do I get a phone call?"

"I do not make rules. The guards must decide."

"Can you make a call for me? Just one." She was desperate to get word to Sara that she was okay. This was probably the most compassion she'd receive until she was released, if she was ever released. It was her only chance.

"I am sorry. I cannot." He dressed her wounds, poured some water on her shirt to dilute the thick bloody residue, and pulled it back onto her body. "Good luck, madam. Guards."

The soldiers reentered the room and roughly led Zak through a small doorway to the back of the building. Two cells lined either side of the narrow space, three occupied by men who had obviously been confined for a long time. Their bodies were gaunt and sickly, their facial hair long and unkempt, and the odor of soured and soiled bodily excretions emanated from them. Zak almost gagged when she passed their cells on the way to her cage.

As the officers unlocked her shackles and cuffs, they teased the men, telling them that she was their new playmate and they should treat her with respect. The prisoners hooted and reached for her while simultaneously pawing their crotches. One of the guards threw a prickly woolen blanket at her as he closed and locked her cell door.

She looked around the tiny space and found only a long drop for a toilet, no bed, no sink, and no water. Human excrement and rat droppings littered the floor of the cell. A small window at the top of the enclosure let in the final rays of daylight. The only good thing about her unit was that she was separated from the men.

Zak began work immediately, using the bottoms of her shoes to clear a spot large enough to lie down. Scraping the debris from the ground, she dug deep enough to find clean dirt and pushed the topsoil into the drop hole. She calculated how much time had passed since they left camp and realized that she'd been unconscious most of an entire day before arriving here. The time coincided with the distance to Mwingi. The trip to Liboi would undoubtedly start as soon as fresh soldiers arrived for the morning shift. She needed to rest, to be strong for the journey and whatever lay ahead. The possibilities were not comforting.

CHAPTER NINETEEN

"God, I can't do this anymore." Sara heaved the cement block she held over her head and threw it as far as she could. "I can't just keep working and pretend everything is normal." She turned to Ben and spread her arms in a hopeless gesture. "Where is she? It's been a week."

"We are trying everything, miss. We will find her."

As tears started falling, she walked away from the work site, unwilling to let the men see her lose control again. Every day since Zak was taken she spent hours stacking blocks for the school and crying, often at the same time. The once-jovial workplace had become a solemn gathering for the dedicated group of men as construction had taken a backseat to finding Zak. They often arrived in the morning with tidbits of news they'd heard in the pubs or on the streets. Every shred of potential intelligence or mere gossip demanded further review. Sara saw to it personally, having hired two full-time private investigators who reported in daily. But still there had been no sighting of Zak, nor had she been located in any police or military facility in Kenya. Fear and uncertainty had taken its toll. Sara's nerves were raw and her emotions fragile.

"You still have the evidence against Wachira, Ben. Why can't you get it to Kibaki?"

"I have sent word whereby I can meet with him. Seeing the president is not so easy."

"She could be anywhere on the entire African continent by now. How can a person as physically distinctive as Zak disappear? Surely she's been noticed. People talk. Why can't we find her?" When Sara became this desperate, the same dire response emerged: *Because she's already dead.*

"Do not think those things. You must keep hope." Imani wrapped her arms around her. She had remained at the camp to help with the school, she'd said. But Sara knew it was to comfort her through Zak's loss. No one ever spoke the words, but the somber mood that surrounded the site was like a wake.

"You're right. I have to do more. I can't give up, ever." She returned to the mess tent and sifted through the thick file she'd accumulated over the past week. For the next hour she reread every piece of information and formulated a new plan. "Imani, come here."

When Imani joined her, Sara said, "What about a newspaper, television, and radio campaign? I'll post a small reward for any credible tips and a huge one for news that leads us to Zak. African people are very diligent. They'll work hard to get good information for the money."

"It could help. But if you say things against the police or the jeshi, the media will not run it. This type of statement will get attention from the government."

"Good, maybe then we can get a meeting with Kibaki. I'm willing to try anything. The longer we wait, the slimmer our chances." Zak couldn't tolerate confinement for very long, even in a weakened state. Her existence was all about freedom, space, and flexibility. Forced containment would be a sadistic form of torture to her soul and spirit. Imani hesitated, her high forehead crinkled with worry lines.

"What are you thinking?" Sara asked.

"You know of Ebony's work. What will happen if we broadcast her name and face across the continent? What of the people who seek to do her harm?"

"I've thought about that. We talked the night she was taken, and I'm not sure she wants to work for that organization anymore. And even if she does, it won't happen if she's—" Sara couldn't bring herself to say the word *dead* out loud. It gave the idea far too much power.

"Then we do this thing."

"And what about Estelle? Should we contact her? I didn't want to alarm her until we had some news. But maybe it's time."

"Ebony's mother, of course. I think Ben has her number."

They sat at the table and sketched out the plan. Sara gave Imani the reward parameters, a missing-person press release, her contact number, and a hefty wad of bonus money for the establishments that agreed to run the story. Imani left to make calls and contacts. After getting Estelle's number from Ben, Sara steeled herself for the phone call she had hoped it would never be necessary to make.

"Estelle?"

"Yes."

"This is—"

"I know who you are, cheri. And if you're calling, someone we love needs help."

"I'm afraid so."

"Don't say anything else. I'll meet you where we last dined in twenty-four hours. And if you have the sat phone, we'll need it."

The line went dead and Sara stared at the phone, thinking how James Bond all this felt. Estelle had obviously been primed on Zak's secret spy protocol. She hadn't mentioned any names, locations, or plans, probably fearing her communications were monitored. Was this the kind of life she would have lived with Zak? No, she stopped herself, this *was* her life with Zak, and she'd take it with all its imperfections and adjustments.

The next twenty-four hours passed with the speed of decades. Sara made arrangements for a charter flight to Nairobi, cutting her travel time from hours to forty-five minutes, packed her bag, then engaged the men in a search for Zak's phone. She had always worn it clipped on her waistband, and so far they'd been unable to locate it in the tents or the area immediately surrounding the campsite. She felt sure the soldiers would not have allowed her to keep it when she was arrested. Ben arranged the group in a tight line from the spot where the paddy wagon was parked. They moved in a slow circle checking the ground and bushes until they'd almost cleared 360 degrees.

Sara was about to give up when Joey called out. "I found it, miss." He waved the phone triumphantly over his head. It seemed to be working properly, and she could charge it on the plane to Nairobi the next day.

The next morning just as Ben was preparing to take Sara to the small Keekorok airstrip, Imani returned. "Many companies are willing to tell the story of a missing American tourist. It was a good idea, Sara."

"Any problems from the government?"

"No, but it is early."

"Estelle is meeting me in Nairobi. I'm not sure what we'll do, but I can't just wait. Keep in touch. I don't know how long I'll be gone. The PIs have my cell number, so I'll call if I hear anything." She hugged Ben and Imani. "And thank you both."

Two hours later when Sara walked into the Stanley Hotel, Estelle was drinking coffee in the Thorn Tree Café. They greeted each other and returned to the private table near the exit.

"Tell me, Sara. From the look of you, it must be bad. It appears as though you haven't eaten or slept in weeks."

"She's hurt, Estelle." The tears started again. She felt comfortable letting her emotions show with Zak's mother, but guilty for not being stronger.

Estelle grabbed at the collar of her blouse and the question squeaked out, "How badly?"

"Very. Claw marks on both sides. It was a lion attack."

"Dear Lord." Estelle's complexion paled.

"She was leading it away from camp, away from me."

Estelle covered Sara's hand with hers. "Don't blame yourself. Zakaria is strong willed, and when it comes to the people she loves, she protects them fiercely."

Sara remembered the many times since they'd met that Zak stood between her and danger. At first it had annoyed Sara and made her think that Zak didn't respect her abilities, but the more she learned about Zak, the more she loved her for expressing her concern in this way.

"Imani took care of her, but she was arrested two days later for the murder of Titus Wachira."

"For three years this man has been her undoing. Now it comes to this." The words were barely audible, Estelle's gaze focused on something far beyond the walls of the tiny restaurant.

"I have no idea where she's being held or even if she's—"

Estelle shook her head and scooted her chair closer to Sara. "There, there, cheri. We're not going to imagine the worst. You and I both know Zakaria is a fighter. If she can't get out of whatever hellhole they've stuck her in, she'll at least find a way to survive it. Trust me on that."

"I know." Sara dried her eyes and took a couple of deep, calming breaths. "I'm glad you're here. You look so much alike. It's comforting… and heartbreaking." She told Estelle about Ben's unsuccessful attempts to obtain an audience with President Kibaki to turn over Zak's evidence on Wachira. She also filled her in on their other efforts—the calls to police and military holding facilities, hospital and morgue checks, the PI reports, and the latest publicity campaign.

"Brilliant. Did you bring her phone?" When Sara nodded, Estelle said, "Let's go to my room. We'll need more privacy for this call."

Estelle closed the door behind them and took the phone from Sara. She scrolled through the incoming and outgoing call list. "Here it is, Stewart, Zak's boss in the Company." She stopped as though she'd misspoken.

"It's all right. Zak told me about her work. But how do you know her boss? I thought she shielded you from that part of her life."

"My daughter isn't the only one with friends in high places. You're okay with all this?"

"It's a process, but right now I just want her back."

Estelle pushed Redial, waited for a connection, punched in a code, and waited again. "I'll put this on speaker, but let me do the talking."

"Ebony?" Stewart hesitated when there was no immediate reply.

Estelle's voice was calm and confident. "Close."

"Estelle, why are you calling? What has happened?"

"I'm assuming this is still a secure line?"

"Yes, speak freely."

"Ebony was arrested for the murder of Titus Wachira and has disappeared."

Several seconds passed before Stewart responded. "By disappeared I assume you mean that you can't find her in any government-sanctioned holding facility."

"Correct. That's why I need your help."

A longer pause ensued. Sara was about to launch into a scathing sermon about the responsibilities of an organization to its employees when she remembered this wasn't just another corporate entity. Human casualties probably weren't even a concern for Stewart. "I'm not sure I can do that, Estelle. You understand the position I'm in here."

"I understand that my daughter has risked her life for you on too many occasions to count, not to mention giving up anything resembling a normal future for this work. And now that she needs help, you are denying her?" Estelle's French-accented voice remained matter-of-fact but her tone held an edge.

"Are you sure she didn't kill Wachira? She certainly hated the man enough."

Estelle's brief hesitation spoke to the uncertainty inside Sara. Even her mother had doubts. "That is not my concern at this point. My daughter's life is. Are you going to help me or not, Captain?"

"My sincerest apologies, but I can't. It would be seen as interference in Africa's political and judicial processes. And if we divulge a connection between Ebony and the Company, it places her and us at great risk. The cost is too high."

Sara started to speak but Estelle waved her off. "Very well, then prepare for what happens next. Like you, I must do what I feel is right."

"Is that some kind of threat?"

Without further explanation, Estelle said, "Good day, Captain." The emphasis on her final word sounded like a curse. She put the phone down and walked to the balcony where she stood for several minutes in silence. When she turned back to Sara, her face was again beaming with purpose. "It's time to call in some favors. How long will it take Ben to get to Nairobi?"

"Six hours."

"We need him first thing in the morning with the evidence. Turn on the TV and let's catch a broadcast of your campaign. And make a big pot of coffee. We'll need it."

Sara made the call and the coffee while Estelle worked the phone. Her first contact was the Director of the FBI. Sara listened in amazement as she explained the situation and that she needed technological and forensic assistance. An agent would arrive in the morning with instructions to do whatever she asked. Her second call was to President Kibaki's office. The response was not as swift, but she was eventually connected to the president. Again, Estelle told the story of Zak's arrest and that they held evidence to support her innocence. After a tougher sell, he agreed to meet with them and at least have his people review the evidence. The meeting was scheduled for two the next afternoon.

"You're amazing," Sara said when she hung up. "How do you know these people?"

"My husband and I were personal friends of the director and his wife. Kibaki respected Frank's work with the children of this country. He still calls me every year on the day my husband died. He questions that Zak killed Wachira and will try to help us locate her. He suspects a deeper political connection aimed at discrediting his administration."

Sara considered her next question, wondering if she really wanted to know the answer. "And what about you, Estelle, do you think Zak did it?"

"I think we are of like mind. My daughter believed she could do such a thing at one time, but I never did. Before I left, I gave her evidence that Wachira was not responsible for her father's death. If she read the reports, she had to release some of the anger she felt toward him. It's hard to hold on to hatred, especially when it isn't deserved. And it has taken so much from her that I'm sure she's ready to let it go. And you?"

"Zak's not a killer. I love her, you know."

Estelle hugged Sara and cradled her head on her shoulder. "I know and she loves you. I realized it the minute I saw the two of you together. She's never had such a look in her eyes before. Don't worry, cheri, we'll find our girl."

❖

By Zak's account, she'd been in this stinkhole for three weeks, every day the same as the one before. It was easy to disappear in this country and much too easy to cover up a long absence. If Ben or Sara or her mother had tried to find her, she doubted they received much cooperation from the government. Besides, no one would look this far from Nairobi. The Somali border area was entirely too dangerous a place to ask questions. Every day she considered her situation and how she might escape as her strength returned.

The food barely qualified as edible, but she forced herself to eat what she could to stay alive. She used half of her daily two-bottle ration of water to irrigate her wounds and keep them from becoming infected. They had healed nicely, considering the conditions, leaving matching red scars on both sides. It could have been much worse if not for Ben and Imani. She thought of them and the time she spent in the bush as a child. It had proved invaluable to keeping her sane during the confinement.

She'd managed to squirrel away some helpful items during her daily outings in the small gated yard. The guards either didn't notice or didn't care that she gathered a few leaves and twigs from the plants with each visit. They served well as tissues and toothbrushes, and she'd begun to fashion a makeshift glove from the remnants to use as a weapon. During the night while everyone slept, Zak slowly rebuilt strength in her arms and torso by exercising against the thick metal bars. Being physically idle during the daylight hours gave her time to think about her situation.

She replayed the information she'd gathered on Wachira and decided that it might be helpful in her defense after all. The man she'd taped and photographed talking to the minister of education after Wachira left that last night had asked about an assignment. The minister had put him off with a prediction that at some later time he could solve two problems for him at once. What if those two problems were Wachira and her?

It would make sense to get rid of Wachira if he was getting greedy or had become a liability. And her vendetta against the police commander was widely known, as was her association with the Ambrosini school project. Who better to take the fall for Wachira's murder? She wondered if Ben had gotten the information to President Kibaki, and if so, whether this mystery man would be of any interest to them. How could they link him to Wachira's death? The connection was the minister of education, but she worried that Kibaki might not want to explore that option and the ties to his vice president.

The Company with its resources could easily identify the man and uncover any other connections between him and the minister of education. But Zak wasn't sure she could depend on Stewart for help. As far as she knew, he had made no effort to intervene on her behalf. While she understood the policy on plausible deniability, the reality sucked. But something else about Stewart bothered her, something buried in the back of her mind.

That night while Zak hung from the steel bars of her cell in the middle of her workout ritual, the memory became clear. She lost her grip and almost fell to the hard dirt-packed floor. Stewart had been the one who told her about her father's death. Zak was on assignment in Venice at the time and had been pulled out immediately. On her flight back to Kenya to meet her mother, Stewart had briefed her on the details. Everything she knew about her father's case came by word of mouth from the Company. She never saw any written documentation, not even an autopsy report.

Stewart told her about Wachira's involvement in the incident. He commanded the police unit that converged on the group of workers and gave the order to fire into the crowd. According to their intelligence, Titus Wachira was directly responsible for Frank Chambers's death. And Zak believed it, all of it. Even after the training she'd received about double-checking facts and never taking anything at face value, she'd failed in the most important case of her life.

Zak fell to her knees over the long drop and threw up, purging the rage and hatred from her system until her throat was raw. She was so grief-stricken and desperate for someone to blame that she hadn't asked to see the evidence. Stewart had lied to her and perpetuated her rage, keeping her captive to her misguided emotions. She'd heard him say many times that the only good agent was one who had something to gain or lose. And Zak was driven by her need for revenge.

Suddenly her past behavior seemed callous and shameful. No wonder she hadn't been able to initiate and sustain a loving relationship. Her heart had been too full of negativity and doubt. Her gut must have known that something was wrong because she'd simply buried herself deeper in her work instead of trying to establish a real life. The fear she'd seen in Sara's eyes on more than one occasion now made sense. Her spiteful grudge against Wachira had taken over her life and replaced it with blind fury. A heart as full and damaged as hers had no room for love.

Oh, Sara, I am so sorry, my love. Her hostility had marred even their single night of lovemaking. But Sara calmed her and showed her that another way existed inside her. She prayed for a second chance to make it right, to shower Sara with the feelings that were suddenly free inside her. Sara filled her heart and she missed her fiery red hair, her chocolate brown eyes, the sprinkle of freckles across her upturned nose, and her luscious lips. But she longed most desperately to be held in her arms, to feel the love and compassion that seemed to ooze from her as effortlessly as breathing. The intimacy she'd experienced during their brief time together would have to sustain her until she was free again. And if that never happened, she would die knowing that she'd been loved and was capable of love.

Her dreams of Sara were halted as the dark African night gave way to another gray dawn. But this one was different. Soldiers were talking in hushed tones in the outer office and there was more activity than a normal day required. Before she could fully focus on their voices, two guards entered the cell area and headed toward her. They motioned her to the back of her cell and unlocked the door. With a wide sweep of his hands one of the men spoke in broken English. "Today you leave Africa. Come."

She was hurried to the showers and provided a relatively clean change of clothes. In three hours' time she'd had a substantial breakfast and was on a plane out of the country. The only information she received from her escort to the airport was a message from President Kibaki. She had been released with a full pardon but was to leave the country immediately without contacting anyone, especially Sara Ambrosini.

CHAPTER TWENTY

As Sara's corporate jet skidded to a halt at Charles De Gaulle Airport, she wondered why she'd accepted Estelle's invitation for a visit. The school was nearly completed after several delays that seemed as much failures on her part as not being able to find Zak. Fortunately, Imani was handling the hiring of teachers, but they still had a lot to do before classes could begin. But Estelle had insisted that she take a break, and Sara hated to disappoint her further.

It was a difficult and a joyous time to have her mother's final wish realized. Sara had grown so much since the project began. And she finally understood what her mother was trying to tell her with all the caveats to her will. Sara realized that she loved teaching and that it was possible for her to both build schools and participate in the education process. The manual construction had also taught her that she was stronger than she imagined, bodily and mentally.

But it hadn't been easy to overcome the obstacles in transforming the dream to reality. She thought of Zak and pain shot through her. Was the effort worth the cost? Her connection to Zak was so strong that she didn't dare think of it often. When she did, she became physically and emotionally weak. The atrocities the jeshi could have inflicted upon Zak during captivity or her eventual death tormented Sara nightly. Only work and trying to locate Zak kept her somewhat distracted. Since Zak's disappearance a month ago, Sara had worked tirelessly to find news of her, but none of the tips she received from the publicity blitz panned out. The private investigators had also come up empty. She seemed to have vanished. Even President Kibaki had failed to provide anything useful.

Estelle and Sara met with Kibaki and turned the evidence on Wachira over, but received no further communication from him. Fortunately, Estelle's FBI contact had made copies of the documentation as a backup in case it was needed later. They also identified the man who met with the minister of education as a known assassin for the African resistance. His bank records in an offshore account led directly to the minister of education.

The only indications that Kibaki trusted any of their information were a short press release two days ago announcing that he had fired his minister of education and the arrival of a plain envelope containing Sara's missing land and building permits. No word of Zak. How would she be able to look at Estelle and not see Zak staring back at her? As she stepped from the plane, she took a deep breath and steadied herself for the jolt she felt every time she glimpsed Estelle since Zak had disappeared.

At the bottom of the stairs Sara stopped, the breath hung in her chest. The vision was too similar, the shards of pain too gut-wrenching. Her eyes clouded with tears and she couldn't stop them. But the figure running toward her was too tall and slender to be Estelle, her clothes too loose. Realization struck like a shot of adrenaline. Zak. She dropped her bag and ran too, initial laughter turning into sobs of joy. She stopped inches away, staring, appreciating, wanting.

Zak raised her hands and cupped Sara's face. "I love you, Sara Ambrosini."

Sara didn't move as the deep timbre of Zak's voice and her words washed over her, leaving her warm and content. If this was the last time she saw Zak, she'd survive now because she knew that Zak was alive and that she loved her.

"Is this what confinement did to you?" She couldn't take her gaze from Zak's face, the sunken cheeks, pale skin, and steel blue eyes rimmed with fatigue.

"It made me realize how I feel and what is important."

"How are you, really? Are your wounds healed? Did they hurt you, mistreat you? Where were you? When were you released? How long have you been here? Why didn't you call?"

Zak smiled, probably amused by Sara's rapid-fire questions, but her tone was touchingly serious. "Did you hear me? I said I love you."

Sara stood on tiptoes and brought their lips together. "Yes, darling, I heard. And I love you. Now kiss me before we both explode."

Their kiss was tentative at first, cautious and tender, but became more urgent as their tongues touched and teased. Sara pressed her body against Zak's and fire sparked between them.

"Ahem, excuse me, but we probably need to take this elsewhere," Estelle said. "This is Paris, but even the French have their limits."

Sara pulled reluctantly from Zak's embrace, unsure of how she felt about Estelle's deceit. She'd spent weeks worrying about Zak's welfare. How long had Estelle known Zak was okay? How long had she been here?

"I can see the questions in your eyes, cheri. Let's go." Estelle motioned to a small office inside the private hangar.

Zak took Sara's hand, and they followed her mother into the office. Estelle turned to face Sara. "I know you're wondering why we didn't call and let you know Zakaria was safe, but we couldn't. It was too dangerous until you were out of the country."

Sara searched both of their faces, waiting for Estelle to clarify.

Zak took over. "I've just been able to piece all the bits together. After you delivered the tapes and photos to Kibaki, he confronted the minister, who admitted to the conspiracy with Wachira. He also confessed that he had his man kill the commander after I left that night. Apparently they'd been waiting for me to confront him alone. His plan to frame me worked perfectly because of my history with Wachira. Once the minister confessed, the president had me released and flown to Paris. They phoned Mother, told her to expect a package, and gave her the date and time of my arrival."

"And why was I left in the dark?"

"Kibaki instructed his men not to allow me phone calls or contact with anyone, especially you. I was taken directly from the holding facility in Liboi to the airport. He needed time to locate the minister's accomplice or accomplices inside the government. We agreed on one week, not a second more. But more importantly, he needed to find the assassin before he found you."

"Me?"

Estelle hugged Sara to her. "Yes, cheri, your publicity campaign to locate Zakaria was getting too much attention. Kibaki joined in the effort but the minister of education instructed his man to silence you. The invitation for a visit was to get you out of Africa. I realize it was bad timing for the school, but we wanted you safe and my daughter needs you."

Sara gazed at Zak. Her muscles were strong and more pronounced against her visibly thinner frame. She had obviously not been fed properly and her face was etched with the shadows of too little sleep. And something else was different as well. It was evident in the depths of her concentrated stare, in her attentiveness to Sara's every move, and even in her touch. This change was more fundamental, more essential. "How are you feeling, darling?"

"Better now that you're here."

"So you've been here a week?" Sara continued her inspection, noting and memorizing even the slightest nuance of change to the woman she loved. The bright blue shirt that exquisitely highlighted Zak's eyes hung loosely from her shoulders, making her appear almost delicate. A pair of baggy blue jeans rested atop the flare of her hips and dipped too severely over her lower abdomen.

"That's what Mother says. The plane trip and the first few days are a blur. I think I slept straight through."

Estelle looked at Zak with the loving eyes of a mother. "She was exhausted but worried constantly that you were in danger and she wasn't there to protect you. It was all we could do not to tell you she was safe."

"I hated keeping it from you. It was like using you for bait while we waited for Kibaki's men to finish their roundup."

"And did they arrest the killer?"

"Yes." Zak hung her head, and her shoulders slouched in a defeated posture. "He followed you to the airport and was arrested there. We got the call just before you arrived."

Sara stroked the side of Zak's face, trying to soothe the worry lines etched across her handsome features. "Don't blame yourself. My God, you were being held captive."

"But if I can't protect you, what good is all this damn training I've had?"

Sara knew that no answer would appease Zak. "And what about your boss? Did he come through at all?"

Estelle raised her hand before Zak could answer. "That's my cue to leave. I'm catching a plane myself. I have an art show in London this weekend, and the two of you need some time alone. My flat is at your disposal. I think you'll find everything you desire there." She kissed them both on the cheek and started toward a small jet that had just arrived. "Love you both. See you soon."

❖

Estelle's flat on the Left Bank epitomized the woman and the artist—light, airy, and alive with color and ambience. The view from the third-floor balcony overlooked a stretch of half-timber homes and shops along the Seine River. Zak barely gave Sara a chance to take it in before she swept her up and carried her to the king-sized bed by the windows. She placed her gently in the center of the yellow satin duvet and started to join her.

"Should you be doing this?" Sara asked.

"Oh, am I being too presumptuous?" Zak slowly backed away.

"Not at all, but you've suffered some pretty serious injuries recently, been held prisoner for weeks, and I just got off an eight-hour flight."

Zak tried to hide her disappointment. All she wanted was to be close to Sara, to hold her and show her how much she cared. "Are you hungry, then?"

"Famished."

"Okay, I'll order something, unless you'd prefer to go out."

"The only thing I'm hungry for is you. I just want to be sure you're okay, physically, because I can't promise to be gentle this time."

Zak settled beside her on the bed. "I'm healed enough and don't want to waste another minute with you." She reached for Sara, remembered the fear in her eyes the last time they made love, and hesitated. "Is it okay if I touch you?"

"Please." Sara opened her arms invitingly and urged Zak into them. "I've missed you so much. I was afraid I'd never see you again."

"Estelle told me how hard you worked to find me. I'm sorry you had to go through that, but thank you for not giving up on me." Zak lightly kissed Sara's eyelids, her cheeks, and her lips. She ran her fingers gently over Sara's bare shoulder and felt their connection.

"I will never give up on you. Don't you know how desperately I love you? Part of me was missing when you were gone. How can that be after so short a time together?"

Zak didn't know how to answer Sara's question, but she understood perfectly. A piece of her heart had been returned today. She stroked a strand of hair from Sara's face and tugged at the French braid that hung down her back. Zak worked the plait apart and fingered her copper tresses loose so they fell over her shoulders. She wanted to experience the feel of Sara's hair brushing across her body like thousands of tiny fingers when they made love.

"Will you make love to me, Zak?"

Zak's eyes filled with tears. "Yes, my love. I want to look at you and feel you close to me." She felt no shame or embarrassment as the tears streaked down her cheeks and landed on Sara's light green dress. She didn't try to control them or explain them away. Part of the joy of this moment was that she truly wanted to experience every feeling possible with Sara. "I want you to know how very much I love you and how precious you are to me. You are my life."

"And you are mine." As Sara cradled Zak's head against her chest and rocked back and forth, Zak felt their connection grow and strengthen.

"May I undress you?" she asked. As she waited for permission, her hand quivered as it hovered over Sara's body.

"You may do whatever you like with me. I'm yours."

Zak straddled Sara's knees and slid her hands under her dress and up the side of her thighs, stretching the fabric out as she ascended. Bunching the material in her fists, Zak pulled it over her breasts and unwrapped her like a greatly anticipated gift. When she lay naked except for her thong, Zak gazed at her with a combination of gratitude and appreciation.

"You are truly gorgeous," Zak whispered as she brushed her lips lightly across Sara's. She hooked her thumbs in the sides of her thong, peeled it down her legs, and threw it on the floor. The short penny-colored curls between Sara's thighs glistened with moisture, inviting her to enter and testing her control. Desire clawed inside like a caged animal, urging her to claim this offering. Zak's body was covered in a light sheen of sexual heat, so pervasive that while it burned deep inside, goose flesh stippled her skin. She'd never wanted anyone so badly that her muscles ached from restraining the passion. But her heart and mind held her in a slow, methodical exploration sweet with sensation and anticipation. This time she had to take it slowly, to show Sara how much she loved her and how deeply her emotions ran.

Sara lay still, her heart pounding wildly against her chest. Zak's reverent gaze touched her like a caress. "Are you okay, Zak?" Several excruciating minutes had passed since Zak undressed her. Neither of them spoke. Zak stared at her like a cartographer plotting newly discovered terrain. No lover had ever spent so much time just looking at her. The vulnerability so nakedly displayed on Zak's face was breathtaking. She never knew that physical desire could be so visually apparent. The attention was flattering yet unnerving.

"I'm just enjoying the real you. My dreams didn't come close."

Sara grabbed Zak's shoulders and pulled her down on top of her. "Kiss me." Zak's mouth was soft and gentle as she complied. Sara pressed harder against the full lips, wanting more contact, more fire, but Zak controlled the pace, easing back and licking her lips with a teasing stroke. "Zak, come on," she urged.

"I need to savor you."

"Savor me later. I need you now. I've waited my whole life for you."

Zak raised up on her elbows and looked into Sara's eyes. "Please. I know I'm asking a lot, but I need to show you something first. Will you let me?" The pleading look in Zak's eyes expanded Sara's sexual appetite into a loving hunger. The pulsation between her legs spread to her heart and the two-pronged aches pounded in unison. Zak stared at her like she was the most desirable woman in the world. Her eyes were dark with desire and an intensity Sara had never seen. She had no idea what Zak needed from her, but whatever it was, she wanted to give it. Denying her anything, ever, was not an option.

"Do whatever you want, darling." Zak unbuttoned her shirt and slid it off her shoulders. When the raised red scars on her sides became visible, Sara stifled her anger. The two sights should not occur side by side in nature: Zak's beautifully sculpted alabaster skin marred by the devastating gouges of a wild animal. But that was her lover, a façade of diffidence and control coupled with an underlying layer of feral instincts and exotic desires.

Zak tossed her jeans onto the floor with her shirt and sat astride Sara, naked and needy. She had never tried to control her baser instincts.

"My wounds don't hurt anymore, so don't worry." She let the cool evening air wash across her skin and moderate the desire to ravage Sara immediately. The woman she loved lay beneath her, offering herself totally and completely. This was the time for Zak to prove she deserved her.

She stretched alongside Sara and scissored her leg between Sara's thighs. The slick wetness that covered her quadriceps signaled her lover's readiness. Zak contracted the muscles of her lower abdomen to stave off her own flood of desire. Lowering herself, she moistened Sara's lips with the tip of her tongue and teased her way inside her mouth. Sara sucked her in eagerly and the sensation tugged at the base of Zak's clit. She lifted her lower body slightly to relieve the direct contact between Sara's thigh and her pubic mound.

"Don't pull away from me, Zak, please." Sara's breathing was already rapid and labored with need. Her nails dug into Zak's butt.

Zak resisted, deepening their kiss and filling Sara with her love. She tenderly stroked her forehead, her eyelids, and the light sprinkle of freckles across her nose. Sara circled her hips against Zak's leg and moaned her encouragement. Zak feathered her fingers down to Sara's breasts, tickling and dancing away before the temptation to devour became too great. The movement against her thigh became more urgent.

"I want you so much, Zak. Soon?" Sara's eyes were filled with the same urgency her body displayed, but her gaze never strayed from Zak's.

"Very." Zak delicately traced the curves of Sara's body from her breasts to her knees, the touch never lingering in one spot long enough to sate. Her own lust would not be denied much longer, no matter how gallant her intentions. It coiled inside her like a crouching predator, ready to strike and consume the object she craved.

Zak licked the base of a breast and almost came immediately. She took the soft mound of flesh into her mouth, and the puckering nipple tantalized her tongue. Pulses of current shot to her aching clit and she tried to close her legs, but Sara wedged her thigh harder against her. Sara moaned and her hips thrust forward, demanding more attention.

"What do you want, Sara? Tell me."

"Make me come, Zak. I need you now."

Sliding her hand down the curve of Sara's hip, Zak followed the natural line to the apex of her thighs. An explosion of heat rose to meet her hand as she cupped Sara's sex. She rubbed against Sara's clit with the heel of her palm and flicked her tongue back and forth across the erect nipple simultaneously. Fire sparked in Sara's brown eyes and begged to be quenched. Zak focused on Sara, watching the subtle changes of her face as her body rushed toward orgasm. Her pupils were dilated behind heavily hooded lids, barely open enough to maintain eye contact. She frequently licked her lips, which were dry from deep, panting breaths, and the pulse along the side of her neck raced. The freckles across the bridge of her nose darkened as her face flushed. Her lips mouthed unspoken words that Zak longed to hear but feared would send her too quickly to orgasm. The beauty of Sara so close to release began to unravel Zak's control. Sara's thrusts were more vigorous, her moans shriller and more exacting. "Zak, please go inside me."

Zak scooted down between Sara's legs, one hand still fondling a breast, the other exposing Sara's clit for her tongue. She circled Sara's opening with the tip of her middle finger, dipping slightly into her slick heat and then withdrawing.

"God, don't make me wait any longer. Do it now," Sara pleaded.

Zak entered her, burying her finger deep inside. Sara arched to meet her hand and kept returning as Zak established a steady rhythm between her breast, clit, and vagina.

"Yes, that's it, Zak. Harder."

The tempo was making it difficult for Zak to concentrate on pleasing Sara without losing it. But the expression on Sara's face told her it wouldn't be long. Sara's fingernails dug into the top of Zak's shoulders and her eyes closed.

"Look at me, Sara. I want you to see me when you come."

Sara complied and with a final plunge of her hand, Zak watched the emotional release play out in her eyes. The single-minded concentration melted into surprise, then shifted to relief, followed by pleasure, and finally settled into a warm, contented look of love.

Only when Sara was in the clutches of orgasm did Zak allow herself to let go. The love in Sara's eyes opened her heart and her body followed. She concentrated on the location of her hands on Sara's body and on how connected she felt to her at that moment. The physical closeness and emotional intimacy she craved was finally hers, and it sent shudders of arousal through her. With Sara's moans still filling the cool Parisian night air, Zak's climax ripped through her so quickly that only a vapor trail seemed to remain.

When Sara's tremors subsided, she urged Zak up beside her and pulled the corner of the duvet across their drenched bodies. She had never been as sexually satisfied yet ravenous. Zak, thoughtful and gentle, made love to her like she was the only woman she'd ever been with. "Thank you."

"For what?" Zak asked.

"For letting me see the tender, loving side of you. It was amazing. Your eyes are so expressive. Don't ever try to hide anything from me again because it won't work. I've seen into your soul." Sara stroked the side of her face and kissed her, never wanting to stop. When she could no longer breathe easily, she pulled back.

"And that's what I wanted you to see, my heart and soul, so you'd know how much I love you."

"But don't think you're getting off that easy, GI Jane." Zak's look of surprise told Sara she had no idea what was coming. "We have details to discuss. I have no intention of letting you get away from me."

Zak rolled over on top of Sara and stared into her eyes. "And I have no intention of trying, so discuss away, my love."

Sara was reluctant to break the mood but she had to know. "What about your work?"

Without hesitation, Zak answered, "Over."

"Could you be more specific, please?"

"They lied to me about my father's death and Wachira's part in it, to keep me blind, loyal, and stupid. When I figured that out, I knew I couldn't work for them anymore. Estelle and I confronted Stewart with the evidence when I got back to Paris. And with the help of your campaign, he didn't object much about letting me out of my existing five-year contract—with full pay."

Sara searched Zak's face for signs of uncertainty or hesitation but found none. "And you're okay with all that?"

"Perfectly, because now I get to have a real life, complete with unemployment, family, and girlfriend issues. I can't wait to get started."

"Don't take this the wrong way, but I might be able to help with the first part, if you're not too proud to accept help."

"I've got a feeling I'll be needing a lot of help from you in a lot of ways, so let's hear it."

"Imani is interviewing teachers for the school in Kenya. She's agreed to stay on as head mistress slash nurse, quite an asset. But after the settling-in period, and a few months of teaching just because I love it, I'll be moving on to other projects. I've been considering hiring a scout, so to speak, to research and do reconnaissance on future sites. Would you be interested?"

Zak slid back down beside Sara. "This isn't just something you made up, is it? I couldn't take a pity position, especially not from you."

"No, my darling. If you don't believe me, check with Randall. He's been accepting applications since I left for Africa. You'd be perfect for the position since you've probably been everywhere in the world at least once."

"Not quite, but I'll consider it, on one condition."

"Name it."

"Let me donate my time to the foundation. I don't really need a salary. Besides, it would be worthwhile just to do something positive and meaningful for a change."

"Salary is negotiable. Can we save the details for later? I have another item that is nonnegotiable."

"I'm at your service."

"I really enjoyed how you made love to me earlier. It was the perfect start to the rest of our lives. But right now I need my African warrior to make love to me. Bring it on, and don't worry about hurting me. I know you never would. And—" Zak started to claim her, and the fire in her eyes stopped Sara. "I'm doing it again, aren't I, babbling?"

"Yes," Zak answered, "but I know how to handle that—food." Sara's objection was muffled as Zak lowered herself on top of her and covered her lips with a searing kiss.

About the Author

VK Powell is a thirty-year veteran of a midsized police department. She was a police officer by necessity (it paid the bills) and a writer by desire (it didn't). Her career spanned numerous positions including beat officer, homicide detective, field sergeant, vice/narcotics lieutenant, district captain, and assistant chief of police. Now retired, she lives in central North Carolina and devotes her time to writing, traveling, and serving.

VK is a member of the Golden Crown Literary Society and Romance Writers of America. She is the author of three erotic short stories and one romantic short story published in Bold Strokes Books anthologies. Her novels are *To Protect and Serve* and *Suspect Passions*. *Justifiable Risk*, VK's fourth book, is currently under way.

Books Available From Bold Strokes Books

Fever by VK Powell. Hired gun Zakaria Chambers is hired to provide a simple escort service to philanthropist Sara Ambrosini, but nothing is as simple as it seems, especially love. (978-1-60282-135-4)

High Risk by JLee Meyer. Can actress Kate Hoffman really risk all she's worked for to take a chance on love? Or is it already too late? (978-1-60282-136-1)

Missing Lynx by Kim Baldwin and Xenia Alexiou. On the trail of a notorious serial killer, Elite Operative Lynx's growing attraction to a mysterious mercenary could be her path to love—or to death. (978-1-60282-137-8)

Spanking New by Clifford Henderson. A poignant, hilarious, unforgettable look at life, love, gender, and the essence of what makes us who we are. (978-1-60282-138-5)

Magic of the Heart by C.J. Harte. CEO Susan Hettinger and wild, impulsive rock star M.J. Carson couldn't be more different if they tried—but opposites attract in ways neither woman can resist. (978-1-60282-131-6)

Ambereye by Gill McKnight. Jolie Garoul is falling in love with her assistant. The big problem is, Jolie is a werewolf. (978-1-60282-132-3)

Collision Course by C.P. Rowlands. Tragedy leaves Brie O'Malley and Jordan Carter fearful and alone. Can they find the courage to take a second chance on love? (978-1-60282-133-0)

Mephisto Aria by Justine Saracen. Opera singer Katherina Marov's destiny may be to repeat the mistakes of her father when she becomes involved in a dangerous love affair. (978-1-60282-134-7)

Battle Scars by Meghan O'Brien. Returning Iraq war veteran Ray McKenna struggles with the battle scars that can only be healed by love. (978-1-60282-129-3)

Chaps by Jove Belle. Eden Metcalf wants nothing more than to flee from her troubled past and travel the open road—until she runs into rancher Brandi Cornwell. (978-1-60282-127-9)

Lightbearer by John Caruso. Lucifer dares to question the premise of creation itself and reveals that sin may be all that stands between us and living hell. (978-1-60282-130-9)

The Seeker by Ronica Black. FBI profiler Kennedy Scott battles ghosts from her past, deadly obsession, and the evil that haunts her. (978-1-60282-128-6)

Power Play by Julie Cannon. Businesswomen Tate Monroe and Victoria Sosa are at odds in the boardroom, but not in the bedroom. (978-1-60282-125-5)

The Remarkable Journey of Miss Tranby Quirke by Elizabeth Ridley. When love enters Tranby's life in the form of a beautiful nineteen-year-old student, Lysette McDonald, she embarks on the most remarkable journey of all. (978-1-60282-126-2)

Returning Tides by Radclyffe. Insurance investigator Ashley Walker faces more than a dangerous opponent when she returns to the town, and the woman, she left behind. (978-1-60282-123-1)

Veritas by Anne Laughlin. When the hallowed halls of academia become the stage for murder, newly appointed Dean Beth Ellis's search for the truth leads her to unexpected discoveries about her own heart. (978-1-60282-124-8)

The Pleasure Planner by Larkin Rose. Pleasure purveyor Bree Hendricks treats love like a commodity until Logan Delaney makes Bree the client in her own game. (978-1-60282-121-7)

everafter by Nell Stark and Trinity Tam. Valentine Darrow is bitten by a vampire on her way to propose to her lover Alexa Newland, and their lives and love are placed in mortal jeopardy. (978-1-60282-119-4)

Summer Winds by Andrews & Austin. When Maggie Turner hires a ranch hand to help work her thousand acres, she never expects to be attracted to the very young, very female Cash Tate. (978-1-60282-120-0)

Beggar of Love by Lee Lynch. Jefferson is the lover every woman wants to be—or to have. A revealing saga of lesbian sexuality. (978-1-60282-122-4)

The Seduction of Moxie by Colette Moody. When 1930s Broadway actress Violet London meets speakeasy singer Moxie Valette, she is instantly attracted and her Hollywood trip takes an unexpected turn. (978-1-60282-114-9)

Goldenseal by Gill McKnight. When Amy Fortune returns to her childhood home, she discovers something sinister in the air—but is former lover Leone Garoul stalking her or protecting her? (978-1-60282-115-6)

Romantic Interludes 2: Secrets edited by Radclyffe and Stacia Seaman. An anthology of sensual lesbian love stories: passion, surprises, and secret desires. (978-1-60282-116-3)

Femme Noir by Clara Nipper. Nora Delaney meets her match in Max Abbott, a sex-crazed dame who may or may not have the information Nora needs to solve a murder—but can she contain her lust for Max long enough to find out? (978-1-60282-117-0)

The Reluctant Daughter by Lesléa Newman. Heartwarming, heartbreaking, and ultimately triumphant—the story every daughter recognizes of the lifelong struggle for our mothers to really see us. (978-1-60282-118-7)

Erosistible by Gill McKnight. When Win Martin arrives at a luxurious Greek hotel for a much-anticipated week of sun and sex with her new girlfriend, she is stunned to find her ex-girlfriend, Benny, is the proprietor. Aeros Ebook. (978-1-60282-134-7)

Looking Glass Lives by Felice Picano. Cousins Roger and Alistair become lifelong friends and discover their sexuality amidst the backdrop of twentieth-century gay culture. (978-1-60282-089-0)

Breaking the Ice by Kim Baldwin. Nothing is easy about life above the Arctic Circle—except, perhaps, falling in love. At least that's what pilot Bryson Faulkner hopes when she meets Karla Edwards. (978-1-60282-087-6)

It Should Be a Crime by Carsen Taite. Two women fulfill their mutual desire with a night of passion, neither expecting more until law professor Morgan Bradley and student Parker Casey meet again…in the classroom. (978-1-60282-086-9)

Rough Trade edited by Todd Gregory. Top male erotica writers pen their own hot, sexy versions of the term "rough trade," producing some of the hottest, nastiest, and most dangerous fiction ever published. (978-1-60282-092-0)

The High Priest and the Idol by Jane Fletcher. Jemeryl and Tevi's relationship is put to the test when the Guardian sends Jemeryl on a mission that puts her not only in harm's way, but back into the sights of a previous lover. (978-1-60282-085-2)

Point of Ignition by Erin Dutton. Amid a blaze that threatens to consume them both, firefighter Kate Chambers and property owner Alexi Clark redefine love and trust. (978-1-60282-084-5)

Secrets in the Stone by Radclyffe. Reclusive sculptor Rooke Tyler suddenly finds herself the object of two very different women's affections, and choosing between them will change her life forever. (978-1-60282-083-8)

Dark Garden by Jennifer Fulton. Vienna Blake and Mason Cavender are sworn enemies—who can't resist each other. Something has to give. (978-1-60282-036-4)

Late in the Season by Felice Picano. Set on Fire Island, this is the story of an unlikely pair of friends—a gay composer in his late thirties and an eighteen-year-old schoolgirl. (978-1-60282-082-1)

Punishment with Kisses by Diane Anderson-Minshall. Will Megan find the answers she seeks about her sister Ashley's murder or will her growing relationship with one of Ash's exes blind her to the real truth? (978-1-60282-081-4)

September Canvas by Gun Brooke. When Deanna Moore meets TV personality Faythe she is reluctantly attracted to her, but will Faythe side with the people spreading rumors about Deanna? (978-1-60282-080-7)